KASIE WEST

SPLIT
SECOND

An Imprint of HarperCollins*Publishers*

HarperTeen is an imprint of HarperCollins Publishers.

Split Second
Copyright © 2014 by Kasie West
All rights reserved. Printed in the United States of America.

Library of Congress Cataloging-in-Publication Data
West, Kasie.
    Split second / Kasie West. — First edition.
        pages   cm
    Summary: "Seventeen-year-old Addie struggles to retrieve her lost
memories and makes a startling discovery that challenges everything she's ever
known about herself, her family, and her world"— Provided by publisher.
    ISBN 978-0-06-211738-0 (hardcover bdg.)
    [1. Psychic ability—Fiction.   2. Choice (Psychology)—Fiction.   3. Family
life—Fiction.   4. Memory—Fiction.   5. Love—Fiction.   6. High schools—
Fiction.   7. Schools—Fiction.]   I. Title.
PZ7.W51837Spl 2014   2013008053
[Fic]—dc23   CIP
                                                                         AC

Typography by Andrea Vandergrift
13 14 15 16 17 LP/RRDH 10 9 8 7 6 5 4 3 2 1
❖
First Edition

To Hannah, Autumn, Abby, and Donavan,
who fill every day with my favorite memories

CHAPTER 1

Addie: Meet me at my house later. If I'm not already dead.

My car sat on the far side of the parking lot, and I couldn't get to it fast enough. The day had been horrible, matching perfectly with the rest of my first week back to school since the whole Duke's-a-huge-jerk-who-had-been-using-me revelation. I could almost handle conversations stopping dead when I entered a room. But the looks of pity had me seething. I did not need pity. If luck were on my side, the winter holiday that began as soon as I exited the parking lot would make people forget. If it didn't, maybe Laila could zap the whole school with amnesia. Ah, schoolwide amnesia, the first happy thought of my day.

I stepped off the curb and realized too late that I hadn't looked first. Tires screeched across asphalt and my hands instinctively flew up, bracing for the impact. The impact that didn't come. At least not yet. The motorcycle skidded my way in slow motion. So slow that I easily stepped out of its way as it moved past. Connor, the driver, let the bike drop to the pavement as he crawled his way off it. Pieces of glass from the shattered side mirror floated by my head. I reached out and touched one with my index finger. It dropped like a brick to the asphalt, where it rocked back and forth—the fastest-moving piece of the world around me—until it stopped.

Back at the bike, Connor slowly ripped his helmet from his head and turned a full circle, searching the ground. His movements gradually picked up speed until he no longer appeared as though underwater. When our eyes finally met, relief washed over his face.

"Addie, I thought I hit you. I was going to hit you."

"I'm fine." At least physically. I had no idea what was happening to me mentally. My ability had always been the same—I could see both outcomes of a choice. In essence, I could see the future. Two futures, really. There had never been any variation to that. It was predictable.

Until now.

Now my ability was acting up. At certain moments, time slowed down around me. The same thing had happened at Bobby's house last week, and I wrote it off as an isolated incident—a fluke that had come out of the extreme stress of the situation. He'd said something about extreme emotions. And it wasn't every day that someone tried to kill you. Everything that day had been weird—the time slowing down, the Search-like vision of Trevor at the hospital. But now I could no longer blame it on that day. I hadn't been almost killed today. I glanced at the motorcycle lying on its side. Well, maybe I had.

A pain shot up the back of my neck and then radiated through my head. I tried not to wince and pressed my palms against my temples, scanning through a pain-relief mind pattern. It didn't help.

"Are you sure you're okay?" Connor asked. "Because you look like you're going to puke."

"I'm fine. Sorry about your . . ." I was about to say *bike*, but then saw Duke, coming toward the scene at a jog.

I spun on my heel and walked as fast as my throbbing head would allow in the direction of my car.

"What happened?" I heard him ask Connor behind me.

"I almost hit her. I should've hit her. One second she was there, the next she was gone."

Just thirty more steps and I'd be at my car. I positioned my thumb, ready to unlock the door, so there would be no delays when I reached it. My head had finally calmed, so I walked even faster. But then his voice was right behind me.

"Addie."

"No." It was a lame response, but the only one my lips would allow passage to.

"Did you get hurt?"

The many answers I could've given to that question flooded my brain: *Not nearly as much as you hurt me. Not nearly as much as I will hurt you if you come any closer. Why do you care? Were you hoping to be the sole provider of painful experiences in my life?*

Of course I didn't say any of those things. I led him to believe he hadn't hurt me. That I had never liked him at all. That when he stopped manipulating my emotions with his ability, everything I ever felt for him vanished. And that was the story I would stick to no matter what. That story let me hold on to a shred of dignity.

"No." I reached my car and pressed the pad, unlocking it. I opened the door and let it act as a barrier between us when I turned to face him. "I'm good." I threw in a smile as proof of the statement.

"The rumors were brutal today. Sorry. They'll die down soon." His ever-present smile made his words seem like the setup to a joke. Unfortunately, I was probably the punch line he'd tell his buddies later: *And then she fell for me again. Ba-dum-bum.*

He ran a hand through his tousled blond hair, pushing it off his forehead and making his blue eyes stand out more. "You still haven't told anyone, right?"

And there it was, the reason he was still coming around. I knew something that could ruin him—he was a Mood Controller. Everyone still thought Duke Rivers, football star, was Telekinetic, which was what he wanted everyone to think so he could play. More specifically, so he could play quarterback, a position the coach would only fill with a Telekinetic. It made all the pity looks even worse this week, because they probably just assumed I was the poor girl with no willpower to resist Duke's charm. If only they knew I had no choice. "I made you a deal. Get your buddies to stop injuring the Norm players and I'll keep your secret. Is that still the arrangement?"

He nodded. "But you think I should tell either way."

Yes! "I could not care any less." I climbed in and pulled the door shut behind me. *Don't look at him, Addie, just start the car and drive away.* I turned my whole body away so I could look over my right shoulder to back up. If I backed over his toes, that was all on him. When I straightened out the steering wheel, I managed not to check and see if he still stood there. I just drove away. Maybe now that Duke Rivers knew I wouldn't spill his secret, he'd leave me alone.

I lay perfectly still as the music flooded my bedroom, attempting to drown out all thoughts. I stared at the words on my ceiling, pretending the answer to what I should do with my life was written somewhere among the quotes painted there over the years. After an hour of staring, my eyes tricked me into thinking some stood out bolder than others, so I read the darker words. Life. Other. Sometimes. Eat.

Not helpful at all.

My door flew open and Laila walked in. "Is this Journey? Are you grieving to Journey?" The lights illuminated. I hadn't realized they had turned off with my lack of motion, but my now stinging eyes proved otherwise. "There are bands of this era that are perfectly acceptable to cry to."

I rubbed my eyes. Was it that obvious I had been bawling all afternoon? "Nobody can sing a love song like Journey." My down comforter puffed up around me, as if slowly trying to swallow me whole. I hadn't put up much of a fight.

There were things I should've been doing: laundry, a half hour of meditation, packing for my dad's house, and then there was the hair appointment my mom had scheduled for me. That was in five minutes. And just like the first three items on the list, I was ready to forgo that one as well. I found the blue strip of hair and twirled it over and over again around my finger. It had faded a lot, but I wasn't ready to give up all the blue quite yet.

Laila stood at my wall monitor, probably searching for the right background music for my suffering. I waited to hear her pick when the room went completely silent. She sat down at my desk and riffled through my drawers.

With every noise, I sensed my desk becoming more and more disorganized. "What do you need?"

"Paper."

"Top right."

She pulled out a clean sheet, and before she could ask, I said, "Pens are in the center drawer."

"Perfect. Time to start a list." She leaned back in the chair, propped her feet, clad in red heels, on the desk, and put the paper on her knees. "It's entitled 'Revenge.' Subtitled 'How to pay Duke back for using not only his ability but his exceptionally good looks against two unsuspecting, perfectly innocent girls.'"

Before I had a chance to object to this pointless exercise, she said, "Number one, figure out a way to make the whole school think he's turned ugly. You know that would kill him. Ooh, I bet we can get a Perceptive to help us. They can just alter everyone's perception of him. It will be awesome. Okay, your turn. Number two."

I smiled. Maybe this would be a good healing ritual after all—just imagining Duke ugly made me a little happier. "How about we get a Persuasive to talk him into doing something really stupid in front of everyone?"

"Kalan would totally do that." She wrote it down and then tapped the pen on her teeth. "What else . . . ?" She stood and walked to my bookcase, tilted her head sideways, and started reading the titles. "Don't you have any books in here about somebody plotting revenge?"

"I'm sure there are revenge subplots in one of them."

She turned to face me and leaned back against my bookcase. "How about we sneak into his room at night and put lipstick on him?"

"How would we get in?"

"A Mass Manipulator can walk through the wall and unlock the front door for us."

"You don't think their security system covers that possibility?"

"We'll find a way."

"Why? I'm sure he showers in the morning. What would putting lipstick on him do?"

"It would let him know we were there, always watching, able to get in whenever we want. Plus I've always kind of wanted to put lipstick on him. He has amazing lips." After she said it, she realized she shouldn't have and dropped her gaze.

I finally sat up and scooted back against the headboard.

"What did you two do anyway?" I asked quietly, not sure I wanted to know the answer. "I guess you kissed?"

"Do we really have to talk about this? He tricked us both, right?"

"He betrayed me and then made you betray me."

"He made you do things too."

I started to nod but then wondered what he had ever made me do, aside from like him. He gave me the feelings, but I was pretty sure I was the one who acted on them. *Stop,* I told myself. I had lost Duke; I wasn't going to let him take away my best friend with his betrayal too. I had to let it go.

"We're not going to do these, are we?" she asked, holding up the revenge list.

"No. But it was fun imagining them. Thanks."

She gave a long sigh, then slid the paper into the slot on the recycle bin. She glanced at her purse on the desk and then started playing with the zipper. "If I had something important to tell you, something that might stress you out, would you want me to tell you now or when you got back from your dad's?"

She probably wanted to go into detail about her and Duke. Get it off her conscience and put it onto mine. I sighed, the slight pressure behind my eyes reminding me that things weren't quite right. My life was a huge mess. "I just need a break right now, from everything. Can we talk about it when I get back?"

She dropped the zipper on her purse, seeming relieved, and turned to face me. "Yes. So what are you packing for your dad's house? Six weeks is a long time."

CHAPTER 2

Laila: You're anal. In case you didn't know.

Addie stacked her clothes by color. On purpose. Her shirts, folded in neat squares, sat in separate piles on her bed. One with shades of red, another greens and blues, and finally neutrals. She gripped a pink-and-brown-striped shirt in her hands, and her eyes flashed back and forth between two piles. It wouldn't surprise me if she imploded from the dilemma of a shirt that fit into two piles. I had an intense urge to grab the stacks and throw them in the air, letting her world of organization rain chaos on us.

"The fate of the universe lies in which pile that shirt belongs to, Addie. Don't screw it up."

She rolled her eyes. "There's nothing wrong with being

organized. I know it's a foreign concept to you, but it will save time later."

"Is that how your ability works? You just store up bits of time and use them when necessary?"

"Yeah, maybe you should try it."

"No thanks. I'm in the business of Erasing time. Taking away minutes. Too bad I can't give those minutes to you so you don't feel the need to do all that." I flicked my hand at her piles of clothes.

She finally decided her shirt belonged in the "shades of red" pile, then she added the stacks to her open suitcase. Her suitcase. Its presence alone made my stomach hurt. This would be the first time we'd been apart in a long time, and I'd been trying not to agonize over it. The suitcase was flipping off my efforts. Hurling it out the window seemed a bit dramatic, so I resisted.

"I still can't believe you're not coming with me. It's not too late to change your mind," Addie said.

My cell phone chimed. *I hope you're at home. Make sure the boys do laundry tonight. I'm working a double shift.*

I laughed. "You're leaving for six weeks. Too long." My brothers would kill each other and burn down the house in half that time. "I'll see you in a few weeks for the game." I grabbed my purse off the desk and flung it over my shoulder.

The letter I'd been carrying around for the last seven weeks made it seem heavier. I wanted to take it out, throw it at her, and run. The problem was, I didn't want to either. It was a letter Addie had written to herself after her Search. I saw the haunted look in her eyes when she came out of that Search before I Erased her memories. She looked miserable. I had no idea what was in the note, but I did not want to bring that look back, no matter how incredibly guilty I felt hanging on to it. Maybe when she got back from her dad's she'd be in a better place.

"Don't leave tomorrow without saying good-bye."

"I wouldn't dream of it."

I hugged her and left.

In my truck, I pulled out the envelope like I had done so many times over the last seven weeks, the tattered corners proving my obsession. Across the front, in Addie's handwriting, it read, "Open November 14." It was now November 21. Miraculously, it was still sealed. The specific date bothered me a little. I hoped there was nothing time-sensitive inside. But considering that date marked the morning after the showdown at Bobby's house, I figured she was just waiting until after that event to make sure nothing changed. Both of our lives had hung in the balance that night, and it made sense that she wouldn't want a single thing to disturb that balance—including this letter. I shoved it back in my purse and started the engine.

I walked in the front door and my brother Eli threw a wadded-up piece of paper at my head. "Grocery list. We're out of food, and I'm starving."

"Don't throw things at me or I'll beat you." I picked up the paper, opened it, and scanned down the list. "Where's Dad?"

"Crashed."

I glanced at the clock on the wall. Nine. "Is Derek in bed already?"

"Yes."

"Did you make him shower? I think it's been a couple days, and he stinks."

"Yes. He showered. You're welcome."

I sat on him and pushed his floppy hair into his eyes. "Thanks, you're the best brother ever." He shoved at me with two hands, but I held on tight.

"Get off me."

I smacked him on the back of the head and stood up.

"Oh! Think something. I'm practicing." Eli was three months away from fourteen and still hadn't Presented. Now every day he felt the need to stare at me while trying to read my mind.

"No." I walked to the kitchen, and he jumped up and followed me.

"Please."

"I hate it when people read my mind." I opened the pantry, inventoried the bleakness, and closed it again.

"Come on. Just think something. I'm getting better."

"Fine." I thought *idiot* really hard, staring at him.

He scrunched his nose, his nearly black eyes squinting with intensity. He looked so much like my dad in that moment that the pit in my stomach that formed whenever my dad was around dropped into place. He gave a grunt of frustration, and then my brother's face was back, young and sad. I used Thought Placement and pushed my word into his head.

"Idiot!" he screamed out in excitement.

"Yep, and you are. Wow, you're getting good." I pointed at him. "Now don't read my mind anymore." I left the bare kitchen. He was right, I did need to go to the store.

"You shouldn't think things like that about your own flesh and blood," he yelled after me. I laughed and continued into the room my brothers shared. Derek was asleep, blanket twisted around his legs. I untwisted it and spread it over him.

I grabbed the laundry hamper and the clothes that were strewn around it off the floor of the boys' room and carried it to the washing machine.

My mom kept a cash card hidden inside an empty detergent box. My dad would never do laundry, so it was perfectly safe at all times. When I went on a last-minute shopping trip like this, it was the money I was supposed to use. I hoisted myself up onto the washing machine and reached to the highest shelf, pulling down the box. I grabbed the card and shoved it in my pocket. Jumping down, I ran full speed into a hard chest. My stomach dropped.

"What are you doing?" His gruff voice grated on my every nerve.

"Oh you know, solving life's mysteries, discovering new math theories, or whatever else a person might do in the laundry room." I opened the lid to the washing machine and shoved clothes in, willing my dad to leave. He didn't. He stood there, studying my face.

My dad is a loser, I thought, over and over. *Don't think about anything else,* I told myself. *Loser, loser, loser.* Sometimes I was glad for the suppression drugs he used on a daily basis that made his ability weaker than it would've been otherwise. But then again, if he wasn't on them, he wouldn't be the financial ruin of our family. I didn't mind if he overheard that thought.

He growled and I smiled, pushing the start button on the washing machine. "Is something wrong?" I asked over the now pouring water. I hoped he couldn't see the outline of the card in my pocket.

His eyes darted down to my jeans. I cursed under my breath.

"Hand it over."

"It's for food. Don't be a jerk."

He grabbed my wrist. "Give me the money, Laila."

"Let. Go." I tensed up, ready to knee him as hard as I could, but stopped when his eyes met mine. They looked so hollow and yet so desperate.

"Your mother will bring home some food tonight." He reached into my pocket and snatched out the card.

"You're pathetic."

He squeezed my wrist harder and I ripped it free, using my shoulder to shove past him. I wanted to love my dad, but instead pity and hatred battled for a spot. I was angry I had let pity win tonight.

CHAPTER 3

Addie: Bored. Entertain me.

I knew what was going on. They were trying to intimidate me. Everything about the Tower was set up for psychological intimidation. From the outside it looked like a fortress. The darkest building in the Compound by far. And the tallest. It was the only passage to the Outside. Para cars were parked beneath, and only cars approved to be seen in the Norm world could exit out the other side.

The third floor of the Tower, where I sat with my mother, was no different in its imposing feel. The furniture was bulky and dark, unlike the sleek, clean furniture found in most places. And the lighting was dim. But knowing they were using intimidation tactics on me didn't keep me from being intimidated. I wiped my sweaty palms on my jeans. We had been waiting for over an hour (driving home the point that their time was more important than ours).

"How much longer?" I asked my mom.

She looked up from her tablet to the closed door. "Soon, I'm sure. Why don't you read?" She pointed to the closed book in my hand. I couldn't concentrate enough to read.

I shrugged and eyed a flickering blue light near the ceiling. "Are they monitoring us?"

"Just security cameras. Why are you so nervous? You went to that football game a few weeks ago."

"Yeah, but that was an overnight pass. We just had to read and sign a contract. This is an extended stay."

"It's not much different—just a backstory, a Norm refresher course, and a mental assessment, plus the secrecy contract."

"Was that supposed to make me feel better?"

She patted my leg a few times. "You'll be fine." The lack of warmth in the assurance didn't garner confidence. But I appreciated the fact that she didn't Persuade me to feel better. Her words could be as powerful as she wanted them to be.

The door slid open with a *whoosh*, and a man who was an illustration in intimidation walked out. He was handsome—tall, black hair, gray eyes, and muscular. But he had a long scar that ran along his cheek, as if he had personally chased down a rule breaker and silenced him. I wondered why he'd never had it Healed. He probably realized its value in his job.

"We're ready for you, Addison." His gruff voice didn't soften his appearance.

Save me, I mouthed to my mom as I left.

She just rolled her eyes. My dad would've pretended to throw me a life preserver.

Scar-Face led me to a large, nearly bare room. Only a table, two chairs, and a bookcase lined with electronics and digital notebooks greeted us.

"Have a seat. I'm Agent Farley with the Containment Committee." He grabbed a tablet and powered it on, then scrolled through a few screens.

I slid into a chair. It felt cold on my bare arms. "Hi. I'm Addie."

"Addison Coleman, please clearly state your claimed ability." He angled the tablet slightly toward me, probably so it would pick up my voice.

"Divergent."

Unlike most people, he seemed to know what that meant, or at least the tablet did, because it didn't complain or ask for a description. After I said it, though, I wondered if that was still my ability. I always assumed I was Divergent, because my grandmother was, but maybe my ability to see the future had to do with Time Manipulation. My recent presentations, coupled with my established ability, seemed to fit better under that descriptor. It was perfectly normal for abilities to grow and expand until we reached adulthood, but for some reason I didn't want to tell him about my expanded ability. What if it wasn't normal?

17

The time to speak up passed with my silence. What would I have said anyway? *Well, I might have this new advancement to my ability, but I have absolutely no control over when or how to use it.* I'm sure that would've caused his tablet to flash red with a big, fat extended-stay-denied-until-more-stable warning. I kept my mouth shut.

He turned the tablet toward me, and the contract came up on the screen. "No telling anyone about your ability, no using your ability in front of Norms, no allowing anyone to guess that you have an ability. Outside this Compound you must act, look, and speak as though you are Normal. Do you understand?"

"Yes."

"Palm here."

I pressed my palm onto the screen and waited while the computer assessed me. I tried to even my breathing and heart rate to let the computer see that I was being truthful in my pledge to keep the Compound's secrets. That the Tower had nothing to fear from me.

"If you break these rules, the consequences can be as severe as a complete memory wipe."

I nodded. I figured they were just saying these things to scare me. Would they seriously perform a complete memory wipe just for telling someone about the Compound?

"Okay then." He smiled now. For the first time. It seemed out of place on his face. "The Norm refresher course is two doors to the left. Please return here when you're finished."

• • •

By the time the class was done, my head felt full of jumbled-together facts. I tried to prioritize them, shifting the unimportant ones to the back of my mind—like how to work a vending machine and public restroom paper towel dispensers—so I'd remember the ones I needed, like how to open locks and turn on lights.

I walked back into the bare room where Agent Farley still sat at the metal table. He turned when the door opened. "All done?"

"I think so."

"Good. I hope you found the class informative. It's important that you blend in."

"It was very informative. My lack of gumball machine skills might've given me away."

Obviously not sensing my sarcasm, he nodded like he completely agreed with the statement. "Enjoy your time away, and don't forget that without your card, entrance to the Compound is nearly impossible."

"Okay."

"Who accompanied you here today?"

"My mom."

"And she will be leaving with you as well?"

"No. I'm going to see my dad."

"Your father . . ." He glanced down at his tablet. "Bradley Coleman. Lives in Dallas, Texas." He ran his finger sideways across the surface, scrolling through several screens. "So his memory of the Compound is still intact."

"Yes, of course."

He raised one eyebrow as though "of course" shouldn't have been part of my statement.

"Do you . . . are there . . . a lot of memories Erased?"

"Only when promises are breached."

That didn't really answer my question, but it was apparent he wasn't going to answer it anyway.

His finger continued across the surface of his tablet. "Just two immediate relatives have left the Compound then."

I stood up straighter, craning my neck to look at the tablet. "Two?"

His finger paused on the screen, and he squinted a little. "No. My mistake. That's a one. Just your father."

"Right . . . exactly. My dad."

He stood and shelved the clipboard with others like it. I stared at it for a moment before his single hand-clap drew my attention back to him.

"Okay then. Here's your mind program, transferred to Norm-friendly tech." He handed me a small, black, sticklike object. It looked like a hologram simulator. I must've had a confused look on my face, because he added, "It's called a flash drive. You slide that white button forward, and it plugs into a laptop or computer. Not a television, though."

I nodded. Really? The stupid video I watched earlier covered manual toilets but not flash drives?

"And here's your backstory and some Norm history refreshers." He pulled a fat orange envelope off the bookcase and handed it to me. "Memorize and stick to your backstory. It's made especially for your scenario."

"Okay."

"I believe you're set."

My mom stood at the end of the hall, speaking to a man in a suit. Her body language registered irritation. Before I reached her, she turned and caught my eye, the tense expression on her face softening. By this time I was close enough to hear the man say, "Have a pleasant day." His words didn't match his tone.

When he walked away, I said, "Did you have to get interviewed too?"

"No." She led the way toward the exit.

"What was that all about then?"

She gave a heavy sigh, and then her gaze flicked to the flash drive I still clutched in my hand. "I was just making sure they were allowing you to take your program, actually."

"Oh." I held it up. "Looks like they are."

"Good."

I pocketed the flash drive. "When's the last time you left, Mom?"

"Wow, it's been years."

"Did they do the whole 'scare you into silence' back then?"

She smiled. "Yes."

"It's so dramatic."

"They specialize in doom."

"Is Dad the first one in our family to leave?"

She flinched slightly. I may not have even noticed if I hadn't

21

been looking for it. My mom's parents lived about ten minutes from us, and my dad's mom died five years ago and was buried in the cemetery downtown next to her husband, who passed when I was seven. My father and I still visited their graves once a year. Did my parents have siblings they weren't telling me about? Maybe Scar-Face hadn't slipped at all. Maybe it really was a number two on his screen.

"Yes. The very first," she said.

Why didn't I have my dad's ability, so I could tell if she was lying or not?

She kissed my cheek and held on to me longer than necessary. I wondered if she was thinking, like I was, about how this would be our first holiday apart. I hugged her tighter, trying to absorb her strength for the next six weeks in the Norm world.

CHAPTER 4

Laila: One a.m. If I have to be awake, then so do you.

It was haunting me—the stupid date on the front of the envelope. Every time I reached into my purse, the envelope seemed to scratch against my hand. And now just the thought of it was disrupting my sleep. Six weeks until Addie came home. I could not carry around the guilt-inducing letter for another six weeks without knowing what it said. Before I could change my mind, I threw back my blankets, grabbed my purse, and ripped open the envelope.

A note on lined paper was folded in uneven thirds, one corner sticking out at a lopsided angle. I smoothed out the page and read the letter Addie had written to herself.

*I promised someone I care about very much that I wouldn't
Erase this path, but I have to. On Friday morning, the
fourteenth of November, however, after certain events occur,
talk to Laila about advanced ability control. Tell her she can
learn how to restore memories. This is the only way I know
how to keep my promise to you. . . .*

I read it through twice, too shocked to comprehend it the
first time. Restore her memory? She wanted me to restore her
memory. I didn't know how to do that. Could I in her other life?

I knew some adult Memory Erasers could do that. Some
could pinpoint memories, selectively Erase certain people from
memories. I was limited for now. Still growing. I could Erase
sections of time. Like two days, three weeks. When I came
into my full ability, I'd be able to do more things. But the note
implied I was able to restore memories now. At this age.

She couldn't have been any more vague. Couldn't she have
written helpful information, like how I managed to do that or
why she wanted it done? Bobby was the only person I knew who
helped people advance their ability. And Bobby was absolutely
unavailable. But I would've never hung out with Bobby. So who
else could I have learned how to advance my ability from?

Great, opening the stupid letter didn't prove any more useful
than carrying it around for weeks.

I reread it.

A smile crept onto my face. I had always pushed my ability to just beyond the limit, scared of the damage I could
cause myself if I went any further. But this note proved it was

possible. No more holding back.

I reached into my desk drawer and pulled out a DAA-approved electronic clip. Maybe putting a few extra hours in on mind patterns would help. But as I went to attach it to my card, I stopped. Doing the same thing I always did would produce the same results. I needed something different. And I knew exactly where I could find just that.

The party was in full swing when I got there. This wasn't like the parties I sometimes dragged Addie to. Even *I* normally avoided these parties. Untested programs filled each wall— a combination of lights and images—broadcasting who knew what kind of garbage into the brains of the watchers. A pattern that wasn't designed for my ability usually made me physically ill. Other people claimed it took them to a new level, but a new level of sick wasn't my idea of enlightening.

But an untested mind pattern created for my ability? That was something I was willing to try. I wandered through the rooms, looking for someone I knew while trying to keep my eyes straight ahead. The patterns of light dancing on the walls were edging into my vision from all sides.

Ahead of me, Kalan sat against the wall, a set of headphones on. I stopped beside her and nudged her leg with the toe of my boot. "Kalan."

She pulled off her headphones. "Hey. What's up? I didn't know you came to these."

"I don't."

"So you're a figment of my imagination?"

I rolled my eyes. "No." I nodded to the wall in front of her. "Do you know if there's a program for Memory Erasers somewhere?"

"No. We don't label them. That's the point. It's freeing not to put yourself in a box."

"Okay." So they were all idiots. "Who provides the entertainment for these things?"

"I'm not sure, but I don't think he attends them."

I sighed and turned to go. Maybe someone else would know more.

"Stay, Laila." Her voice was smooth and steady. It made me want to sit down and join her. It almost made me forget Kalan was a Persuasive.

"Did you really just use your ability on me?"

She smiled. "This is where we practice. We try to reach further. You should practice."

I sat down next to her. "And does it work? Are you advancing?"

She threw her head back and laughed. "Not really. But it's fun."

I shook my head. No help whatsoever. I started to get up, but she grabbed hold of my forearm.

"I need your help."

I looked at her hand on my arm and she let go. "With what?" I asked.

"I need a memory Erased."

"You want one of your memories Erased? Fine. Tell me when it happened and how long the event was."

26

She cleared her throat and looked at her hands. "No. Not one of my memories. Someone else's."

I sat up straighter. "What? No." Addie may have thought I just Erased whenever the need arose, but I had my limits.

"I know you've done it before. I saw you kissing Patrick one day by the lockers. I asked him about it the next day, thinking you two were together, and he looked at me like I was crazy. He thought I had imagined it."

"Well, that's none of your business, is it? Those are memories of me I took back. I didn't take out anything that belonged to him."

"This would be a memory of me you're taking. I swear."

"Kalan, no, I can't. I won't. Sorry." I stood and left her sitting by the wall alone with her mind pattern.

I continued to search, pausing at an open door. Someone in the room had caused everything, including the people, to float about an inch off the floor. That was impressive, even for a Telekinetic. I didn't know many who could move more than one thing at a time, let alone an entire roomful. A guy in the center of the room, the only one not floating, caught my eye. I had no idea who he was, but as soon as he saw me looking, a big smile spread across his face, and everything fell with a bang.

"That was less than a minute," someone called out.

"I was distracted," he said, turning his smile back to me.

I gestured him over with my head, and he bounded over like an eager puppy.

"How'd you do that?"

He shrugged one shoulder and leaned close. His breath

27

reeked of stale smoke. "I'm talented."

"Who sold you the program?"

"What program?"

I sighed. "The one that helped you do that."

The guy looked over my shoulder to someone behind me. "Great party."

I turned to face the host. I didn't recognize him—short, red hair—but he would have answers. "Hey." I caught up with him as he continued to walk down the hall. "Where did you get these programs?"

"They're DAA."

"Whatever. They are not. I'm looking to buy some myself."

The guy gave me a hard look, and by the way he studied me I wondered if he was a Discerner, like Addie's dad, trying to find out if I was telling the truth.

He must've decided I was, because he said, "His name is Connor."

"Connor Bradshaw?"

"I think so."

Huh. I vaguely knew Connor. We had shared a class or two over the years. He was cute in a scruffy, just-rolled-out-of-bed kind of way. I knew Connor sold minor Enhancers, which were discouraged but legal—a couple of weeks ago he had offered me a block enhancer at a party—but I had no idea he sold illegal ability patterns as well. Nice. Connor, like every other guy, would be easy to manipulate. I was one day away from answers.

CHAPTER 5

Addie: Adult parties are even stupider than teen ones.

I sat in the bedroom my father had appointed for me in his new house. Aside from being plain, the room wasn't bad. My feet were propped on the desk, while I painted my toenails two different colors—black and orange. More out of boredom than holiday spirit. I obviously had no friends in Dallas, my dad had no cable, and I had brought only two books, both of which I'd read—one on the drive over and the other yesterday. What had I been thinking? Two books for six weeks? Not smart. But despite my boredom, this trip was exactly what I needed—time to be alone, rest my ability from the strain of classes, and figure out how to move forward.

My dad poked his head in my room and said, "I have a

pre-Thanksgiving party for work tonight. Did you want to come?"

Would I have to speak to people? was what I wanted to ask, but instead just shrugged.

"I think my boss has a daughter your age. Or maybe it's a son. I don't know, either way there will be a teenager in the vicinity." He must've seen the hesitation on my face, because he clasped his hands together and said, "I'll make you a deal."

"What kind of deal?"

"If you come with me to this work thing, tomorrow morning I'll take you to the most amazing bookstore you have ever seen in your life."

Considering the only bookstore I'd ever seen was a small, one-room, secondhand dive, he knew it wouldn't be hard to impress me. He also knew it was an offer I couldn't refuse. He smiled before I could even respond, obviously using his ability of Discernment to read the feelings written all over my face.

"Do I have to dress up?"

He looked me up and down, lingering on the ratty cuffs of my jeans. "Maybe a little bit. Would a skirt be out of the question?"

"I can probably handle a skirt."

"Okay, it sounds like we've come to an agreement then. Can you be ready to go in an hour?"

"Sure."

As we drove to the party, I began to wonder if my dad had invited me to meet friends and up his odds that I'd want to stay with him after Christmas. He'd hinted that he wanted me to stay longer, through the school year, but I figured I'd picked my mom's house for a reason. There must've been something about this life I didn't like. What would be the point in changing my mind now, after I'd gone through all the work of making the decision?

"What's up, kid?" my dad asked, patting my knee.

"Nothing."

"We don't have to stay long, okay?"

He picked up on the wrong anxiety, but I appreciated his concern anyway. And not staying long sounded great. "Thanks."

We turned onto a street where large houses loomed out of the darkness. Birds I couldn't see squawked in a noisy chorus from treetops. What kind of birds were so active in darkness?

The circular drive was full of cars when we pulled up. My palms were already sweating from the thought of the small talk that was about to ensue. I repeated my cover story in my mind as we exited the car. The taller-than-necessary front door stood partially ajar, and the noise of the party flowed down the walk-way. We let ourselves in, and my dad greeted several clusters of people as we made our way into the heart of the home.

"Ah! Coleman!" a broad-shouldered, gray-haired man called from across the room.

My dad waved and closed the distance between them. "Jenson. Thanks for having us. This is my daughter, Addie."

"Hi, Addie." He pumped my hand several times and then looked around. "Hmm, mine is roaming around here somewhere

31

and would be much better company than us old folks." The longer he searched the room, the more irritated he became. "Give me a minute." He pulled out his phone and dialed a number. "Are you upstairs?"

My dad and I exchanged a look, and I tried not to laugh.

"Could you please come down? I want you to meet someone."

Great, I was forcing someone to attend a party against their will. Perfect start to a friendship.

He hung up the phone. "While we're waiting, why don't you get some food? Here, let me show you the good stuff." He led the way to a table set up with food, and soon I had a heaping plateful in one hand and a soda in the other. So I had no free hands when his daughter joined us downstairs and we were introduced. She was really pretty, taller than me, with dark eyes and hair and a perfectly put-together outfit.

"Stephanie, I want you to meet Addie. Her father and I work together. Why don't you show her around?"

"Sure." She gestured for me to follow, and I did. When we were far enough away from our fathers, she said under her breath, "Okay, this food is nasty. My dad is a vegetarian and thinks tofu should be in everything. Believe me, you don't want anything to do with it." I followed her into the kitchen, and she dumped the whole plate into the garbage. "If you're hungry, I can find you something real."

"No, I'm good."

She smiled a perfect white smile. "So this is the kitchen." She pointed through an arched opening. "And that's the living room . . . and . . . did you really want the grand tour, or was that my dad's idea?"

"It was your dad's idea."

"That's what I thought. Come on, I'll show you the most important room. Mine."

Stephanie's room was like a yearbook of her life—pictures everywhere. And where there weren't pictures, there were pom-poms and cheer trophies. A large football poster hung on the wall, a heart drawn around one of the players. I walked closer and looked at the guy, surprised when I recognized him. Trevor. Dark wavy hair, high cheekbones, amazing eyes. He was just like I remembered him from the football game a couple of weeks ago . . . and from my weird vision or hallucination or whatever it was I had in the hospital. I was trying not to dwell on it. With his poster image staring me right in the face, my heart racing to life, it was hard not to think about it.

Why had I had such a realistic vision of someone I'd barely met? *Because your stupid ability is acting odd,* I told myself.

My fingers brushed the smooth surface of the poster, running down his face and then tracing the red heart drawn there once, then twice. "Is this your boyfriend?"

"Trevor? No. My ex. We were off and on for a while, but he has issues, and I'm tired of dealing with them."

"Issues?" I dropped my hand and shook it out, looking back at Stephanie.

"He got hurt last year and can't get past it."

Now my heart was thumping against my ribs for different

33

reasons as I remembered exactly why and how Trevor had gotten hurt. I turned away from her so she wouldn't see my face redden with a surge of anger toward Duke.

"I was so supportive for the longest time, even threw him a big party to help him get over his fears." She shook her head like she wasn't going to continue.

I cleared my throat, pushing my emotions down. "What happened?"

"I don't know. He shut me out after that."

"That sucks."

"I know. I'm just done with guys for a while."

Especially football players, I thought about adding, but instead said, "Me too."

"Oh yeah?"

"Long story."

"You want to know the worst part? We have the same friends, so I'm constantly running into him."

"I hate that." Running into arrogant ex-boyfriends was not high on my list of things I enjoyed doing either. I continued around her room, looking at more pictures. "Oh hey, that's Rowan, I know him."

She curled her lip. "You know Rowan?"

"Well, I don't know him very well, but my friend Laila knows him." *Or at least is well acquainted with his mouth.*

"Hmm." She shook her head. "Never heard of her." She grabbed a laptop from her desk and plopped onto her bed with it. "So are you going to Carter High now? I haven't seen you before."

"No, I'm just visiting my dad for the holidays."

"Your parents are divorced?"

"I guess it's not official or anything, but yeah."

"Oh, so it's fairly recent then?"

"About two months."

"Sorry."

I started to say, *It's okay,* but it didn't feel okay. "Yeah."

"My parents have been divorced for seven years."

I sat on the edge of her bed. "Does it get any easier?"

She gave me a look of empathy that seemed very sincere. "It totally does. I promise." She nodded her head toward her computer. "Do you ever chat online? We should exchange info."

"Sounds good."

Her computer dinged, and she glanced at it, then let out a sigh. "This is what I'm talking about."

"What?"

"Party at Trevor's the day after Thanksgiving. Sharing the same friends with your ex sucks." She typed a response in the chat window. "Do you want to come with me?"

At first I thought she was narrating her own typing, because she wasn't looking at me, but then she glanced up with a questioning eyebrow raise.

"Me?"

"Yeah. It would be nice to have a new face around. A friend who's mine and not one I share with Trevor. Maybe you can help me buffer some of the awkwardness."

I laughed. "I'm not a very good awkwardness buffer. I kind of create awkwardness."

"Even better."

I shrugged and my general loathing of parties almost made me say no thanks, but then I remembered my multicolored toenails and the extreme boredom awaiting me at my dad's house. And how when I had nothing to occupy my mind, it did a great job occupying itself with Duke. "Why not?"

CHAPTER 6

Laila: Know anything useful about motorcycles?

I walked up the drive to the open garage. Connor stood staring at a holographic image of a motorcycle. He slid the holograph simulator across the counter so the glowing image moved to fit perfectly over his real bike—the ghostlike replica giving the metal a hazy appearance. Then he picked up an engine part off the counter beside the simulator and turned it, trying to replicate the placement of the part.

"What happened to your bike?"

He looked up, surprise making a momentary appearance on his face before he went back to his task. "It had an unfavorable meeting with the pavement."

"Poor bike." I watched him for a little longer. A lock of hair fell across his forehead, and he pushed it out of his eyes. It was obvious he had been doing that all day by the grease streaks that lined his face. He had amazing hair—the perfect amount of body and shine.

I shifted on my feet, moving my hand to my hip. This would work a lot better if he looked at me, but his bike had all his attention. I finally got impatient. "I need something."

"What?"

Since the guy at the party had been reluctant to give his name, I figured Connor wouldn't openly admit he had ability advancement programs. I had to be careful in how I approached this: start with what I knew he had, then work my way up to the other things I needed. "I'm not sure. You offered me a block enhancer a few weeks ago at a party. I want it." It wasn't like I didn't want the block enhancer. After my dad had taken the grocery money, I needed something to keep him out of my head. My own mental blocks weren't strong enough yet.

"Give me one minute." He popped off a dented section on the front of his bike and sighed. "These aren't easy to get here."

"Maybe you should stop playing with Norm toys, then."

"This is not a Norm toy. It's a hybrid. If it were Norm-made, it would be gas-powered. It just has the body of a Norm bike. I think they look so much better."

I gave his holograph-cloaked bike a once-over. "Paint-covered metal, so beautiful."

He ran his hand along the seat, the tips of his fingers glowing blue as the light hit them. "Can't think of anything more beauti-ful." He met my eyes then, with his muddy green ones, like he expected me to challenge that statement. I didn't care what he thought was beautiful.

"If you get me the blocker, I'll give you and your bike some privacy."

"Funny."

I took a lap around his garage. It was like a collision of old meets new. The sleek shelves and high-tech tools next to the old, greasy parts. A case of oil sat on the shelf. So his motorcycle wasn't Norm, but he had something that was. Out the window, in his side yard, I saw the offender—a beat-up truck. He really did like Norm toys. I didn't understand people who collected old things. Didn't they appreciate how far we'd come? Whatever. It was none of my business. I just wanted his help.

I sat on a stool nearby. Now he was going slow on purpose. To make a point. I could tell by the way he studied the part in his hand, then looked at the image over and over. If he would just look at me more, I knew I could get him to do what I wanted. A small smile, a flip of my hair. Men weren't hard to manipulate. I was so tempted to Erase the last five minutes and step into the garage again for a do-over. This time he wouldn't be in control. I would.

"Do you ever sit still?"

"What?"

He pointed to my knee, which was bouncing all over the place.

"Most people don't make me wait." And by *people* I meant *guys*.

Connor wiped his hands on a towel and said, "I'll be right back. Stay."

I rolled my eyes.

He came back with a case and opened it, revealing several neat rows of electronic clips.

"Which one did you want? I forget."

"A block for Telepaths." I stood and peered over his shoulder into the case. "Does it work?"

He shrugged. "I'm just the middleman, Laila. I haven't tried all these. But my customers are usually very happy."

I pulled my card from my pocket. "I only have ten."

"Well then, I guess you're out of luck."

"How much is it?"

"Twenty."

"Bill me." I handed him my card, and he pressed the chip into my palm. He ran my card down a black strip on the inside of the lid, then handed it back to me. His case was full of other chips and drives. They were a good excuse to ease my way into what I really wanted to talk about. "Do you have anything for ability advancement?"

His eyes flashed to mine and then back down again. "Nope."

So he was going to be difficult. "Do you know anyone who does?"

"I only sell what I'm given. I don't ask questions."

"No questions? That's not very smart. Didn't think you were

such a brainless follower, but I guess I was wrong."

His eyes revealed only mild humor, not the anger I was hoping my comment would inspire. Anger was so much more telling. "I know what I need to know, and the rest is none of my business and definitely not any of yours."

"Who's your supplier?"

"Confidential."

"I'm not trying to take over your business, Connor. I just need information."

"You're looking in the wrong place." His hand hovered on the lid of the open case. "Now, did you need anything else?"

I had done this all wrong. He obviously had information, and I'd put him on the defensive. I lifted my hand ever so slightly and concentrated hard. Ten minutes. That's all I'd take back, and then I'd try again. I'd be sweeter this time or more flirty. Act innocent, not demanding. I searched for the paths in his mind that I needed to block. His mind felt stiff. Usually I had no trouble quickly blocking the few active paths where I could feel the short-term memories had been stored. But as I tried to perform that task on him, the energy in them didn't die. It only waned slightly and then sprang back to life.

He tilted his head. "Is that a no?"

I tried not to visually react to my failure, even though I wanted to demand how he'd done that. I hid my shock by studying the items in his case. "What are those?" On a raised portion, a variety of different metal devices were displayed. On closer inspection, I saw one even looked like a fly.

"Way out of your price range."

"But . . . are they listening devices?"

He pointed to the row of winged bugs. "These are listening devices. This row is tracking devices."

"They look so real."

He slammed the case shut. I tried a memory wipe one more time, but it didn't work. Tucking the chip into my pocket, I left his garage. What was wrong with me? Was I losing my ability? No. That was impossible. He must've been using something that protected him from Memory Erasers. Did he know that was my ability?

I'd get information from him. I'd just have to find another way.

CHAPTER 7

Addie: Must reread the Compound secrecy agreement.

I was under the table, because it was the only quiet corner of the bookstore. I found three books right away that I wanted, but apparently my dad was a browser. My dad was right—the bookstore was amazing, and normally my dad's browsing wouldn't have been a bad thing. I would've explored every corner of the place. But today was kids' day or something, because a million kids who didn't know how to use indoor voices had taken over the store. So with my purse as a pillow, I started reading a graphic novel under a table.

"What are you doing?"

I lowered the book to see a little boy staring at me between the slats of a wooden chair. "I'm reading."

"That's a boy book."

"A boy book? It is not."

"Is too."

"Says who?" Why was I arguing back?

"It's about shooting. Girls don't like shooting books."

"Well, I do, and I'm pretty sure I'm a girl." I pointed to the book he held. "What do you have?"

Apparently thinking that was an invitation to join me, he pulled out the chair and plopped on the floor in its place, then held up the book. *Spaceships*. "I'm learning to draw. My brother is teaching me."

At least he was a kid with good taste and seemed to be able to talk at a normal volume. "That's cool."

He offered it to me. I took it and flipped through a few pages, which illustrated steps to drawing different spaceships.

"This one kind of looks like the *Millennium Falcon*, don't you think?"

He squinted at the picture. "Yeah, but the *Millennium Falcon* has a dish thing on top."

"True, but you could always add that."

I shut his book and handed it back. "Have fun drawing. Those are going to be cool."

"Girls shouldn't know what the *Millennium Falcon* is either." I could tell he was trying to be funny. I looked at him closer. He couldn't have been much older than eight.

"Who are you hiding from?" he asked.

"Nobody . . . everybody. I just wanted a quiet place to read."

I glanced around. "What about you? I bet your mom is looking for you."

"My mom's not here. She's at work. I'm here with my brother. He brings me to story time every week."

"That's nice of him. So, don't you think he's worried about you?"

He looked up as if considering this and then furrowed his brow. "Ew, there's gum under here."

"Come on, I'm going to help you find your brother, okay?" This place was huge, and I could imagine his brother frantically looking for him in the mob scene. Plus, I obviously wasn't getting any reading done. I slid out from under the table and tucked my books under one arm.

"What does he look like?"

"Who?"

"Darth Vader."

"Huh?"

"Your brother, of course."

"Oh, uh . . ." He screwed up his face. "He has brown hair and big muscles."

I laughed. "Okay, that might help." We walked the entire perimeter of the upstairs area and didn't find his brother anywhere, so I led him toward the stairs.

"There he is!" The little boy pointed over the railing.

I followed his gaze, prepared to see the brown-haired, big-muscled guy, and felt my mouth open a little. "Trevor." My heart gave a flip that surprised me.

It shouldn't have surprised me. Trevor was even cuter in

person than in his pictures in Stephanie's room and a lot cuter than I remembered him being at the football game. Not the obvious cute. In fact, taken individually, his features were a little off: his lashes too long, his nose slightly crooked, his cheekbones too high. And yet as a whole, they made him uniquely attractive.

"Trevor!" the little boy yelled.

Trevor looked up, pointed at him, and then pointed at the ground beside him. As in, *Get your butt down here.*

"Looks like you're in trouble," I said.

"He pretends like he's mad, but he never really is."

I laughed.

"I better go." He rounded the railing and took off down the stairs at a run. Halfway down, he turned and waved good-bye to me. I saw his misstep, the way his heel nicked the edge of the stair, causing him to lose his balance. He was going to fall the rest of the way down the wooden staircase. My breath caught, but then the world slowed.

The boy flew in the air, slowly careening backward, ready to land on his spine. I let go of my books, and as they swam toward the floor, I rushed forward and positioned myself below him. Then I directed him toward my lap, wrapping both arms around his waist and bracing my feet against the stair below me. It was a good thing I did, because the minute I touched him, he plopped into my lap. His momentum jerked me forward a little, but I was able to maintain my grip on the stair with my shoes.

I sat there for several deep breaths, not letting go, while the world around us took its time returning to normal speed. Then I

46

panicked. I'd just used my ability in a store full of Norms. It was over, wasn't it? I was in huge trouble. But when I looked around, nobody was even paying attention. Nobody was looking at us. Well, except Trevor.

He took the stairs two at a time and, when he arrived in front of us, squatted down. "Are you okay, Brody?" he asked, smoothing the boy's hair out of his face.

"I almost fell."

"Yes, you did. You scared me."

I let go of Brody's waist and he slid off me sideways, leaving Trevor and me face-to-face without a barrier. He met my eyes, his chest brushing lightly against my knees. "Are you okay?"

My heart beat out of control from where it seemed to have taken up residence in my throat. I stared at him in shock. This was my vision in the hospital. The wooden staircase, Trevor and his question. Why? Could I see the future without Searching now? Why had my brain picked this moment? I leaned back on my elbows as a wave of pain struck behind my eyes, causing Trevor's image to blur. I tried not to cringe. "I'm fine. Just need to catch my breath."

He looked up the stairs and then back to me. "You came out of nowhere."

"No, I was on my way down too. You probably didn't see me. I'm just glad he's okay."

He stayed kneeling in front of me, but reached a few feet to my right and picked up my purse. I had no idea how it ended up there. I had probably let go of it halfway down the stairs. I wasn't

47

sure if it was his hair or his deodorant that I got a whiff of as he stretched to reach it, but it smelled amazing.

"Thanks," I said, breathless, when he handed me my purse.

He nodded and stood, then held out his hand. I took it, letting him help me to my feet.

He ruffled Brody's hair. "You sure you're okay, kid?"

He scrunched his face up, and I held my breath. Once I had pulled him onto my lap, had he been able to see the world in slow motion around us like I had?

"Your books," Brody said. "Where'd they go?" He looked down the stairs, like he would find them in a heap at the bottom. I knew they were at the top, confirming that I hadn't been on my way down at all and had been way too far away from Brody to catch him like I had.

"I put them down up there, when we saw Trevor, remember?" I pointed.

"No, you didn't."

"I'll get them for you," Trevor said.

"That's okay," I objected, but he was already walking up and up and was probably realizing just how far I had come in less than a second. When he finally reached my books, I noticed they were scattered, as though dropped in a hurry. He squatted down and picked them up one at a time and then shifted his gaze between them and Brody and me for a few beats before coming down again.

"Thank you," I said, taking them from him. The confused look on Trevor's face made me know I needed to quickly get his mind off the books and what he had witnessed. "Well, good to meet you, Brody. Have fun drawing your spaceships."

I walked down, and they followed.

"Have we met before?" Trevor asked.

Apparently, I wasn't very memorable. "Yes, we sort of met at a football game a couple weeks ago."

"So how do you know my brother?"

"I don't. We just met here." I pointed up the stairs.

"She was under a table reading comics," Brody said with a smile.

Trevor's already lowered brows got lower.

"She wanted to be alone," Brody whispered loudly.

Trevor studied me for a moment. "A football game?" Then recognition came into his eyes. "You're Duke Rivers' girlfriend."

He must've been a Duke fan. Like every other football player seemed to, he probably thought Duke was amazing. I knew something that would make him hate Duke in under a second flat. I had the strongest desire to share it with him. "No, no, no . . . no," I said both to answer his question and to stop myself from saying what I really wanted to.

He smiled. "Are you sure?"

"Sorry, it's just . . . we broke up." *And he and his buddies screwed up your shoulder.*

He nodded, then looked at his brother. "Well, Brody, we better let . . . um . . ."

"Addie," I filled in for him.

"Addie?"

"Short for Addison."

"We better let Addison go. Tell her thank you."

"Thank you, Addison," Brody said.

Trevor took a step back. "Maybe we'll see you around." He gave one last glance up the stairs to where my books had been, his eyes flashing suspicion. Was this why my brain had warned me about this moment, about Trevor? Because he was someone I needed to be careful around? Make sure nothing about the Compound slipped?

"Yeah, maybe." I waved and then turned on one foot and made a beeline for the nearest bookshelf. Once safely behind it, I leaned against it and tried to quell the pounding in my skull.

At home later, my head still ached. I tried a few mind patterns, which helped a little, then headed for my bed, thinking a good nap would heal me completely. It didn't. I tried to analyze when and why this was happening. The added ability wouldn't have weirded me out so much—abilities grew and expanded all the time—if it didn't come along with this massive headache.

I rubbed my temples and watched the light on my ceiling dance as the heater blew the drapes. I hadn't Searched anything since Bobby's house. What if I just tried a simple Search, two minutes? The choice: Should I get up and get some water or should I stay in bed and stare at the ceiling? I would Search that easy choice.

I took a deep breath and drew on the energies. I felt the cold glass in my hands and the memory of water trickling down my throat. It layered with the other memory of staying where

I was, the pillow fluffed up around me. Just when I thought I had nothing to worry about, a pain so intense I had to push my palms to my temples radiated through my head.

I rolled onto my stomach and pressed my face into the pillow. It took a few minutes for the pain to dull. I took a deep breath and forced the tension out of my shoulders. Then I rolled out of bed.

After I walked to the kitchen and took my first drink of water, my dad came in through the garage door.

"You're home," I said. It sounded more like a sigh than the happy declaration I was going for.

He set a bag of groceries on the counter. "Not feeling well?" It must've been pretty obvious.

"Headache." I thought about all the things that might happen if I told my dad what was going on with my ability. Would he send me home to have tests run? "I've been getting them lately." I chose my words carefully. I didn't want him to worry if this really was nothing. "Is that normal?"

"When do they come on?"

"Right after I Search." I left out the part about being able to slow down time.

"That can be normal." His eyes looked worried. I may not have been a lie detector, but his look seemed to oppose his reassurance. "Why don't you rest your ability for a few weeks and we'll see how you feel then?"

I thought about pressing him. But resting my ability sounded nice. I needed a break. This had to work itself out.

CHAPTER 8

Laila: Your hot ex-boyfriend is annoying.

Take-out bag clutched firmly in hand, I headed for the door of the diner. I'd almost reached it when I saw his blond hair out of the corner of my eye. Duke. I stopped, then backed up and plopped down at the table across from him.

"Where's your fan club?"

He met my gaze, and a smile formed on his lips. Was that just habit, or was he seriously happy to see me? Because I'd be the last person I'd want to see if I were him. "Laila."

"You remember my name? I thought I took care of that."

His smile faltered for a split second. Then he must've decided I was joking, because it was back in full force. Why hadn't I ever

Erased any of Duke's memories? Guilt. I didn't think I deserved to have Duke look at me normally after what I'd done to Addie. And yet here he was, looking at me like nothing had happened. The boy had nerve.

"You're going to have a nice future working for the Containment Committee, since you seem to have absolutely no problem wiping unsuspecting people of their memories."

It's what everyone assumed a Memory Eraser would do—work for the CC. Erase the memories of Norms who had found out about the Compound. "Such a noble profession," Mr. Caston had claimed one time when we were forced to fill out a Your Future form in class. I had written *Designer,* and he had clucked his tongue and shook his head and said, "What a waste of a perfectly usable ability. Not everyone gets something that can translate into such a noble profession." Blah, blah, blah. He could take my noble profession and combine it with his noble profession and save the world with them. My ability was for me and the memories I wanted to keep to myself.

"This coming from a boy who had to feed his girlfriend emotions in order for her to stay with him."

He glanced around, then asked, "Where is Addie?"

"Went to stay with her dad for the holidays."

He took a bite of his burger. "I hope I had nothing to do with that decision."

You had everything to do with that decision, jerk. That's what I wished I could say, but I didn't want to give him the satisfaction.

"Why would you?"

"So why'd she go then?"

I tried to think of something that would really bother him, because I knew that despite what Addie thought, Duke still had lingering feelings for her. Once Addie let someone in, she was impossible to forget. There was something about her that crawled inside a person and built a nice comfy home there, her goodness expanding until it filled every limb. Without her, there was only hollow emptiness. And I knew Duke was feeling that. I could see it on his face when he said her name.

I also knew that Addie had feelings for him. I would not let him hurt her again. Because he would. It's who he was. He slithered around in a person until he found what he wanted and then took it, leaving a different kind of hollowness, the kind that felt like something had been stolen. "Not that it's any of your business, but she's visiting a guy she knows there."

"She is?" Even though his smile remained plastered on his face, I could see in his eyes that my statement had hit the mark.

I fished in my memory for the name of that cute cowboy she had her eye on. "Trevor."

"Trevor? She knows Trevor?"

"They started talking after that football game." Addie would kill me if she knew I was blatantly lying like this, but whatever, it was worth it for the new look on Duke's face—defeat. I sighed. No, I wasn't doing this for her, I was doing it for me.

I stood.

"Wait."

I lifted my hand slightly. Speaking of keeping my memories

54

to myself: A five-minute wipe should do it. Right before I sent the burst of energy his way, I remembered how my ability had failed on Connor. That worry sank in for a brief second, and then I gave a push. I felt the paths in his mind easily close and smiled. I was fine. A thrill that I had long ago come to associate with power trickled through my body. Power was an amazing feeling.

I let my hand fall limply back to my side. Maybe I *was* the type of person who could work for the Containment Committee. Twisted. I had about three seconds before Duke would come back to full awareness. Feeling a little sick to my stomach, I turned and left.

Just as I reached the door, Duke called, "Laila! Hey."

I turned. "What?"

"I didn't even see you there. Where's Addie?"

"Not here."

At first I didn't notice the tugging on my emotions. I thought maybe my anger toward him was just softening to pity; that maybe I was feeling bad for just wiping our conversation from his memory. But when a surge of joy pumped through my chest, I snarled. I marched to his table. "Knock it off."

He shrugged and held up the last bite of his burger. "I seem to be missing more of my burger than I remember eating, so turnabout's fair play." The smile didn't leave his face, and again a surge of happiness shot through me. It felt so good I almost melted to the seat in front of him. It reminded me of how he had manipulated me in the first place. This feeling. I loved this feeling. And then I knew he could help me.

"I need your help."

"Excuse me?" He popped the last bite of burger into his mouth.

"You need to convince Connor Bradshaw to tell me some things."

"Is there a question in there somewhere?"

"No. You owe me."

"Tell me what exactly we're convincing Connor of and I might consider helping you."

"You'll see. It's something for Addie." It was low of me to use his feelings for Addie against him, but being low didn't bother me. Especially if it yielded results. "Meet me in front of your house on Saturday at noon." I stayed there for five more seconds, letting the happiness he offered snake through my arms and extend to my fingertips. Then I pushed away from the table and walked out the door. The happiness that had been dancing patterns inside my chest was gone, and I realized how seldom that feeling existed in me and why I had been so desperate to keep it.

CHAPTER 9

Addie: Is there such a thing as death by water bottle?

"Are you sure Trevor is going to be okay with you bringing me?" I sat in the passenger seat of Stephanie's car the day after Thanksgiving, wondering if this was a good idea. Especially after the show I put on for Trevor at the bookstore. I wondered if I should tell Stephanie that I ran into him the other day. Is that what friends did? But I didn't want to make a big deal about it. I didn't want her to think I was trying to make a play for her ex or anything, no matter how much she claimed she was done with his issues. And really, it was no big deal. We had run into each other. We barely talked.

"Trevor won't care at all that I'm bringing you. He's like the nicest guy ever."

"I thought he had issues."

"Oh, he has issues, but he keeps them to himself, remember? That was one of the issues. He doesn't talk to anyone, really, at least not about anything deep. Not even Rowan. And speaking of Rowan . . . ," Stephanie said. "You said you knew him."

"Yes."

"He'll be here, I'm sure. But a word of warning—he's not exactly my favorite person."

I had sensed that from our last conversation about him. I tried to remember Rowan's personality from the football game. He seemed nice enough, maybe a little hyper. Laila liked him a lot. "Why?"

"Let's just say that when Trevor and I were together, Rowan didn't want us to be. He constantly sabotaged our relationship. I think he was jealous."

"Why?"

"He was mad I took Trevor away from guy dates."

"I see."

"So anyway, if my witchy-ness comes out around him, I'm sorry, I can't help myself."

I laughed. "I completely understand."

We weren't the first ones to arrive. Several cars were parked in front of his house, which was good. The more people, the less I had to talk. Stephanie had to park a few houses down. She cut the engine, smoothed her hair, straightened her skirt, reapplied her lip gloss, and then got out of the car. It was a lot of primping for someone who claimed to be over the person we were about to see.

We walked up the path, and the sun reflected off something in the tree, catching my eye. At first I thought it was a bird, but that made no sense considering birds weren't metallic, and when I looked again, it was gone. Stephanie knocked on the door.

Trevor answered. "Hey, Stephanie," he said, and then looked over at me, his eyes widening slightly in surprise. "Oh, Addison. Hi."

My cheeks warmed. "I hope it's okay that I came."

"Of course."

"I didn't realize you two knew each other already," Stephanie said, an edginess to her voice.

"We don't, really," I answered quickly. "We have a mutual acquaintance. Duke Rivers."

"Come in." He stepped aside, and we walked into the house. The smells of nutmeg and cinnamon hung in the air as Trevor led us down the stairs into a large rec room. The smells reminded me of the sorry attempt my dad and I had made at Thanksgiving dinner yesterday.

"Steph!" Rowan called out from where he sat in a beanbag. He did a back roll out of it and came rushing over. "Hey."

He stuck his hand out to me. "I'm Rowan."

I shook his hand. "Yeah, we met at a football game a couple weeks ago."

He looked confused. I rolled my eyes, knowing he probably only remembered one thing about that night. "I was with my friend Laila."

"Laila . . ." He trailed off, obviously coming up empty.

What the . . . ? Hadn't he kissed Laila all night? I didn't

think that was easy to forget.

I tried to give Stephanie a look that would say, *Maybe he is a little weird*, but she had already slipped away. I assumed it was because she didn't want to hang out with Rowan.

Trevor pointed. "We're getting ready to start the movie. You can go get some food and then pick a seat."

"Is there water somewhere?"

"There's a fridge right outside that door, in the garage. It's full of water and Coke and stuff."

"Thanks."

I walked into the garage, and the heavy door automatically shut behind me. I waited for the lights to come on with my movement but then remembered they didn't have sensors here. It was pitch-black, and I couldn't see a thing. I kneed a few solid objects before I finally thought to pull out my phone for the light. I found the wall and flipped on the switch. With the lights now on, and my phone out, I dialed Laila's number.

"Are you dying without me?" she answered on the second ring.

"What have you done?"

"You're going to have to give me a time range, because I've done a lot of things."

"You Erased his memory, didn't you?"

"How did you find out?"

"I just talked to him."

She grunted. "I don't believe he told you. Why were you talking to him, anyway?"

"Because he's at this party. Wait, who are you talking about?" I asked at the same exact time she did.

"The fact that you have to ask, Laila, really scares me. How many memories have you Erased? I'm talking about Rowan."

She gave a little laugh. "Oh yeah. Rowan. How is he?"

"Clueless. Who were you talking about?"

"Maybe Duke."

"You Erased Duke's memory?" I tried not to register the tiny bit of hope that sprang up inside me over that thought. If he couldn't remember me, I didn't have to feel like such a fool every time I saw him. Instead I concentrated on the overwhelming amount of indignation I felt about it.

"Just five minutes of them."

"Why, Laila? Why would you do that to someone without their permission? That is so wrong on so many levels."

"Duke deserved it. And as far as Rowan goes, it was the humane thing to do. I couldn't leave his memories of kissing me intact, or he would've searched the world and come up empty. No girl would've ever lived up to me. It would've been tragic. This way he has a chance at happiness."

"There is something very wrong with you."

She laughed.

"Stop Erasing memories."

"You're no fun."

"I better go. I'm at this lame party."

Laila blew air between her lips. "You think all parties are lame."

"Exactly." I smiled and hung up. When I turned around, my breath caught in my throat because Trevor stood just inside the door. His face was relaxed, so I wasn't sure if he'd heard my conversation, including the part about Erasing memories, or if he had just walked in.

"I was looking for the water."

"It's in the fridge." He pointed, then went there himself. He handed me a water and pulled out a few sodas.

"Thanks."

"Not a problem," he said, and then headed to the door.

"It's an inside joke," I blurted out, pretty sure he had at least heard the last part of my conversation.

He turned back around. "What?"

"I think all parties are lame. I'm kind of antisocial. So it was just a joke. Your party is fine."

He nodded. "All parties *are* lame, but what am I supposed to do when people invite themselves over?" He leaned his shoulder against the wall, his eyes shining with a teasing smile.

"Hey." I laughed. "Stephanie invited me. I promise."

"Well, you did recently save my brother. . . ." His relaxed position became a little tense with the mention. Was it the thought of his brother falling that caused the change in his demeanor, or did he suspect my secret? It was hard to believe that someone without any knowledge of the Compound could come to any sort of real conclusion. But he had witnessed me move faster than any human should and then possibly overheard me asking Laila about Erasing memories.

My mind flashed to the man in the Tower with the scar across his cheek. Crap. Did Trevor overhearing my talk with Laila count as me telling someone? I looked around as if someone could be watching me, right now, in Trevor's dimly lit garage. Was that even possible?

The way Trevor trailed off about me saving his brother made it seem like he expected me to finish his sentence, fill in the blank he wasn't seeing. When I didn't say anything, he opened the door. "The movie's about to start." And with those words, he walked inside.

I followed after him and looked around for Stephanie. She was squeezed in between two girls on the couch, laughing and talking. So much for feeling out of place. Rowan came up next to me, popping the tab on his soda and taking a long drink. "Hey."

"Hi."

"Did you have a good Thanksgiving yesterday?"

"Yes. Ate too much, slept a lot. The norm." But really it wasn't the norm. It was odd. My first holiday away from my mom. My dad acted weird and nervous and kept asking me if I wanted anything else. Maybe for the next little while I'd celebrate holidays away from both my parents. Twenty years or so should do it.

I probably sounded more bitter than I meant to, because Rowan said, "Well, if you want something out of the ordinary, you should let me show you around town."

"Um . . . yeah, sure."

"You want to sit down?"

"I think I'll just stand for a while."

He gave me a once-over, almost like the reason I didn't want to sit with him would be written somewhere on my body. "Where did you say we met again?"

"At a football game. I go to Lincoln High."

"Ohh. That's right. Duke's girlfriend."

"No." I said the word with some hostility, then sealed my lips to keep from adding more.

"Well, that's good. I was going to say that I was surprised Trevor invited you here. He's not a fan of Duke's."

"He's not?"

"At the last football game he found out Duke and some of his lackeys have been playing dirty. Purposely injuring the competition. Trevor was one of the victims. Ruined his career."

"Purposely?" How much did they know? Was it possible they knew about abilities? Was that why Trevor seemed so suspicious when he saw me save his brother?

"Cheating. Hitting after the whistle. Just dirty plays. And Trevor had a lot of respect for Duke, so when he found this out, it really bothered him."

I took a relieved breath. Those were all things any Norm could do. "So he doesn't like Duke." Maybe the suspicion I'd sensed in Trevor was really just his feelings about Duke. Maybe seeing me reminded him of Duke.

"That's an understatement. No worries, though, he's a good Southern boy, so he'll be polite to you."

I started to respond that he *had* been nice to me when I

realized what Rowan was saying—that it was an act. Was Trevor forcing himself to be kind to me? He probably really wished I hadn't been invited to the party.

The television went blue and the movie started. With a wave, Rowan took his place back on the beanbag.

I settled into a chair along the back wall, crossed my arms, and tried to watch the movie. Every time Trevor laughed, a wave of frustration washed through me. He was going to judge me because of Duke? I finished my water and had an overwhelming desire to throw the empty bottle at the back of Trevor's head. Why was I having such a strong reaction to him? I didn't care what he thought of me. I resisted releasing the bottle in the air, by twisting it around and around in my hands. Soon, the paper around the bottle had turned to a shredded mess.

After the movie, Stephanie craned her head around. She pointed to the now empty cushion on the couch next to her like she wondered why I hadn't sat there. I was new at this friend-making thing. I walked over and sat down.

"I wondered where you disappeared to," she said.

"I sat back there."

She introduced me to her friends, and then they picked up whatever conversation they had been having before I sat down . . . something about comics?

"Graphic novels are cool," I said. When all three of them stopped and looked at me, I realized they must've been on the other side of that opinion, so I added, "What did you think of the movie?"

That did the trick, and they started talking again. A couple of empty soda cans sat on the coffee table in front of us, and I wondered if Stephanie would get the hint I was ready to leave if I started to clean.

I gathered some cans and then headed to the garage, where I saw a large recycle bin. When I came back in, Trevor and Stephanie were talking. I observed her body language for a minute, the way she leaned toward him, how she twirled a section of her dark hair around her finger and laughed too loudly at whatever he said. She was not over him. But it was more than obvious he was over her. He looked at anything but her, his arms were crossed over his chest, and for every small step she took toward him, he took a step back. If they talked for too long, he would eventually back into the wall. Despite his body language, though, he was doing exactly what Rowan had claimed he did—being friendly by smiling and nodding at whatever she was saying. Poor Stephanie. It sucked to be in a one-sided relationship.

"Addison!" I turned at my name and saw Brody barreling toward me. I was surprised when he wrapped his arms around my waist.

"Hey. I didn't know you lived here," I said, teasing him.

"Yeah, Trevor's my brother, remember?"

"Oh yeah. How could I forget? How's the drawing going?"

He took hold of my hand and pulled me toward the hall. "Come see. I drew the *Millennium Falcon*. It's so cool."

"Okay, slow down, we wouldn't want you falling down any stairs."

66

He gave a little giggle. "You were fast that day. Really fast. Trevor says you were at the top. How did you do it?"

"No, he just doesn't remember. I was already walking down."

"That's what my dad said, but then Trevor said, 'Dad, she's beautiful. I remember where she was standing.'"

My cheeks heated up with the compliment at the same time that my stomach clenched at the implication. Not only did Trevor suspect something, but he was telling people. Great.

"You have a good little memory, don't you?" I wondered how good. Did he remember time slowing down? When I had touched him, he came into the moment with me while the world around us continued to swim. Was it possible he couldn't see what I saw?

"Yup," he said innocently, and led me down the hall.

"Where are we going exactly?"

"Trevor's room."

I stopped and jerked him to a halt with my abrupt movement. "Can you just bring your drawings out here? I probably shouldn't go into your brother's room."

"Okay, wait here."

"Waiting." The hall was filled with family pictures taken over Trevor's and Brody's lifetimes. Not just formal ones, of them stiffly posing for a camera in a studio, but candid ones as well. Camping, boating, barbecuing. A lifetime of memories. Could those memories be gone in the blink of an eye if the Compound found out that Trevor might be onto something? Surely Scar-Face didn't mean a complete memory wipe. He just meant the memories about the Compound, about abilities. Didn't he? I wasn't ready for my memories to be wiped either from one little slipup. Trevor needed to believe I was completely Normal. How could I convince him of that?

CHAPTER 10

Laila: What's that lame saying about a pen and a sword?
It might be true.

The difference between Duke and other Mood Controllers was that Connor wouldn't be anticipating Duke's ability. And if, like the rest of the school, Connor still thought Duke was Telekinetic, then maybe it could work to our advantage. It was the first time in the last two weeks I was glad I hadn't announced to the whole school what Duke was, like I had wanted to.

"What's Connor's ability?" I asked Duke as we drove to his house.

"I'm not sure. He was in a lot of Bobby's classes, so maybe he can manipulate mass."

The way he said Bobby's name so casually made me flinch a little. As if Bobby was still just his neighbor and best friend, not a convicted murderer. I cleared my throat and shook off the feeling. "I thought you knew everyone's ability. Addie said you printed off some roster from the school computers."

"Yeah, but I was only interested in certain abilities. I didn't pay attention to the others."

He was only interested in the abilities that would get him what he wanted—a look at his future. I tried to hold back the growl rising up my throat. "When you get home, look it up for me."

"I would, but I destroyed that list."

"Then get another one printed off."

"One, it's not as easy as you make it sound. And two, you'd have to fill me in on some more details in order for me to become that invested. Last time I schemed, it kind of blew up in my face. I'm sure you remember."

He parked in front of Connor's house and shut off the engine.

How could I forget, seeing as how I was one of the pawns in his scheme? My phone chimed, and I read the screen. It was from Eli: *Think of something.* I smiled. I had told him last night that if he asked me that one more time I was going to think of his death in vivid detail. I texted back: *Ha-ha. You wish you could read my mind from five miles away.* As much as the thought of him reading my mind at all bothered me, I really wished he would at least pick up on something here or there.

I looked over at Duke. "When did you Present?"

"I was twelve. Worst day of my dad's life. He wanted a Telekinetic son. He got me."

I wasn't exactly the type that people opened up to, so I wasn't sure what to do with that information. "Whining makes you less attractive. Don't do it anymore."

He laughed.

I glanced up the drive. Once again, the garage door was open. Connor was tinkering around inside. The boy loved his bike. I took a deep breath and shook out my hands. I wasn't used to talking to a guy without the safety net of being able to Erase whatever I wanted to when the conversation was over.

"So what do you want me to do again?" Duke asked.

"Trust. He needs to feel trust. Comfort. Ease." I cleared my throat. "And a little lust never hurt anyone."

Duke shook his head. "I don't think he needs my help with that one. Isn't that the one emotion you have control over?"

"He doesn't like me. He'd rather date his motorcycle."

"Is that a first for you?"

"Shut up. Just do it. And for the love of all that is living, try to be subtle about it."

He leaned close to me. "If I remember right, you didn't suspect anything."

I shoved him back. "Stay out of my bubble, pretty boy."

We got out of the car. I kept at least a foot of space between Duke and me as we walked up the drive and into Connor's garage. He didn't seem as surprised to see me this time. "I don't give refunds," he said, wiping at an already shiny piece of metal on his bike.

"I don't want a refund. Just a friendly chat."

71

"Hey, Connor," Duke said, his annoying smile painted across his face. "Nice bike."

I should've told him not to talk. To just stand to the side like the shiny little toy that he was. I didn't even know why I bothered bringing him. Connor had probably mastered blocks for all the abilities, like he had with mine.

"Thanks," Connor said, and I could've sworn his tone was a little less edgy than his original greeting. Maybe Duke would be useful after all.

I turned my back to Connor and mouthed the word *Trust* to Duke, who gave a slight nod.

"It *is* a nice bike," I said. "Looks like she's all fixed up from her meeting with the pavement. Addie told me what happened. Crazy. You're lucky you didn't hit her."

"I don't think luck had anything to do with it," he said.

What did he want me to do, tell him he was awesome because he managed to avoid hitting my friend at the last second? I ran my hand along the seat, testing his reaction. When he didn't flinch, I threw my leg over and sat.

"What do you want, Laila?" Connor asked evenly.

"Just what I always wanted." I met his eyes. "Information." *Come on, Duke, make him feel trust.* "What would it hurt? I won't even mention where I got it from."

"They're not stupid. They'll be able to make that deduction."

"It's not like I'm some narc. I'm a customer. A paying customer."

"A partially paying customer."

"I'll pay you back. That's not the point, though. The point is that I need help and I'm willing to pay for it."

"Ability advancement. That's what you're after?"

I felt Duke's gaze shift to me in the background, but I didn't turn to look at him. "Yes. Just a name. I'll figure out the rest on my own."

He tilted his head at Duke, and for a second I worried that maybe he felt Duke crawling inside him, but then, without looking at me, he said, "Get off my bike."

I used his shoulder, acting like I needed it for the task. As I did, I gave a quick glance back to Duke. I could tell by the set of his perma-grin and the intense look in his eyes that he was concentrating hard on his task. I squeezed Connor's shoulder as I straightened up and then dug a pen and scrap of paper out of my purse. "Just a name."

He grabbed the pen and paper and began writing. I tried to keep the heightened beat of my heart to myself, but it sounded like it was broadcasting to the ends of the earth.

"I will give you information on one condition."

"Sure."

"When you go, you take me with you."

"Fine," I said, even though I didn't mean it. He handed me the paper and I looked at it. "This is just an address."

"I'll give you the name when we go." And then he said, "Hey, Duke."

"Yeah."

Before Duke could even finish the word, Connor threw the

pen at him like a knife, end over end. It stuck into his shoulder for a beat before falling to the floor. "Telekinetic, huh?"

"Ouch," Duke said, rubbing at his shoulder.

"Don't ever try to mess with my head again," he said to Duke, "or I'll mess with yours. And believe me when I say you don't want me inside your head."

I grabbed Duke by the arm and left before Connor had a chance to change his mind. We headed down the driveway to the car.

"He drew blood," Duke said, pulling his hand off his shoulder and showing me his bloody palm.

"Remember what I said about whining."

"I didn't even think it was working, but . . . he drew blood."

I held up the paper. "But we got what we came for." My ability was about to be maximized.

"You're welcome."

CHAPTER 11

Addie: Saving Norms from themselves is exhausting.

"Addison?" Trevor walked down the dimly lit hall. "Is everything okay?"

"Hi." I whirled away from my intent study of his past, displayed in frames on the wall. "I mean, yes. I'm fine."

"The bathroom is at the very end on the right."

"Huh? Oh. No, I'm not looking for the bathroom. I'm waiting for your brother. He wanted to show me some pictures he drew."

He looked over my shoulder to the door behind which Brody had disappeared and smiled. "He likes you."

Trevor's smile seemed so genuine that despite what Rowan

had implied, and how I had just witnessed the evidence of its use on Stephanie, it made me smile. "He's cute." I pointed to the bedroom. "Your brother." I bit my lip, not knowing why I felt the need to add the qualifier to that statement. Of course I was talking about his brother.

Trevor looked at his hands and then back up at me, through his amazing lashes. "He doesn't like a lot of people."

"Well, I have a slight advantage. . . ."

"You saved him."

"I was going to say that I know what the *Millennium Falcon* is, but I guess saving him worked too."

He laughed. "*Star Wars* knowledge is a big advantage." He tilted his head as if remembering something. "So you really were under the table at the bookstore reading comics."

I scrunched my nose. "Yes, and just because your brother and I like the same books doesn't make me immature."

"No. I'm impressed. I . . ." He hesitated, like he wasn't sure if he wanted to share whatever he was thinking. I remembered Stephanie saying he was private, so it surprised me when he continued. "I draw comics. Or attempt to."

"You do? Online somewhere?"

"No. Nothing so public."

"Wow, that's cool." How could he be impressed that I read them, when he wrote them?

"So are you moving to Dallas then?" he asked.

I took the hint—he was ready to change the subject. I'd have to ask him more about his comics later. "No. My dad lives here.

76

I'm visiting for the holidays. I just needed a break from things."
I regurgitated the story the Compound had approved, like I was
reading it off a paper. For a minute I thought he would call me
on it.

But he only nodded and didn't ask for any clarification.

"Duke. I needed a break from Duke." Why was I telling
him this? That definitely wasn't in my packet. Maybe because
I wanted him to know I wasn't a fan of Duke either. Maybe
because he had just shared something personal with me. Maybe
because I hadn't been able to talk to anyone about it. Even
though I tried not to hold it against her, Laila had been a part of
the heartbreak, and I didn't feel comfortable talking to her about
it. Probably because every time I tried she got this guilty expression on her face and couldn't stop saying sorry. It was easier to
talk to a total stranger—especially this total stranger, for some
reason. "He was using me." I hadn't said that out loud before. It
still hurt.

"For what?"

Oh crap. *Well, Trevor, he wanted me to tell him his future.* I
couldn't say that. So what might a Normal guy use a Normal
girl for? My face went red as I thought of the main possibility.
"Not for that. We weren't . . . He just needed help . . . with his
homework and stuff." Oh my gosh, that was lame. I'd just made
myself and Duke sound like total idiots. "He's not a good guy."

"No, he's not. I'm sorry."

"*I'm* sorry. About your shoulder."

He rubbed his shoulder with my mention of it.

"And I didn't know Duke was in on the whole cheating scheme until recently." I was getting way off my script, but I didn't think the Compound accounted for Trevor actually knowing some of the same people I did. It's not like I could pretend they didn't exist. But I should have avoided the subject altogether, because Trevor's eyes went tense.

"In on it?"

"I mean, the plan, whatever that was."

"To purposely injure people . . ."

"Right." Warning lights went off in my head. I had just been talking about what Rowan said—the dirty plays, hitting after the whistle—but Trevor seemed to think I meant something more. What did he think he knew, exactly? And how could I make him unthink what he thought he knew? I suddenly realized why Laila was so quick on the draw with her ability. "They're bullies. They need to grow up."

He looked at me for so long I wanted to squirm under the stare, tell him, *Whatever you're thinking is probably right. Someone intensified your injury by using an ability.* Finally, he said, "Duke can go—"

Brody burst out of the room holding a sketchbook. I held Trevor's stare for a moment, trying to let him know that I understood how he felt about Duke. That I agreed. Brody tugged on my arm, breaking my gaze.

I looked at the drawing. "Wow. You are really good."

Trevor tousled his hair. "He's the best."

• • •

The next morning I sat on a bar stool in the kitchen, my laptop open, flash drive plugged in, ready to start a session. But I had distracted myself with a pencil. I kept dropping it over and over again, trying to slow its path to the ground. Slowing down time didn't seem to be about concentration, because no matter how hard I stared at the pencil, gravity still pulled it to the ground just as fast as always. I knew my dad wanted me to give my ability a rest for a couple of weeks, but the more I thought about that advice, the worse it seemed. I'd never taken a day off from exercising my brain from the time I was five. I just needed to work through this.

I stared at the pencil. Maybe it didn't work because the pencil wasn't in peril. That seemed to be the commonality in all the events where time had slowed around me. Bobby had said something about strong bursts of emotions advancing an ability. Maybe that's when my ability was advancing—when my emotions were heightened.

I stood and walked to the sink, turned on the tap, and flipped on the garbage disposal. "Okay, pencil, your death is imminent." I held the pencil, tip down, above the sink. Just as I dropped it, my dad walked in, and my heart doubled its beat. The pencil's path to the sink slowed and I swiped it out of the air, slammed it on the counter, and turned off the garbage disposal. I cringed and kept my back to him. I should've just let it fall. Outside the window in front of me, a little girl rode by on her bike at normal speed. My head burst with pain. I leaned into the counter.

"What are you doing?" His voice sounded normal, and I let

out the breath I'd been holding.

Gritting through the pain, I grabbed a dirty plate inside the sink and ran the sponge over it a few times before I spoke. "Cleaning this plate."

I turned off the water and returned to my computer before he had too much time to assess. Double-clicking on the brain icon, I settled in for some mind expansion, trying to ignore my pounding head.

"Are you okay?"

"Fine." My mom had always warned me not to push my ability too hard too soon. She was right. I had obviously damaged something. This was not good. I loosened my shoulders and tried to relax. If heightened emotions were bringing out this ability, I just needed to learn not to let my emotions take over.

"Is your head still bothering you?"

"Yes."

"Have you been resting your ability?"

"No, not really."

He let out a frustrated sigh.

"I know. I will." Starting now. My program filled the screen.

"What is that?"

"Oh, just a morning routine. Mom sent it with me."

His face hardened for the briefest moment. "Is it a new one?"

"Sort of. I got it a few weeks before I came."

"You're not even supposed to have that here."

"They approved it." I pointed to the black stick in the computer. "That's why it's on a flash drive."

"This isn't resting."

"I don't really consider this work. It's a part of my daily routine."

"Have you been doing it every day since you've been here?"

"Not every day."

"Can I see it?"

I pulled it out and handed it to him. He flipped it over in his hand several times and then held it up to the light. I didn't understand what he was looking for, but then he said, "Can I . . . will you . . ."

I waited. My dad rarely hesitated on a sentence.

"I'd like to speak with your mother about this." He pocketed the flash drive without asking my permission and pulled out his phone while he walked away. Nothing worse than parents just laying down the law without explanation.

I sat, frustrated for a moment, then followed after him. If he wasn't going to tell me why he did that, I'd find out on my own. And by "on my own" I meant "eavesdropping."

I pressed my ear to his closed door and advanced my hearing. He was midsentence. ". . . had discussed this. No more experimental programs. Let it go, Marissa, she's developing fine." Long pause. "No, but I want to. I still think we should." Another long pause. "Of course she'll be angry, but better now than later." He grunted. "That's not true. And if we're going to talk about unfair advantages, I think you have them all, from her friends to her school."

I was so lost, but that didn't stop me from listening.

"No, I told you I'd wait, and I'll wait. But we need to tell her soon. . . . . Stumble upon it? I don't think so. I pulled some strings and got it moved into Pioneer Plaza just in case for some reason she ended up at the local cemetery with a friend."

Cemetery? What was going on? I wanted to burst into the room and force my dad to tell me what he was talking about. But at the same time all my limbs were frozen with the thought that they were keeping something huge from me. The last time they'd sat me down, it was to tell me they were getting a divorce. I wasn't sure I could handle their secrets on their terms anymore. My dad hung up the phone, and I backed away from his door.

I dialed Stephanie's number and slipped into my room.

"Hi, Addie."

"Hey." I shut myself in the closet for the added layer of sound protection, not that I thought my dad would spy on me, but just in case.

"How are you?"

"I'm okay. I have a question. What's Pioneer Plaza?"

"Pioneer Plaza? Downtown?"

I fingered the sleeve on one of my hanging shirts. "I guess."

"It's a park that has all these bronze statues of cowboys and bulls. I think it's supposed to be like a tribute to the pioneers who settled Dallas or something."

What? "Do you think you could take me there sometime this week?"

"I have cheer practice all week. I would take you after, but it's probably not a good idea to go downtown after dark. How about next week?"

"Yeah. Okay." But next week wasn't soon enough for me. Maybe I could borrow my dad's car and go by myself . . . and get lost and mugged and kidnapped. Well, maybe not those last two, but definitely the first one.

It took me a minute to realize Stephanie was in the middle of a sentence. I tried to catch up. She was telling a story about cheer and some girl named Lindsey. I was completely lost until she said, "So Lindsey thinks Trevor might still like me. What do you think?"

"Do you still like him?" I already knew the answer, but I wondered if she had admitted it to herself yet.

"I don't know anymore. I don't want to, but we have this history together, you know? And it's hard to just erase history."

"True." *It's actually very easy,* I thought. "You want my honest opinion?"

"Yes, of course."

"I think you should give yourself some space from him. Let yourself live without him for a while. I bet you'll realize you're happier that way." I didn't want to say, *Because I saw the way he was with you, and it wasn't promising.* That would've been heartless. But she had to feel it. One-sided relationships didn't feel right. And she'd see that once she got into a healthier relationship where someone appreciated her more.

She sighed. "You're probably right. Thanks for listening."

"Anytime."

"I gotta run. My dad is calling on the other line."

"From downstairs?" I asked with a laugh.

"Yes, he's such a weirdo," she said, laughing as well.

"Have fun."

"Bye, Addie, and thanks again."

I hung up and looked at the phone for a minute, then dialed Laila's number. It had been a few days since I'd spoken to her.

"Addie. Hey."

"My dad just stole my flash drive and is keeping a secret hidden from me at a park full of bronze bulls," I said without a formal greeting.

"Whoa. What?"

"My dad is keeping secrets from me, and they have to do with a DAA program, a cemetery, and pioneer statues."

"What kind of secrets?"

"If I knew that, they wouldn't be secrets."

"Oh, the secret kind of secrets. Why didn't you clarify?"

I smiled. "I have to figure it out. Do you happen to still have Rowan's phone number?"

"Rowan . . ." She trailed off, and I could tell she was trying to remember who he was again.

"You know, the guy whose memory you Erased."

"Oh, Norm Rowan with the exceptionally good kissing abilities."

"Too much information, but yes."

"Yeah. Why? He doesn't seem like your type."

"I don't like him, but I'm going to see if he'll take me to the fake bulls." I hadn't planned on asking Rowan; I had hardly talked to him at all. But he had offered to show me around town, and I decided to take him up on that.

"Good call." Laila gave me Rowan's number. "And since we're on the subject, I've been thinking about trying to advance my ability."

"Um, we weren't on that subject at all."

"Wait for it. It really does relate. Connor."

"The guy who almost hit me with his motorcycle?"

"Yes."

"What does Connor have to do with DAA programs and bull cemeteries?"

"Well, he has nothing to do with cemeteries, but Connor is the one who always sells me the black market programs."

"You mean tries and then fails to sell you those programs."

"Uh, sure, okay. I got Connor to tell me who the creator of these advancement programs is. Now I just need to meet him . . . or her."

I closed my eyes. "Do you hear yourself talking right now? Bobby advanced his abilities and he almost killed us, Laila. Killed us. And now you're saying you're going to meet someone else, like Bobby, who has the same screw-the-system-and-the-rules attitude and ask him to help you? Is that really what you're saying?"

She hesitated for only one beat before saying, "Yes. That's what I'm saying. What are the odds he's another Bobby?"

Sometimes talking to Laila made me feel like an adult, because I had the overwhelming desire to scold her. I took a deep breath. "Why do you want to advance your ability, anyway?"

"Who doesn't want to advance their ability?"

"I think I damaged mine," I blurted out. Fear tightened my chest as I admitted that out loud.

"What?"

"I don't know. Something is happening with my ability. It's weird, and when I push it, my head hurts really bad. And now I can't even Search without getting the worst headache ever. What if I lose my ability? What if my ability advanced too early and now I'm broken?"

"Calm down. It's probably just stress."

"What if it's not? What if I pushed myself too hard? You need to just wait, Laila. The DAA program is supposed to be the most natural. Your ability will advance when it's supposed to advance."

"I may or may not actually do the DAA program on a daily . . . or weekly basis. There are other ways, faster ways. People do it all the time."

"I can slow down time."

"What?"

"It started at Bobby's, and now at random times, out of nowhere, time slows down. I can't control it. And when it's over, I get the worst headache."

"Slow down time? Awesome. So that must be your advancement. It makes sense, because you've always been able to manipulate time in a way, kind of walk forward through it."

"It's not awesome. I can't Search anymore, and I can't control this."

"It's just your growing pains. You'll be fine when your mind settles into it. See, this is what I'm talking about. I want that."

"You want to slow down time?"

"No, I want to restore memories."

"Restore memories? How do you even know that's how your ability would advance?"

"I don't." She said it, but I heard the hum in her voice that meant she was lying.

"You do. How?"

"I don't. I just think it would be cool."

"Why are you lying to me? I'm so tired of people lying to me. Do I not deserve the truth? Do I look like someone who can't handle it?"

"You told me I could restore memories before I Erased yours."

CHAPTER 12

Laila: Remind me to think before I speak next time.

All I could hear were Addie's quiet breaths. In. Out. This was not something I should've told her over the phone. What was I thinking? "Addie?"

"What do you mean I told you? Why would I tell you that?"

I cringed. I should stop and wait to tell her the rest when I saw her.

"Tell me," she said, her voice strong.

"Because you wanted me to restore yours. You wouldn't tell me why. You actually didn't even tell me that I could restore memories. You wrote yourself a note. In that note you told me."

"If I wrote myself a note, why do you seem to know its

contents and I know nothing?"

Because I'm selfish. "Because I didn't want to stress you out any more than you already were. I just wanted to learn how to restore memories and then surprise you with it when I came next week."

"Surprise me with the fact that you've damaged your mind by hanging out with Bobby-like criminals?"

"It sounds like brain damage can happen regardless of who I hang out with."

Addie went completely silent, and I squeezed my eyes closed.

"I'm sorry. You don't have brain damage. You're going to be fine. Talk to your dad about it. He'll probably know what to do."

"He told me to rest."

"See. There you go. Rest." She didn't sound like she thought that would help, but her dad was smart. She probably did need rest. The Bobby situation got to her more than it did me. Her headaches probably had more to do with that than anything. I hadn't had a single headache since that night. And besides, her note was proof to me that I was fine when my ability advanced before, in the other version of her life. I would be fine in this version too. "Just trust me. You wanted me to restore your memory. I'm going to figure out how. Do you trust me?" I shouldn't have asked the question, because I wasn't sure if she did anymore. Not since Duke.

"I don't want you to get hurt. Will you just use the DAA program? I can wait if it takes a while to work, Laila."

I couldn't help but notice she hadn't answered the question. "Yes, I'll use it."

"And the note?"

"I'll give it to you when I come."

"Okay."

"I'll talk to you soon."

She hung up. She knew as well as I did that I wasn't going to wait. I didn't have awhile to sit around and wait for the DAA's program to work. I wanted to advance my ability now. I laced my heeled boots and applied some gloss.

As I parked the truck, a motorcycle rumbled up behind me. I should've known who it was by the confident way he dismounted, but I couldn't tell for sure until he took off his helmet and ran his fingers through his shiny hair.

I stepped out of the truck. "You even made it sound like a Norm motorcycle."

"I knew you'd come here without me even though I told you not to," Connor said, ignoring my comment.

"How did you know I'd come tonight, though?"

He reached into the bed of my truck and pulled a tiny metal device from beneath the rim. "Tracker." He pocketed it. "And they're expensive, so I'm glad it didn't get lost."

Anger surged through me. "You were tracking me?"

"Does that bother you, princess?" He took off his gloves and tucked them in his back pocket. "I don't trust you."

"Then next time just shove the tracker down my throat, for more accurate data."

"I would've, but I wasn't sure you'd end up here in forty-eight hours, and like I said, these things are expensive."

"Well, for the record, I don't trust you either." It was a grade-school comeback, but I couldn't think of anything else to say. "And I don't need you here tonight."

"I'm not here for you. I'm here so you don't ruin my relationship with my supplier."

"I wasn't even going to mention your name. But I'm pretty sure he'll know who sent me now, since, you know, he'll see you."

"Just let me do the talking and shut those pretty little lips of yours."

"Little? I've actually been told they're quite full, which makes them very hard to shut."

"You are infuriating."

"I was thinking the same thing about you."

By this time we were at the door, and Connor knocked. When no one answered, he started to leave. "Guess he's not here."

"Okay, see you later." I rang the doorbell several times, and Connor sighed and rejoined me on the porch. Eventually, the door slid open. A man in his midtwenties answered. He didn't look like I expected he would. He was clean-cut, shaven, with unmarked skin. First he looked at me, and I could tell he liked what he saw. That would help. Then he looked at Connor, and his stance relaxed.

"Oh hey, man. What's up?"

"Can we talk inside?"

"Sure." He stepped aside, and I walked in first. I didn't need Connor here, and I wanted him to know that.

"Are you here to pick up another pack already? That was fast."

"No." He pointed to me. "I'm here because of her."

"I can see how she might be compelling, but you know that's not how I work."

"I know." ˉ

I cleared my throat. "Look, I would've found you with or without Boy Wonder here. I'm here for information. I want to advance my ability. I want you to help me. It's as simple as that."

He laughed. "I think you've mistaken this for the DAA. Does this look like the DAA to you?"

I knew his question was rhetorical, but I looked around anyway. Cases like Connor's covered tabletops, and several laptops were open and running through mind patterns. "It looks like an illegal operation that the DAA wouldn't like. Last I checked they prefer to be the sole provider of ability advancement. The Bureau seems to agree with that concept as well."

He glared at Connor. "Did you bring a narc into my house?"

"She's just a spoiled brat looking for something to occupy her time."

Spoiled? I had to clamp back the laugh that wanted to escape. If only. Whatever. It beat him knowing the truth and feeling sorry for me.

He walked back to the door. "Is this some sort of juvenile lovers' quarrel? I don't know why you felt the need for a witness. Get out." Suddenly, his face changed to that of a greasy-haired older man with a goatee.

I tilted my head. "You're a Perceptive." He had made me see him the way he wanted me to see him. Now I wondered which of his faces was real.

"Very good. You have brains in that gorgeous head of yours. Now use them to get out of my house."

I crossed my arms. "No. I'm not going to turn you in to any sort of authority. I just want to advance my ability. You are obviously exceptionally advanced in yours. Teach me."

At this point, Connor grabbed my arm and dragged me toward the door. I twisted out of his hold. "Don't touch me."

"This is my life you're messing with."

"Wait," the Perceptive said. He had added a tattoo of a cross to his neck . . . or maybe took away the illusion covering the tattoo, I still couldn't tell. "What's your ability?"

"None of your business."

"You just made it my business."

"I did? You're entering into an agreement with me?" I plopped down on the closest chair. "Good. When do we start the training?"

He looked at Connor as if he thought Connor had any sort of control over me.

"Come here." He beckoned me to follow him, and I did without a glance in Connor's direction.

He led me into a room filled with digital images projected onto the walls. People, places, words. It was overwhelming and made me a little dizzy. I leaned against the wall.

"What is all this?" A metal bird sat perched on the desk, and

I studied it. "Is that a listening device? Are you recording this?"

"Sit," he told me.

I sat.

"Put your palm on that black pad there." He pointed to a palm scanner on the desk.

"Why?"

He raised one eyebrow, and I put my palm on the black pad. Nothing happened. I glanced around the room at the images. I didn't recognize any of the people, and as I continued to watch, I realized the places all looked unfamiliar as well. These were images from the Outside. "Did you hack into the Containment Committee surveillance?"

He didn't answer. After a few minutes, he said, "You're clean."

"I could've told you that. We didn't need the dramatics."

"Okay, here are the terms. Five hundred bucks a lesson. Any indication, even the slightest hint, that you are going to talk, this"—he pointed to his face—"disappears with your money."

"Five hundred bucks? Impossible. I can't."

Connor let out a laugh, and I shot him a look.

"Those are my terms," he said. "Take them or leave them."

The room was so high-tech, possibly a room straight from the Bureau's own computers. Maybe he had hacked information from the Department of Ability Advancement as well. His ability was more advanced than that of any Perceptive I'd ever seen. I wanted him to teach me. Needed him to. He was good. "My brother is almost fourteen and he still hasn't Presented. If you can help him too, then you have yourself a deal."

His dark eyes were hard and held my stare. He was the first to break contact and reached into a drawer, pulling out an electronic clip. "He can't come here, but I'll do you a favor. Tell your brother to stop using the DAA program and use this for a week. It will be my little gift of good faith to you." He held it out to me. "I'm Face, by the way."

I took the clip. "Laila."

As we walked down the driveway, I glanced back at the front door. It was shut tight. I wondered which face was his real one. This was definitely a problem in the having-anything-to-blackmail-him-with department.

Connor chuckled.

"What?"

"Nothing."

"You don't think I can get five hundred dollars?"

"I know you can't. You are broke." He said the word *broke* with two syllables. He grabbed his helmet off the seat of his bike. "Maybe you can ask your daddy for some money."

Considering my daddy asked me for money on a weekly basis, that wasn't happening.

He pointed to my pocket, where I had stored the electronic clip Face had given me. "You're going to let your brother use that?"

I wasn't sure yet. Addie had said the DAA program helped. Maybe I should just have patience and let him continue with that. "Are you saying I shouldn't?"

He shrugged.

"Oh, that's right, you're just the middleman. You don't ask questions."

"I was just going to offer to buy it off you. Since you need money and all."

It was tempting. I was a long way from five hundred dollars, and any little bit would help. But I wanted to help my brother. "No thanks."

"So what's your next step then?"

"Nothing that involves you." I opened my truck door and climbed inside without waiting for a response. I had no idea what my next step was. I was broke no matter how many syllables the word had.

CHAPTER 13

Addie: There really are bronze bulls. Lots of them.

I stared at the black screen of my cell phone long after we hung up. I wanted Laila to restore my memory? Why? Was there something I had learned in the other life that I needed now? Maybe whatever it was that my parents were keeping from me. Or maybe why my head felt like it was going to explode when I used my ability.

I slid my finger across the screen. There was nothing I could do about that now. The only thing I had control over was figuring it out now. I hit the Call button.

"Hello," Rowan answered, and I could tell by his tone he had no idea who was calling.

"Hi, Rowan, it's Addie."

"Addie! Hey. The answer is yes, and what time should I be there?"

I laughed. How could Stephanie hate this guy so much? He was hilarious. "I need someone to take me to Pioneer Plaza."

"Pioneer Plaza? I don't even know if I know how to get there. Hey," he said to someone who must've been in the room with him, "do you know where Pioneer Plaza is?"

"Yes," the other person, who sounded suspiciously like Trevor, said.

"Addie wants to go."

"Why?" Trevor asked.

"Because she's funny."

I smiled. I rarely got described as funny—that was Laila's trait. Weird, yes. Funny, no.

"We can take her, right?"

"Sure," Trevor said.

I bit my lip, trying to contain a smile.

Back to me, Rowan said, "We'll be by to get you in ten minutes. Text me your address."

"Ten minutes? I didn't mean tonight."

"Well, you're getting tonight."

I hung up the phone, texted him my address, and ran to the bathroom.

"Please, Mr. Bull, don't trample me," Rowan said. He had wedged himself beneath the bronze hoof of one of the many bull statues that trailed through the park in downtown Dallas.

"I wish that bull was real," Trevor said.

"Hey, Addison is the one who dragged us here, remember?" Trevor raised his eyebrows at me. "So true."

I gave Trevor's shoulder a small push, and he laughed.

"Okay, take another picture, Addie," Rowan said.

"Sure thing." I snapped a picture with my phone, and then Rowan ran off to find the next statue. I couldn't for the life of me figure out what I wasn't supposed to know or see here. They were just bronze statues. I had discreetly studied each one as we walked down the line, but there was nothing out of the ordinary—if bronze statues were considered "ordinary."

"I think he was born with more energy than the rest of us," Trevor said, nodding to Rowan, who was now trying to climb on top of a horse.

"It would seem that way."

His gaze lingered on the blue stripe in my hair, and he asked, "What's the story with the blue?"

I let out a breathy laugh. "A long one. My one and only attempt at rebellion." I twirled it around my finger a couple of times, my hair, straight like it had been for weeks, feeling a little frizzy out in the humid air. "Have you ever done something stupid?"

"Today? Or ever?"

I laughed. "Does that mean yes?"

"Haven't we all?"

"Something you regret, though. Something you wish you could take back."

We walked over a hill, and a field of gravestones stretched out in front of us. My breath caught. This was what my father had been referring to. It wasn't visible from the road at all.

"I'm fairly cautious. Most of my regrets have to do with things I didn't do versus things I did."

It took me a moment to remember what we were talking about and another one to settle my heart. Crap. We had to stay until I looked at every gravestone. How could I make that seem natural? I had to keep him talking. "So what haven't you done lately that you wish you did?"

"Most recently would have to be when I came to talk to Duke after the football game a couple weeks ago. . . ."

Ah, here it was again—the sore subject I wished he wouldn't associate with me. "Oh?"

"I had just overheard some things Duke said in the locker room."

"Right. So you probably wanted to lay him out."

He smiled. The first one of the night directed at me, and it made my insides flip. He had an amazing smile. "Something like that."

I thought back to that night with Duke. "So instead you were super nice? That doesn't make sense."

"My mom always tells me that if I feel like punching someone, first I have to say something nice to them. Out loud. If I still feel like punching them, they probably deserve it."

"Duke totally deserved it, though."

"But you were there. I wasn't counting on that."

My insides flipped again. I wasn't even sure what that meant, but it sounded good. I grimaced. I needed to stop this small crush I seemed to be developing on Stephanie's ex-boyfriend. Especially considering she wanted to take the ex out of the equation. I was being dumb. Duke was a jerk, and now apparently my heart wanted to fall for the first guy who talked nice to me. Trevor was just being a gentleman, I reminded myself. He was nice to everybody.

But either way, his regret was now mine. Duke needed someone to lay him out. Not just Laila's attempt, which only ended in a cut lip, but a full-on, Trevor-delivered knockout. Duke was a big guy. I looked at Trevor's arms, wondering if he could pull it off. It was hard to tell; they were covered by a jacket, but they seemed thick enough. When I looked back up again, I realized he had caught me assessing. My face went hot. "Sorry. I just wondered if you could do it." Why did I have to say everything that came into my brain? I could've just pretended he had a piece of lint on his jacket or something, but I always thought of those excuses a beat too late.

"I could," was all he said.

Quiet confidence. Trevor oozed it.

My phone beeped, and I pulled it out. *Do you happen to have five hundred dollars lying around?*

No, not at the moment, I texted back. *Is your dad in trouble again?*

No. It's for an investment.

Of course it was. I knew she wouldn't listen to me about dropping the ability advancement plan. "Sorry," I said to Trevor.

He shrugged. "It's okay." He pointed to a headstone fifty

feet away. "Rowan is going to jump out from behind that head-stone when we get close. It would make his day if you actually screamed."

"If you hadn't told me, I'm sure I would've done a better job of it."

He put a hand to his chest. "My big regret of the day."

I smiled and read all the headstones as we passed by. "Is this a historical graveyard or something?"

"Yes."

A historical graveyard. "Any famous people buried here?"

"Mostly Civil War heroes. But there are others." He gestured toward one of the larger headstones in the cemetery, a huge cross. "That guy was some famous writer."

"Really? Awesome. Which one?" I pivoted so we were now heading toward that grave.

"A dead one."

"Ha-ha." Just when we almost reached the writer's grave-stone, I stopped, a cold chill trickling down my body as I read a different headstone. *Adeline Coleman*. My grandmother's name. She had died five years ago—the exact year listed on the stone in front of me. This was impossible. I had visited my grand-mother's grave at the cemetery in the Compound many times in the last five years. This couldn't be hers. Somebody else had the same name as her . . . and died the same year she did . . . and was buried in the same town where my dad lived. It was just a coinci-dence. A really big, nearly impossible coincidence. Crap. It wasn't a coincidence at all. This was the secret my dad was keeping.

He'd had his mother's body moved out of the Compound.

"And here I thought Rowan was the only thing that was going to scare you here," Trevor said. His hand lightly touched my elbow, as if he could keep me up with the whisper of a touch. "You okay?"

It felt as if all the blood from my body were draining out my feet. I pointed at the gravestone. "This isn't historical."

He turned his attention to the words written there. "Adeline Coleman," he read out loud.

"That's my grandma's name."

"Your grandma is buried here?" Trevor sounded as confused as I felt.

"No . . . I . . ." I trailed off.

He studied the headstone again. "Were you named after your grandma?"

A memory seemed to slam into my mind. I sat on the couch with my grandmother the Saturday after I Presented. Her arm was wrapped around my shoulder as she stared at my test results.

A smile had taken over my whole face. "My dad must've known I'd be Divergent. That's why he named me after you."

She set the paper down on the coffee table and turned toward me. "It's not an easy ability to live with—knowing things that others possibly never will—but you're strong, Addie. I know you can handle it. I couldn't be happier to share an ability with you."

"And a name."

"They aren't exactly the same."

My ten-year-old heart raced. "Our abilities? Can you do something different?"

"No, our names."

"Oh. Right." Sometimes I forgot because everyone called her Addie too. But she was right; our names weren't exactly the same.

A loud "BOO!" shouted in my ear, pulled me out of my memory. Rowan laughed when I jumped, but the scream Trevor asked for was lodged somewhere beneath all the disbelief in my chest.

"Ah, you guys are no fun," Rowan said, draping an arm over my shoulder. "What're we all looking at? Adeline Coleman. Do we know her?"

"It's her grandmother's name," Trevor said.

"This is your grandma's grave?" Rowan asked. "So you've been here before. And here we thought we were giving you the grand tour."

"No . . . I haven't. I . . ."

Trevor brushed his hand over mine, and I realized I was gripping his forearm in a clawlike vise. "You okay?" he asked.

I quickly let go, turned on my heel, and walked back the way we had come. I pulled out my phone and dialed my dad's number.

"Hi, baby. It's getting late. Where are you?"

"Pioneer Plaza Cemetery."

He went quiet.

"What's going on?"

"Addie, we'll talk about this later. This isn't an over-the-phone kind of conversation. I need to talk to your mother. This is something that will take some explanation."

"Is it her? Is it grandma? That's all I want to know right now."

"Later."

"Dad. Just one answer."

"Addie—"

"Don't I deserve to know that much?"

"Yes."

The cold air nipped at my cheeks. "Yes I deserve to know, or yes it's her?"

"Both."

I hung up the phone. I had never hung up on my dad, but I didn't care. My mind raced through my grandmother's funeral. I remembered watching them lower her casket into the earth. I remembered throwing a rose down with her, barely seeing it fall through my tears. So they moved her here? But why? Was he making some kind of statement? One that said, *I'm never going back*?

I had to call Laila. She'd know what to do. I walked half a block away and dialed her number. A chorus of birds squawked in the tree above me, and I moved out from under it, not needing to add bird crap to my night. Laila didn't answer.

I slid my phone into my pocket.

"What's going on?" Rowan asked when I got to the car, where they were waiting.

"Is everything okay?" Trevor asked.

"I don't know."

"You didn't know she was buried here?"

I met Trevor's eyes, mine stinging with frustration or sadness or something that didn't feel good. He took a step forward as though tempted to comfort me but then stopped. "Come on, we'll take you home."

CHAPTER 14

Laila: I think I sold myself short.

Eli elbowed me. "How come I can only read *your* mind? You're not cheating, are you?"

We cut through the park and headed toward the gaming arena where I had asked Kalan to meet me. I only hoped she still needed that favor. "Why would I cheat?"

He sighed, somehow knowing that my lack of answer was my answer. "That's not going to help me, so don't."

"Maybe you're trying for the wrong ability. Have you ever thought of that?"

"My early indicators said I have a tendency toward Telepathy."

"Yeah, well, maybe your early indicators were wrong. Do you

want to try some of my tracks and see if they feel right?"

"I had absolutely no traces of mind blocking."

I knew this. I was just trying to make him feel better about his lack of progress. "Just relax. It will come when it's supposed to."

He kicked at the ground as we walked. "Or maybe it will never come."

I sighed. "I have something for you. Remind me when we get home." I hadn't given him the program from Face because I wasn't sure I could trust it. It was one thing to take a risk with my own ability, but to do it for him was completely different. But how could I screw up something that hadn't even Presented yet? I'd tell him what it was and give him the choice.

"Hey, there's Leonard," Eli said as we got closer.

I followed his finger and saw his friend, Kalan's brother. Kalan stood next to him. The only reason I had agreed to bring Eli here was because I knew she'd be here. "Have fun," I said. "I'll be over there on the bench. And don't take all night. It's getting late, and I'm not your taxi."

"So what's the definition of someone who drives me anywhere I want to go, then?"

I smacked him on the back and then shoved him for good measure. He laughed and ran off.

"Kalan!" I waved, and she looked my way, then came to join me.

"Hey. You wanted to talk?" she asked.

We reached the bench and sat down. "Two things. One, I

need a list of all the students and their abilities from the office. Well, actually, just one student in particular." Kalan worked in the school office. I knew she could get it for me.

"Laila, it's winter break. The school is on lockdown."

"That should make it easier, then. Nobody there to ask questions."

"The word *lock* is in lockdown for a reason."

"What if I could get you the code to the office?"

"A code to the office is the least of my worries."

I sighed and watched my brother and her brother step on the platform and get scanned into the game. A huge holographic three-headed monster popped up between Eli and Leonard. They immediately got to work fighting it.

"Whose ability are you looking for, anyway?"

"Connor."

"Connor Bradshaw?"

"Yes. Do you know it?"

"No. Anybody else and I might've known, but Connor is . . . a loner."

I growled. This was supposed to be easy. I would advance my ability. I would give Addie her memories back. I would stop feeling guilty. The end.

"So what's the other thing?" she asked.

"Did you still want someone's memory Erased?"

She took a gasp of air. Then she nodded twice, her eyes shining with held-in tears. I had thought long and hard about this. She was asking for a memory of herself back. I could do this for her. But I wasn't exactly one for charity. Of course I needed something in return.

"I'll do it for five hundred dollars."

She was quiet for a while, then said, "Three hundred and the list from the office. That's the best I can do."

I cracked my knuckles. I was the one who'd brought it up, but without the full amount, was it worth it? The tears in her eyes tugged at my guilt. What had happened to her? "Did someone hurt you?"

She wrung her hands together until red marks streaked her skin. "He doesn't deserve to remember how much."

Three hundred bucks. That was over half the money I needed for Face, for lesson one. Kalan was right. It was her memory. She was asking me to get it back for her, to help her, that was all. "Okay. Whose memory?"

CHAPTER 15

Addie: I would make a horrible spy.

I waved good-bye to Rowan and Trevor, then walked into the house. My dad wasn't in the main room, so I knocked once at his bedroom door and walked in. The sink water in the bathroom was running. I sat on his bed and waited, arms crossed.

His keys, wallet, and cell phone sat on his dresser, reminding me he had recently taken something of mine. I moved the stuff on his dresser, looking for my flash drive. It wasn't there. I went to his nightstand and searched through his top drawer, digging beneath a notebook. I didn't like to invade my dad's privacy, but I was angry about finding my grandmother's grave and sick of the secrets my parents had been keeping from me. I wanted my DAA program back.

The handle to his bathroom door rattled, and I quickly shut the nightstand, empty-handed, and turned around. I'd have to find it later. I leaned back against the nightstand, trying to act casual, knowing that "acting" was impossible to do around a lie detector.

He cursed quietly under his breath. "You scared me."

I didn't say a word. I didn't have to lie about how angry I felt.

He sat down on the bed and patted a spot next to him for me to join him. I stayed where I was.

"So your grandmother is buried here."

"Why?"

"Because I'm not going back there. She's my mother. I wanted her here."

He wasn't going back. That thought stopped me for a moment. It had been my original thought as to why he'd had her moved here, but I still couldn't believe someone, especially my dad, would want to leave the Compound forever. "You're not going back?"

His determined gaze softened. "If you need me to be there for something, I will be there. But other than that, this is my home now."

I nodded. That admission alone made the divorce so much more real to me. "I didn't see Grandpa's grave. Why didn't you bring him here as well?"

He looked at his hands. "That one might take awhile."

He should've told me this before. "You thought I'd be angry?"

"It's not that."

"Then what? Because I'm trying my hardest to understand why you wouldn't tell me this."

"It's complicated."

"No, not really. You open your mouth and you say, 'Addie, I've decided to move my parents' graves into the Norm world, where I can see them on a more regular basis.' It's easy."

"Did you want me to tell you that before or after I dropped the divorce announcement on you?"

I opened my mouth to speak and then closed it again with a sigh. He was right. It was complicated.

"Am I forgiven?"

My mind flashed back to the Tower and the scar-faced man with the tablet who said I had two family members on the Outside. Was it possible he meant my grandma? "If that's the whole truth, then yes." I met his eyes. "Is it?"

"Yes."

"Seriously, Dad, I can't stand finding things out like this. If there's anything else, just tell me. I promise I can handle a lot more than you think I can."

"I know." He grabbed my hand and squeezed.

"I'm glad you have her here. I know you and grandma were close." I squeezed his hand back. "Like us, right?"

He smiled. "Right."

I stood to leave but then remembered what I had been sitting on, his nightstand, and what I had been trying to find inside it. "What about my flash drive? Why did you take it?"

"You don't need that."

"Why?"

"I promise your ability will develop perfectly naturally without it."

I sighed. "Fine."

Only it wasn't fine. I wanted that DAA program. When I got to my room, I pulled out my phone and dialed my mom. It was a little late, but I figured she'd be okay even if I woke her.

"Hello," she answered after the third ring.

"Hi, Mom."

"Addie," she said with a happy sigh. "How are you?"

"I'm okay. Just found out about Grandma tonight."

"Yes, your father called me a little while ago. I'm sorry we didn't tell you. It's just been kind of an ordeal." She must've noted my lack of reassurance, because she added, "There really was a reason. We wanted to wait until both graves were approved for the move, and then your dad was going to take you to see them."

"Why hasn't Grandpa's grave been approved?"

"Because he was a Bureau member, and there are more strings to pull if a person held the title of agent."

"Oh." I had almost forgotten that my grandfather worked for the Bureau. There were a lot of things I didn't remember about him. He had died ten years ago in the line of duty. I was sure the Compound didn't want to let go of a hero, even if he was a dead one. I glanced at my closed door. "Dad took my flash drive."

"I know. I'm trying to talk to him about that."

"What does he have against it?"

"He's always thought natural development was the best.

We'll figure something out soon, okay? Why don't you get some sleep?"

"Okay. Good night, Mom."

"Good night."

An hour later, I lay in bed staring at the ceiling, my brain buzzing. It wouldn't let me rest. *Two relatives have left the Compound*, the man in the Tower had said. He had used the word *left*. As in, of their own will. That couldn't possibly be referring to my dead grandma.

Scar-Face had slipped, and he knew it. It was hard to believe my dad had lied to me again, to my face like that, but it was the only thing that made sense. So who else was living out here? Someone related to my dad? Was it possible he had a sibling or something? I got up and listened outside my dad's door. The deep, even breaths of sleep reverberated through the thin wood. Unlike Laila's dad, mine was a very light sleeper. I had to try anyway.

The knob turned smoothly, but the hinges protested with a loud squeak as I pushed open the door. I paused, holding my breath. His breathing was still even. The thick carpet pushed between my bare toes as I stepped into the room. His phone still sat on the dresser. I just wanted to see the list of contacts he kept stored in it. All I could hear was my heart pumping blood in a swooshing rhythm. I tried to keep myself calm. I didn't need my ability acting up right now.

I took the ten more steps to his phone and swiped it up before

I could talk myself out of it. Then I swiftly walked out into the hall. I let myself recover for a minute and then took the stolen phone to the living room.

I slid my finger across the black screen, and four empty boxes appeared like a slap to the face. Oh yeah, password. Laila had made it look so easy when she'd stolen Poison's number from her dad's phone a few weeks ago.

What number combination would my dad use? I started with the four corners and the screen flashed red. I tried my birthday. Nothing. Then his birthday. And holding my breath, I tried my mom's birthday. It didn't work, and the phone locked me out for fifteen minutes. Great. This could take all night.

I was right. Two hours later I still couldn't figure out the stupid password, and I had already fallen asleep twice on the arm of the couch. Now I was locked out again. I leaned my head on the arm and rested my eyes for just a minute. When I opened them again, the gray of early morning tinged the living room. Was I really going to have to wait until he decided to come clean?

I replaced my dad's phone and went to bed.

CHAPTER 16

Laila: Is a guy touching my shoes
a good enough reason to kill him?

The next day, Kalan showed up at my house. I opened the door, expecting her to say she'd changed her mind about wanting me to Erase someone's memory. Instead she handed me an envelope. I looked inside. "Cash? You don't want to use your card?"

She looked over her shoulder, then said, "It's less traceable this way."

I felt as seedy as my dad in that moment, and a shudder went through me.

"The list is in there too, but it's not my fault Connor hasn't claimed an ability."

"What?" I pulled out the list and flipped through the pages

until I found Connor Bradshaw. Next to his name it stated, "Unclaimed."

"Maybe he doesn't have an ability."

My eyes shot to hers. "Of course he has an ability. He's Para."

She bit on her thumbnail. "Maybe he wasn't born with the potential to develop one."

I gave a single laugh that sounded shakier than I meant for it to. The statement touched a nerve. "Have you ever heard of that happening to anyone?"

"No. But I looked up his transcript, because I thought maybe I'd be able to tell his ability from the classes he's in."

"And could you?"

"Not really. He does awful in his Para classes but aces all his Norm classes. That boy has issues."

"Obviously." I refolded the list and shoved it back into the envelope. Useless.

"Anyway, I fulfilled my half of the bargain. Here's your half." She handed me a piece of paper with a name, address, and date on it. "His bedroom is on the second floor, second window on the right if you're looking at his house from the front."

"Parents? Siblings? Are they around a lot?"

"Yes. He lives with both his parents and has two sisters." She shrugged when I sighed. "Good luck."

"This won't have anything to do with luck."

She smiled. "And that's why I asked you in the first place."

I stared up at his window. He had just shut the blinds. Mike Petty. We were in the same science class. He seemed nice

118

enough, but whatever. In and out with as few people involved as possible—that was the easiest way to Erase a memory. That meant no parents, no siblings.

The tree in front of his house seemed climbable had I been in the habit of climbing trees. I looked down at my feet. Why had I worn my heeled boots again?

I walked up to the tree and gave it a little kick with the pointy toe of my boot. The lowest branch was reachable, so I grabbed hold and tried to hoist myself up. My shoes slid all over the bark.

This wasn't happening with shoes on. I unzipped my boots and pulled off my socks, leaving them at the bottom of the tree. The cold grass seeped into the bottom of my feet, causing goose bumps to form on my legs. I took a deep breath and reached up. Two scraped palms, one cut ankle, and many breathless curses later, I was perched on the branch closest to his window. I tapped on the glass.

Mike's face appeared, and I waved. He opened the window. "Laila?"

"Let me in before I fall."

He powered up the screen and reached out a hand for me. I let him help me inside.

"What are you doing here?" he asked once I stood inside his room. It was littered with clothes and smelled like moldy grass.

"I needed the winter break homework assignment for science."

"And you couldn't have called?"

"That would've been easier."

He laughed and gave me a once-over.

"If you're done looking, get it for me so I can go." It would've been so much easier if his back were to me—if he were looking through his backpack or something. That way I could spend a little time rooting around for some older brain paths. The easiest memories to Erase were the most recent. Kalan wanted three weeks ago. I would have to count backward for that.

"And if I'm not done looking?" He took a step toward me.

I rolled my eyes. "Not happening."

He took another step forward.

"Ugh." I gave a frustrated sigh. "Seriously?" With an ability like mine, knowing how to make someone unconscious in under ten seconds came in handy when I needed time to get away after an Erase. I should've just used it right away.

I let him reach me. Even let him put his arm around my waist, then I pinched hard on the pressure point between his neck and shoulder, enhancing the effect with my ability to cut off brain connections, and he went down. I might've tried to soften the fall, but he deserved it.

I didn't have to touch a person's head to Erase their memories, but it made it easier. And because I had to concentrate a little harder for this one, making sure I got the right path, I placed my hands on his head. Three weeks ago. The short-term memories buzzed around, and I felt past them to the stored memories. It may have been harder to find and Erase long-term memories, but it was easier to cover them up. People generally didn't notice when they forgot what happened on a certain day several weeks ago. It didn't strike them as weird. Whereas if they lost the last five minutes, that was odd to them. I performed both kinds of wipes on Mike, because he couldn't remember I was here.

I opened one of the magazines next to his bed and placed it next to him. Hopefully, he'd just think he fell asleep reading. It was why I'd waited until night to do this, so his brain would trick him into thinking he just forgot.

I took one last look at Mike's unconscious form and then looked back at the window and my scraped palms. I should've held out for the five hundred dollars. I stepped out onto the branch, reached inside his window, and pushed the button to lower the screen. As it powered down, I held on to the branch above me and walked toward the trunk. When I reached it, I sat down to try to swing to the ground. That's when I saw Connor standing at the bottom of the tree, holding my boots.

"I thought these looked familiar," he said.

"You keep track of my shoes?"

"Mike is a customer."

"That doesn't explain the shoe fetish." I sat on the branch. "Make yourself useful and catch me." Without waiting for his answer, I pushed myself off the branch. I thought this might give me a clue as to what his ability was. The momentum of my fall knocked him over, but he softened my landing.

"Ouch," he said, pushing me off and getting back to his feet. He brushed off his pants. "For someone who doesn't trust me, you had no problem flinging yourself at me."

"Flinging myself? Please. That didn't require trust. I landed on you. It required aim." I made sure to look at his face as I said,

"Besides, I figured, with your ability, I'd be fine."

His face gave away nothing, not even a hint of surprise or confusion. So did that mean he had an ability that would help him in a situation like that? What ability would that be? Time Manipulation? Maybe he could speed up his reaction time to things. I once heard of a guy who could increase the blood flow to his muscles, making himself stronger when he needed to. Maybe he had an obscure ability like that.

"You and Mike, huh?" He nodded toward the window.

"Ew. No."

"Then what?"

"None of your business."

Connor moved to the tree and reached up to the lowest branch.

"What are you doing here?" I asked. "Tracking me again?"

"Like I said, I have a delivery."

"Might want to wait. He's not exactly up for visitors right now."

Connor climbed the tree like he was in the habit of climbing trees. I pulled on one boot and zipped it up, then used the tree to balance while I pulled on the other. I walked to my car, but before I had the chance to get in, Connor called out.

I turned to see him standing at the base of the tree. "What?"

"What did you do to him?"

"He's fine. I'm surprised he's not up already. Just a little pressure point."

"Is he going to remember you were there?"

He knew my ability? Anger flared up in me. "Who told you?"

"You're not exactly secretive about it," he said and walked toward his motorcycle. I shoved him in the back and he whirled around and grabbed my wrist. "Don't start what you can't finish, princess."

"I finish whatever I start."

He smirked then, like he was humoring a child.

I ripped my arm free from his grasp and controlled the urge to kick him in the leg like a four-year-old might. "How come I can't Erase your memories?"

His humoring smirk was gone, replaced by fiery eyes—the first look of anger I'd ever seen him display. It was more intimidating than I thought him capable of. "You've tried to Erase my memories?"

As if he didn't know. He had easily blocked my attempt. "Go die, Connor." I turned and walked to my car, slamming my door shut. Why did I let him get to me so much? Maybe because he was the only guy I'd ever met who none of my abilities worked on—not my memory Erasing or my looks. He was the only guy I couldn't control.

CHAPTER 17

Addie: Must learn what qualifies as a life-or-death situation.

My ringing phone woke me up. I groaned and pushed the hair off my face. "Hello."

"Addie, hey, it's Stephanie."

I smiled. "Hi, Stephanie. How is cheer practice going?"

"Fine. Just two more weeks and then we get winter break. I'm so ready for a break."

"You guys have a short break."

"Does Lincoln High get a longer one?"

"We have six weeks off. But we don't get as long in the summer."

"So like year-round school then?"

"Yep." I yawned. "So what's up?"

"I was wondering if I could drag you shopping with me today."

"For what?"

"Winter formal. I need to buy a dress."

"Oh. Sure. Who are you going with?"

"I haven't been asked yet, but I'm still hopeful. If I don't get asked, I might just go with a bunch of girlfriends for fun. You should come too."

I rolled onto my stomach and looked at the clock on my nightstand. Ten a.m. "To your winter formal?"

"Yeah. Come on. We'll buy you a dress today too."

"Sounds awful."

She laughed. "I'm coming to pick you up. Be ready in thirty minutes."

"Did you know he was going to be here?" I don't know why I bothered putting that in question form. It should've been an accusation, because I knew it was true.

"Maybe." She took a sip of her drink and stared at Trevor from where we sat by the indoor fountain in the middle of the mall. "It's a fund-raiser the football team roped him into doing with them. Calendars or something to raise money for new uniforms."

He was at a table set up in front of a sports store with about eight other guys, taking money and putting it in a metal box as people bought calendars. "So how did you know they roped him into it? Have you been talking to him?"

She smiled like she had been caught doing something she wasn't supposed to. "We may have talked last night. I know you told me we needed space, but I couldn't help it. I miss him."

A twinge of jealousy squeezed my heart as I wondered who'd called who. I scolded myself for the thought. I had no claim on Trevor and no right to be jealous. Maybe I had read him wrong at the party. If he was still talking on the phone with her, maybe he did still like her. "You can do what you want, Steph; it was just a suggestion."

She let out an airy squeal. "Okay, so what should we do right now? Should we go talk to him or buy a calendar or something?"

I laughed. "No, we should sit here and stare at him from across the mall like creepy stalkers."

"Do you think the football players are shirtless in the calendars?"

I scanned the table of players, several of whom were pasty white and fifty pounds overweight. "Ugh. I hope not."

She laughed. "So true." She stood, apparently deciding it was now time to stop staring and start talking. "Let's go." She held her hand out for me, and I let her help me up. Then she tucked her arm around my elbow. "This is so fun. Thanks for coming with me today."

"No problem."

"I still think you should buy that blue dress. It looked amazing on you."

"Well, after seeing you in that black dress"—I gestured

toward the shopping bag she held—"I don't think I'll ever wear a dress again."

"Whatever."

We arrived at the table and waited behind several customers before we were finally in front of Trevor. He looked up like he wasn't surprised to see us. He had probably noticed us staring at him for the last half hour by the fountain.

"Hi," Stephanie said.

"Hey. How's it going?"

"Just shopping for dresses for winter formal." She lifted up her bag a little. I knew what she wanted him to do. She wanted him to ask her who she was going with. It was obvious.

He didn't take the bait, and I couldn't tell if it was intentional or not. "Nice."

"Have you guys been doing good today? Raising a lot of money?"

"We've been busy. I think the team will do well." He rolled a pen between his hands. That wasn't a good sign for Stephanie— he wouldn't even meet her eyes. Although that wasn't a good sign for me either—he was looking at a pen. *Stop analyzing him,* I told myself. It was none of my business.

"Well, I want to buy one." Stephanie set her drink on the table and started digging through her purse.

He took a calendar from a box on the floor beside him and put it on the table. "Did you figure out why your grandmother's grave is at Pioneer Park?" He looked at me with the question.

That single look sent my heart pattering a million miles a

minute. Stephanie gave me a sideways glance. Crap, I knew I should've told her. I just didn't want to make a big deal out of nothing.

"Apparently, that's where she's been. I just didn't realize it was so close." I didn't feel like I could tell the truth without an explanation, considering most people didn't have graves moved.

Stephanie's wallet was slightly too wide for the narrow opening of her purse, and when she finally tugged it free, it smashed into her drink. As the cup fell, Trevor tried to save the calendar in its direct path and ended up knocking the entire metal box of money off the table.

The box flew toward the floor, money floating out of it slowly because time had changed to a crawl. I shouldn't have done it, but it was my instant reaction to grab the box, closing the lid as I did, and shove it back on the table. Only a few stray coins hit the ground. I quickly removed my hands from the box, but it was too late. I met Trevor's stunned eyes.

Stephanie was too busy scooping the ice back into the fallen drink to notice. "I'm so sorry. The calendar is soaked. I'll totally pay for it."

But Trevor was still looking at me.

"That was a close call," I said.

He lowered his brow, then turned his attention to the two quarters on the floor by my foot. I reached down, picked them up, then placed them on top of the cash box.

"How did you do that?"

"Do what?" I asked. "I saw that your elbow was going to

knock it off the table. I just stopped it from happening." My head throbbed, and I tried not to lean on the table for support.

"No. My elbow *did* knock it off."

Stephanie held out a ten-dollar bill. "Here. For the calendar."

"You don't have to buy a damaged calendar, Stephanie. It's no big deal." He handed her one that wasn't wet and took her money, carefully removing the two quarters from the top of the box and lifting the lid. The money inside was a mess, sideways and jumbled. He straightened a few piles. Then he looked at the ground again and back at me.

"Well, we better get going." I tugged on Stephanie's arm, but she gave me that look like she wanted to stay and talk and I wasn't helping. "There are people waiting to buy calendars." Sure there were seven other guys sitting at the table, but still, I just wanted to leave. I couldn't believe I hadn't let a stupid cash box fall on the ground. So glad I used my ability to save a metal box from certain destruction.

"Yeah, we better go," Stephanie said. As we walked away, she bit her lip. "Is something going on between you two?"

"What? No! I asked Rowan for help. Trevor tagged along. Really, it was no big deal."

She brushed at a wet spot from the spilled drink on her shirt. "I should've stayed and talked to him. I was hoping he'd ask me to the dance."

"You have to leave him wanting more," I said, remembering Laila giving me that advice at some point in the past. "Always understay your welcome."

"What does that even mean?"

I laughed. "I have no idea." Just as we were about to round the corner, I heard my name.

"Addison!"

I turned to see Trevor walking toward us.

"Can I talk to you alone for a minute?" he asked when he reached us.

"Yeah, sure," Stephanie said, the hope in her voice so apparent.

"Um." He looked at Stephanie, and I could tell he didn't want to hurt her feelings when he said softly, "I meant Addison."

This was one of those dramatic moments in books where the main character was supposed to say, *Anything you need to say to me, you can say in front of my friend.* But that was the problem. I knew what he wanted to say, and he absolutely couldn't say it in front of my friend. So instead I tried to put him off so Stephanie wouldn't be hurt any more than she already was. "We're kind of in a hurry."

But he took the drama that was supposed to be mine and used it. "It will only take a minute, but I can just ask you right here. What are—"

"No!" Great. Now I was going to look like the biggest jerk. "Sorry, Stephanie. I'll be right back." I marched past him and into the empty tiled hall that led to the bathrooms. I faced him.

He squared off in front of me. "What are you?"

"Excuse me?"

"Tell me I'm crazy." He looked into my eyes, and the intensity

130

of his stare, the set of his mouth, the angle of his brow—it all seemed so familiar. Like I had been here before with him staring at me like that. It caught me off guard, softened my resolve, and I hesitated. I had to look away. I knew what my father said about lying and how one of the first indicators was when someone couldn't look you in the eyes.

"You're crazy," I said to the wall over his right shoulder.

"While looking at me."

He must've known the lying rule too.

"I have to go. Stephanie's waiting, which, by the way, you should really ask her to winter formal. It would make her day."

"Addison." Why did he call me that? And why did I like it?

He put his hand on my shoulder. I met his eyes again, my heart beating in my throat. His normal friendly exterior was stripped away, replaced by a vulnerability that made me want to tell him everything. "You're crazy," I whispered, then walked away.

CHAPTER 18

Laila: Never give anyone the benefit of the doubt.

I counted the money again, even though I knew it hadn't magically multiplied overnight. I sighed, shoved it back into the toe of my boot, then threw the boot in my closet. It would have to be enough. I would make it be enough. Face wasn't beyond manipulation.

A shrill scream came from the backyard, and I smiled and looked out my window. A minimal amount of snow had fallen overnight, and my brothers thought they could go sledding on the tiny hill in the back.

I grabbed my scarf, slipped on a pair of wedges, and went to watch them. When the first few runs didn't work, they decided to gather up as much snow as they could to form a trail just wide enough for the sled. After an hour of hard work and me making fun of them, they actually managed to get in a few decent slides.

"Look, Laila, despite your lack of help, we are the masters of the snow," Derek called out.

"Was there mastering going on? I missed it."

Eli threw a snowball at me. It landed perfectly, so that the cold ice leaked beneath my scarf.

I jumped up, shaking off the snow. "Can you read my mind now, Eli?"

"I don't have to, but you'll have to catch me first, and I don't think any running is going on in those shoes."

He had a valid point. I pretended I was going to chase him, and laughed when both he and Derek squealed like little girls and ran away.

It was one o'clock. I told myself I would go over to Face's at two and try my luck. I went inside to make some hot chocolate.

"I'm going out," my dad said just as the door shut, cutting off any chance I had at a response.

"Okay, good to see you too," I said to nothing.

I filled the kettle and put it on the stove. My phone dug into my thigh, and I pulled it out and looked at it accusingly. I didn't want to call Connor. It was none of his business what I was doing. Sure he had helped by introducing me to Face, but I definitely didn't need him there this time. Then why did I feel like I owed him the call to let him know I was going over there today?

My phone rang, and for a second I thought it would be

Connor, as if he'd read my mind and knew I was going. But then the caller ID flashed my mom's number.

"Hello."

"Hi. I thought I'd be able to come home between shifts, but Susan called in sick and overtime pays the bills."

"Okay. What time will we see you then?"

"Late. How are things there?"

"Fine. The boys are masters of the snow."

"I thought they'd like that. Do we need anything?"

"No."

"Let me talk to your father. I couldn't reach him on his cell."

I looked out the window, but his car was already gone. "I would, but he just left like the responsible parent that he is."

"Laila, give him a break."

"You give him enough breaks for all of us."

"If you had his ability . . ."

"Lots of people have his ability and seem to handle it a hundred times better. And he's not even trying to break the addiction. If he would just do one addiction program . . ." My mom sighed, and I felt guilty. She had enough to deal with. "You're right. I have no idea how it feels to hear people's thoughts." And saying it reminded me it was true. Maybe I'd be exactly like my dad if I were bombarded with people's innermost thoughts.

"Thank you for trying to understand. I gotta run."

"Bye, Mom."

I scooped chocolate powder into some mugs and then poured the hot water over the top. "Masters of the snow, come get your hot chocolate," I called out the back door.

They ran in and attacked the offering. I tugged on Eli's arm. "So . . ."

He knew what I was asking. I had given him the new electronic clip the night before, and I wanted to know if it was working.

"Haven't tried it yet."

"What are you waiting for?"

"Confidence."

I had told him the risks of programs not approved by the DAA. Apparently, that was harder for him to overlook than it was for me. "Well, make sure you tell me if you decide to do it."

He nodded and took another swig of his hot chocolate.

"I'm going out." I headed down the hall, and Connor's face flashed through my mind again. Fine, guilt, be a stupid pest. I dialed his number.

"What?" he answered, and I almost hung up, any feeling of obligation gone.

"I'm going to Face's today. Two o'clock. I don't need you there." Then I hung up and ignored the phone when it rang. I reached my bedroom and stopped, horrified, in the open doorway. My entire room was ripped apart. All my clothes pulled from the drawers, my mattress resting crooked on my bed, the contents of my desk spread across the floor, my laundry basket upended.

"No . . . no, no, no, no." I walked farther in. I knew it was gone, but that didn't stop me from opening my closet, grabbing my black boot, and reaching all the way to the toe. Empty. Even though I knew exactly which boot it was in, I checked the other one just in case. Nothing. I threw my boot hard at the wall, and it bounced off and hit me on the leg.

I hated my dad. More than hated him, despised him.

I rushed back down the hall and paused by the kitchen. "If Dad happens to show his face here in the next hour or so, call me."

Eli put down his hot chocolate. "What's wrong?"

"Nothing."

Once in my car, I began dialing my dad's number every minute. By my third try, I was sure he had turned off the ringer, but I kept at it anyway. Then I started calling his usual hangouts. Then actually driving to his usual hangouts. Apparently, he was smart enough to go somewhere new today. I couldn't find him anywhere. When I showed up at Face's house, an hour late, Connor was there. Great.

I must've thought about that money at some point today when my dad was around. It was my own fault. I had to protect myself better. Keep him out. Keep everyone out.

At least now I knew I could make money with my ability. I looked at the house. Maybe I could make Face some promises of future payment. My time was running out. I was seeing Addie in one week. I hoped to have advanced my ability by then so I could restore her memory. Maybe it wasn't too late to start on the DAA track.

I took a deep breath and stepped out of the car. Connor

must've been inside, because only his motorcycle was parked along the curb, his helmet hanging off a handlebar. I knocked on the door and put my flirty face on. This time a man with curly red hair answered. Three rings pierced one eyebrow.

"Is Face here?"

"You're looking at him."

"Oh. Right." I noticed two things I hadn't before. One was a small blurry spot on the right part of his neck. His image was a little flawed. Not that anyone would notice if they weren't looking, but it reminded me that there were ways to see through lies. "Not your best look."

"I don't take votes."

The second thing I noticed was, "Your voice is the same."

"Eh. Too much trouble to change it. I have to be very familiar with another voice, and it's hardly worth the effort. Most people think it's a different voice just because it's a new face."

"Most people are slow. It's obvious."

I didn't see Connor anywhere, but I didn't care. I did my best work alone. Especially when I had nothing to work with except my flirting abilities.

"It's good to see you," he said. "I'm short on cash."

"Well, that's the thing. I had your money, but it got stolen, so I was hoping you could do this first lesson on good faith and I'll have it for you next week."

"Well, here's my thing, I don't have good faith in anyone except Mr. Cash. I get along well with him. And until he shows up, I won't do a thing."

I Erased his memory twice and started over, each time trying something a little different, to no avail. In the end, I Erased myself from his day completely and went outside. An invisible hand felt like it was trying to take my life by squeezing my throat. I crawled in the back of my truck and lay down, staring at the cloudless sky. Maybe this was pointless.

I heard the scuffing of feet before the voice. "And just like that it's as though you never existed." Connor's head appeared over the side of my truck.

I didn't move.

"Face didn't even remember you were there. Craziest thing I ever witnessed."

"You need to get out more."

"Why would you need to advance your ability when you can do that?"

"Are you mocking me? Because I'm really not in the mood."

"Bad hair day?"

My hands clenched into fists. "Just leave. I'm not going back in there, so you don't have to worry that I'm going to ruin your life."

"Why do you want to advance your ability so badly, anyway?"

I finally looked at him. The smug look on his face just made me angrier. "What about 'leave' don't you understand?"

"Mainly the whole 'leave' part."

"Fine. I'll leave." I stood and thought I could get out the same way I got in, over the side. But my foot missed the tire, and I went down hard on my knee. My leggings ripped, and I could feel the moisture from the blood before I saw it. With my knee throbbing, I stood and opened the driver's-side door. Before I could shut it, though, Connor was there, holding it open with one hand.

"Just leave me alone." My hands shook, and I clenched them into fists so he wouldn't notice.

Without a word, he grabbed my leg and used it to turn me toward him.

"I will head-butt you if I have to. I've done it before."

"You are so stubborn." He took hold of the gaping hole in my leggings and ripped it open further.

He placed his fingers on the bloody mangled mess that was my knee, and we locked eyes. A tingling warmth stretched across my knee, and before I realized what he was doing I almost shoved his hand away. But right as I put my hand on his, it hit me. He was a Healer.

The tingling warmth turned into a searing pain—like fire tearing through my flesh. I squeezed his hand and gritted my teeth. The pain died, and I quickly let go.

Aside from the blood and ripped pants, my knee looked perfect. He had regenerated my skin. Healing was a rare ability. It was no wonder Connor kept it to himself. But that still didn't explain why he failed all his Para classes when he was obviously very good at it. I pulled my leg away from him. "You should really ask permission before you use your ability on people."

"You're welcome."

"Move so I can shut the door."

"Who stole your money?"

"It's not polite to eavesdrop, you know."

"You're such a loudmouth it's hard not to."

I placed my foot on his chest and was about to shove him out of the way so I could shut my door when he grabbed hold and yanked me off my seat. I landed on the running board that ran the length of my truck and now had to look up to see him.

"You think you're tough, princess?" He was so close I could smell the musky scent of his deodorant. I glared at him. As if I needed someone else to show me I had no control today.

I'd show him how much control I had.

I looked down and then back up through my lashes. "I'm sorry. Thank you for Healing me. It's just been a really bad day." Step one: Seem vulnerable. Check. I wrung my hands together and then "accidentally" let them catch the bottom of his shirt. I pulled back when I realized, giving a little laugh. "Sorry." I reached out and touched his chest with my apology, pretended to hesitate, then put my hand back and left it there. Step two: Contact. Check. "It was my dad."

"What was your dad?" His breath came quick now, and I could feel the rise and fall of his chest beneath my hand.

"He stole the money. For suppressors."

"Your dad stole your money?"

I nodded. Step three: Share something personal. Check. He leaned toward me. So the impenetrable Connor wasn't as immune to me as I thought he was.

Step four: Draw his attention to my mouth. I bit my bottom

lip. His eyes flicked to my lips and then back to my eyes. Check. And step five would normally be: Reel him in for a fun, forget-all-my-problems make-out session. But since I couldn't do step six with him—Erase his memories—I had to stop there. His eyes again went to my lips, and this time my heart picked up speed. I took a deep breath to control it.

"What's your dad's ability?" he asked.

Crap. In my attempt to play him, I had told him something real.

I stretched up a little, toward his face. He leaned closer. His breath touched my cheeks. It smelled hot and sweet. I blinked and reminded myself that I was proving I had control over him, not the opposite.

If I knew one thing about Connor, it was that he had a lot of pride. If I wanted to assert my control and make sure he never, ever came this close to kissing me again, I just had to do one thing. Make him feel stupid.

"My dad didn't steal my money." I gave a single laugh. "But you should see your face right now. You totally bought that."

I thought he'd jerk away, be angry, but the smugness in his eyes made me think that he was the one playing me.

"Can I ask you something?" Connor said, still not moving away from the space where our breath mingled.

I felt myself nod, even though I had meant to play stoic.

He moved a millimeter closer. His bottom lip brushed ever so softly against mine and sent a chill up my spine. "Can I have my shirt back so I can go?"

Horrified, I looked down at my hand. It held a tightly clutched fistful of his T-shirt. So had I been the one pulling him toward me the whole time? I let go and stepped back up into my truck, swallowing the bitter taste of humiliation.

"Laila," he said, but I didn't give him a chance to finish. I slammed the door and pressed my thumb against the starting pad.

CHAPTER 19

Addie: Can cardboard have blocking capabilities?

It took two days watching my dad every time he pulled out his phone to finally figure out his password. So that night, after giving him plenty of time to fall asleep, I retrieved his phone again and brought it back to my room. I sat cross-legged on my bed and entered in his code. The wallpaper on his phone was a picture of me sticking my tongue out at him. It almost made me feel bad about stealing his phone to get information. Almost.

I clicked on Contacts and held my breath. My name was first on his list, followed by several people I didn't recognize. Probably coworkers. But just in case, I wrote down the name and address of any contact I didn't know. Then there were some names I did recognize from back home, friends of my parents. My mom was in there, which shouldn't have seemed weird, but it did. By the time I got to the end of his list, I had written down five people altogether. I could handle researching five people.

I zipped my hoodie higher against the chill in the air and looked up and down the street again for the bus. The schedule had said one stopped every fifteen minutes, but I'd been standing there for twenty and hadn't seen a single bus pass. Considering it was the middle of winter, it could've been much colder. It was Dallas, after all. But standing outside in my light jacket with the wind blowing was causing a chill. I pulled out my phone and checked the map again. Maybe I could walk to one of the addresses from here. The little red dots on the map, indicating each location, assured me I couldn't.

The sound of a car idling on the street made me look up. The passenger-side window rolled down, and Trevor leaned over. "Addison. Hi."

"Hi."

"Do you need a ride somewhere?"

"No. I'm good."

He looked at the pole next to me, and I did as well. A sign showing the bus schedule was posted there. "This is the downtown bus."

I nodded. Two of the addresses were downtown, and I figured I should go there first.

"Are you going to the cemetery again?"

That's right. The cemetery was downtown. Maybe Trevor could drop me off, and I could walk from there. "Yes."

He moved his head once to the side, indicating I should get into his car.

I hesitated for one second, then opened the door. He moved a duffel bag from the passenger seat into the back, and I sat in its place. "Thanks." I buckled and ran my hands over my thighs, trying to warm up.

"No problem." He flipped his blinker on, then pulled onto the road.

A chill ran down my body. He reached forward, turned a knob on the dash, and then aimed one of the vents at me. Warm air hit my neck and cheeks.

I picked a subject before he had a chance. "How is your comic coming?"

He shrugged one shoulder. "I'm thinking about letting my brother take over. He's already a better drawer than I am."

"He is good. But I'd have to see your work to compare."

"You already told me you were impressed I drew comics. I wouldn't want to risk you changing your mind by showing you the product."

"True. My opinion is right up there with the top comic critics in the world." I paused. "Wait. Are there such things as comic critics?"

He laughed. "Yes, there are actually."

His smile was contagious. It made me want to smile back. He glanced over at me after changing lanes, and I quickly averted my gaze. My eyes landed on his duffel bag in the backseat.

"Oh no. You were on your way somewhere, weren't you? I'm sorry. You can take me back. Really, I don't mind waiting."

He didn't slow down at all with my suggestion. "It's okay. I was just on my way to the gym. I can go later."

My eyes went to his arms with his mention of the gym. This time he wore a T-shirt, and I could clearly see this trip must've been a daily routine. I looked away before he caught me staring at his arms again. "Aren't you cold?"

"My sweatshirt is in the back." It was quiet for a while. He pulled onto the freeway. After driving in silence for several miles, he said, "I'm not crazy."

"I know." Not this again. Tension immediately spread across my chest. "You brought a sweatshirt, so clearly you're not."

"That's not what I mean. I know what I saw. You can move fast. Beyond fast."

"Fast?" I put on my best skeptical voice. "What are you talking about?"

He took in two deep breaths and stared straight ahead. "I know what I saw."

My eyes stung. Why had I gotten in the car with him? I didn't like this at all. Trevor was a nice guy, and I felt terrible making him feel this way. "I don't know what to tell you."

"The truth would be nice." He pulled into the right lane and exited the freeway.

I wished I could tell him the truth. But I knew I couldn't. "If you believe that's what you saw, there's not much I can say."

The statues came into view. He parked the car and turned toward me, his eyes pleading.

His stare nearly undid me, almost made me confess to every lie I'd ever told in my life. When my head started to swim, I realized I hadn't taken a breath since he faced me. I blindly reached for the door handle, fumbled with it for a few seconds, then pushed myself out of his car.

"Thanks for the ride. I'll see you later," I said, then quickly shut the door and walked toward the cemetery. I reached the first tree, ducked behind it, and let my breathing return to normal. Trevor had some kind of hold on me, and I couldn't figure out what.

The first address on my list was one of my dad's coworkers. I recognized him from the Thanksgiving party we'd gone to at Stephanie's house. So after politely telling him I had the wrong address, I headed for the second red dot on my phone map, an apartment building ten blocks from the cemetery.

The apartment number was 314, so I waited by the elevators to head up to the third floor. They were taking forever and I was feeling impatient, so I found the door marked Stairs instead. The stairwell was dimly lit and in need of a paint job—maybe the reason they kept it dimly lit. The echo of every step I took bounced off the walls. I made it to the third floor and stepped out into the hall.

A sign indicating that 314 was to my left was mounted on the wall. I followed it. I knocked on the door. Nobody answered. I knocked again, harder this time. Just as I turned away, the door swung open.

"Hi, I was—" My sentence stopped in my mouth as I turned back to face the man now standing in front of me—my grandfather.

My supposedly dead grandfather.

I bit back a scream, and my heart doubled its speed. I stuttered out something incomprehensible.

His mouth curved into a smile, and he said softly, "Addie." Then he pulled me against him in a crushing hug.

My arms, not sure what to do at first, stayed stiffly at my sides. But as memories filled my mind and my eyes filled with tears, I wrapped them around his waist.

"You're . . ." *Alive,* I wanted to say, but my throat closed up and the tears spilled from my eyes.

He pushed me out by my shoulders and took my face in his hands, searching every inch of it. "Look at you. You're so beautiful. So, so beautiful."

My cheeks went hot. He looked just like I remembered him—white hair and blue, smiling eyes. A few fresh tears found their way down my face.

A movement out of the corner of my eye caused him to let go of my face and both of us to turn.

"And who's this?" he asked.

I quickly wiped at my cheeks. Trevor stood at the end of the hall.

He walked forward. "Sorry, I just didn't want to leave you

downtown alone. Are you okay?"

"I'm fine. I'm good. You can go now."

My grandfather spoke up. "Does your father know you're here, Addie?"

"No."

"Stay." He shut the door in my face.

Great, was he going to go call my father? I turned to Trevor. "Thanks for the ride, but really, I'm good now."

He looked at the door, as if thinking I was anything but good, standing there staring at a door. "Who is that?"

"My grandfather."

"When's the last time you saw him?"

Why did Trevor have to be so observant? "It's been a while."

The door swung open again, revealing my grandfather holding a walking stick and wearing a pair of headphones. The cord to the headphones hung down his chest and was plugged into nothing. He used the stick like a metal detector wand as he held it inches away from me, running it up one side of my body first and then the other. He did the same to Trevor. So weird.

"Okay, you're good. Come in." He gestured to both of us to follow him inside.

"Actually, Trevor was just leaving."

"No, please, both of you come in."

Trevor didn't wait for a second invitation and walked by my grandpa and into the apartment. I sighed and followed him. My grandpa glanced up and down the hall, shut the door behind us, and bolted and chained several locks. I noticed the keypad to an alarm next to the door as well, but he didn't set it.

"Addie. It's so good to see you."

I was so confused, and anger was beginning to build in my chest. My dad had kept this from me.

He led us into the living room, which was a cluttered mess of books, newspapers, and modified kitchen appliances. A computer sat on a table in the corner, a recent picture of my father and me filling the screen, only broken up by the icons. There were so many questions waiting to spill out, but there stood Trevor, taking everything in.

"This is Trevor, by the way. I met him here, in Dallas." I hoped my grandfather understood what I was trying to say, because I couldn't very well tell him, *He's a Norm, so don't say anything incriminating.* Not that it mattered. I had already done enough incriminating things to last a while.

"Trevor." My grandfather shook his hand. "We don't talk out in the open. If you have questions, you ask them in the box."

"The box?" Trevor said.

He gestured to the sliding glass door, and through the windows on his back patio, I saw a large cardboard refrigerator box standing upright. A dark line in the shape of a door was cut into one side of the box. I had memories of him with my grandmother when I was young—pre-ability young. I remembered him being really fun. But was a six-year-old's version of fun a seventeen-year-old's version of slightly left of normal? I wasn't sure. And that thought made my heart heavy.

"I have questions," Trevor said, starting toward the door.

I grabbed onto the back of his jacket. "No. You don't." I had questions. I could start with the easy ones. "How long have you lived here?"

"Ten years."

That's when he died—ten years ago. So he'd been living here ever since? He was the family member Scar-Face had referred to. He had to be. So the Compound knew that he had left. But did they know he was here?

"Do you want something to drink? Only water. I make my own special filter to take out the stuff the government adds."

"I'm good," Trevor said.

We stared at each other in silence then. My grandfather smiled proudly at me as he fiddled with his headphones.

I looked at the box, then back to my grandpa. If it got him to answer some questions, I could go stand in a box for a few minutes. "I think I want to go to the box." Trevor started to follow, and I turned on him. "I need to talk to him alone."

Trevor nodded, then sat down.

By the time I got to the back patio, my grandfather was already inside, and the flimsy cardboard door stood partially ajar. I walked in, and he pulled it shut behind us. For a second I thought I'd see wires and lights, something to show it was actually shielding us from the supposed eavesdroppers, but it was just the inside of a really big box. I looked up. There wasn't even a ceiling. Nice. I took a deep breath. "You're alive." I didn't know why I was stating the obvious, but it seemed important to say out loud.

He got an apologetic look on his face. "I am."

"But why? Why did you pretend to be dead? Why did you come here?" I asked.

"I had to get out of there. That place controls everything. Every memory you have is theirs. How do you even know what parts of your life are real?"

"What?"

"I'm a Healer. They can't steal my memories. My brain heals itself when they try to shut off the paths. They can't even give me new memories. So I know things. I know what they do. I couldn't live there anymore."

"What who do?"

"The Containment Committee. The DAA. They're after them."

"After who?"

"The people without abilities."

"The Norms?"

"No. The people in the Compound without abilities. They don't want them diluting the bloodlines. They steal them. Reassign them."

He was crazy. I was standing in a box talking to my crazy, supposed-to-be-dead grandpa. I was trying to separate the crazy from the bits of reality.

He looked over my shoulder. "Have you told Trevor?"

"Told him what?"

"Told him about the Compound?"

"Of course not. That's illegal. No."

"If you want to borrow my box to tell him, you can. Because they might be listening. They follow all the Paras living Outside."

"I don't think they have the resources for that, Grandpa." I sighed. This was pointless. My grandfather was paranoid and delusional. Was this the real reason he'd retired from the Bureau, the real reason he came to live on the Outside? Because he was crazy? "The Compound knows you're not dead."

"I know."

"Do they know you're here?"

"I've moved all over. I'm safe now. I managed to evade them several years ago."

I nodded slowly. I wondered if he really had, or if they knew exactly where he was and considered him harmless. "It was good to see you."

"You'll come see me again?"

"Yes, of course." A realization hit me. "Dad moved Grandma here for you."

"I told him not to. She loved the Compound. She was like you. Divergent."

"I know." I started to leave, then stopped. "Grandpa?"

"Yes?"

"Did she have any other powers?" Maybe she'd kept things from me too. Just like my dad.

"Like what?"

"I don't know. Anything else to do with manipulating time? As she got more advanced?"

"She could see two futures." He said it in awe.

"I know. Divergence. But anything else?"

"Why? Can you do more?"

I started to say yes. I wanted to tell him, to tell an adult who might be able to help me understand. But as I looked at him and then at the box that surrounded us, I didn't really think my grandfather would be able to help me understand much. "No. Just the two futures thing."

I walked out of the box. Day had turned to dusk outside— pink clouds streaked the sky. I used to think the Perceptives made the sunsets more beautiful than they really were, but seeing the brilliant sunsets over the last few weeks made me realize that not everything beautiful was an illusion.

Back in the apartment, Trevor sat hunched over a newspaper. I thought he was reading it at first but then saw he was drawing on it. He stopped when he saw me and threw down the pencil.

"My turn in the box?" He said it with a smirk on his face. The kind that said he knew I wasn't going to let that happen.

I smiled back. "Nice try."

My grandfather slid the door shut. "Let me get you kids a snack before you go." The hope in his eyes brought out the guilt in me.

"Okay. We can probably stay a few more minutes."

He smiled and excused himself into the kitchen.

I sat next to Trevor on the couch and leaned my head back on the cushion, closing my eyes.

I could feel Trevor staring at me, probably waiting for me to explain to him what was going on. That was impossible, though.

Even if I wanted to, I couldn't. So I opened my eyes to tell him once again that I couldn't, but he wasn't staring at me. He was drawing again. Oh. Good.

He cleared his throat. "'Man Rescues Infant. In a feat of heroism some like to attribute to a rush of adrenaline, a man in Dallas climbed five floors in under five minutes and rescued a baby from a building engulfed in flames.'"

"What are you talking about?"

"It's the article. In the paper. Your grandpa has the headline underlined." He held it up so I could see. The only thing I saw was the head Trevor had drawn, its mouth wide open, eating the *M* in "Man." He was a really good artist. I didn't need to read the article, though. Maybe it was a Para, but not necessarily. Ordinary people did amazing things every day.

"What's your point?"

"My point is, you can do that. I saw you in the bookstore with my brother. You saved him."

I stood and walked to the window, looking down onto the street. "Listen, whatever you thought you saw, you need to forget it, because it's only going to cause both of us problems."

"I can't do that. I overheard some of the Lincoln High football players talking in the locker room a couple weeks ago—soothing emotions, tearing muscles—and I tried to explain it away. But then you come here from Lincoln High. And you can do that." He pointed at me like "that" was something visible on my body. "And I can't help but think what they said was true." He rubbed his shoulder. "It's personal. I need answers."

No wonder why Trevor hadn't been easy to deter. He had heard something unexplainable. My appearance had brought him an explanation. I looked at his shoulder, and thought about what Duke and his teammates had done. "I'm sorry about your shoulder," I said, sitting down again. "Duke's a jerk. But I can't give you answers. It's too . . . dangerous."

He ran his hands through his hair in frustration.

My grandpa came into the room, carrying a tray of cut vegetables. I grabbed a carrot stick and took a bite.

"I grew these veggies myself using my own special fertilizer."

I resisted the urge to spit out the chewed-up piece of carrot in my mouth. Trevor raised his eyebrows at me and mouthed, *His own fertilizer?* I tried not to laugh.

Trevor stood. "Thank you for your hospitality, sir, but I need to get going. Do you need a ride, Addison?"

I looked at my grandpa, then shook my head no. I didn't need to hold Trevor up from his plans any longer. I could take the bus back. "No, I'm good."

My grandpa held the platter out to Trevor. "Take some food for the road."

His hand hovered over the vegetable tray. Finally, he settled for a couple of cucumber slices, which he immediately palmed. At the door, he fumbled with all the locks and left.

I watched him go. Then my gaze drifted to the picture Trevor had drawn on the newspaper. Was that article about a Paranormal? Was that the kind of story that would alert the Containment Committee? And why did my grandpa have the article underlined? What if he brought other people here to the box to try to warn them with his crazy theories? He wouldn't. Would he? If the CC thought he was harmless, that seemed like the kind of thing that might change their minds and bring them straight to his door. Or maybe he really had managed to evade them.

The toaster on the table started beeping. Nope, he was harmless.

My grandpa eyed it. "I think you should go after him."

"Why?"

"Because he seemed upset." He nodded toward the toaster. "And because there's a Containment car downstairs waiting to intercept him."

It may have been crazy talk, but I'd rather be safe than sorry. I ran out the front door after Trevor.

CHAPTER 20

Laila: Self-torture sounds better without the word *self*.

It had been three days since my father stole my money. Three days since I'd seen Connor and humiliated myself. And for three days, I had been trying to talk myself out of having to face him again. But I had a theory—maybe I didn't need to learn to advance my ability. Connor was a Healer. Maybe he could Heal Addie's blocked paths. Reopen her mind to her memories. Maybe she didn't need me to do it at all.

I decided I must be a fan of self-torture. Especially because the last thing in the world I wanted was to ask Connor for a favor. If it were anyone but Addie, I would've walked away by now.

Only he wasn't at home or in his garage. I texted him: *Where are you?*

He made me wait five minutes before he texted back: *Founders Park. By the metro.*

I drove the twenty minutes to Founders Park, stepped out of the car, and put my aloof face on. I liked to be in control of every situation I could. There were too many times my father asserted his power. I wouldn't give up mine when I had a choice. Definitely not for a guy.

I walked past the statues that flanked one corner of the block. As the Compound started changing faster and faster, someone with too much sentimentality, in my opinion, had sanctioned that the oldest area of the city remain forever unchanged. Old cars, old houses, old streetlights, and statues of our founders. Essentially an entire city block wasted. Prime property sitting unused and antiquated. It had turned into a museum of sorts, mostly occupied by schoolchildren taking field trips—a practical study of the Outside world. And even schoolchildren didn't care to see it. Most of the time it was all but abandoned, like now. Especially during school holidays.

I found Connor sitting on a park bench in front of an old transit car. "I haven't been here since I was eight. I thought someone had gotten smart and torched the place. Guess I was wrong."

He didn't look over. "Funny."

"I thought so. Was it the delivery or the subject matter that didn't work for you?"

"More the insulting nature than anything."

"I see." I sat down next to him and studied the metal boxlike thing that used to serve as mass transit. I couldn't imagine getting around like that. All smashed together with so many other people in your space. "I need a favor."

"Are those the only four words you know?"

"Now that joke didn't work at all, because I had already said many words before I jumped into the whole favor thing. If I had led with it, then maybe."

He rubbed his eyes and stood. "The answer is no."

"You haven't even let me ask."

He didn't say anything and walked to the next display—a row of old motorcycles.

"What's with your obsession with Norm things?"

"It's good to be educated. You never know whether you'll end up out there."

"I will never end up out there."

He got out his phone and took a picture of the motorcycle. "Are you Clairvoyant now?"

"No, but some things are nonnegotiable. Me living on the Outside is one of those. I can't imagine always being surrounded by—"

"I'm half Norm."

I started to laugh but then realized he was serious. "You're half Norm?"

"My father is Norm, my mom is a Mass Manipulator."

"Really? And you're a Healer. That's . . . amazing really." Not just the fact that he was a Healer, which was rare, but that he

160

was so skilled in his ability. It didn't seem diluted at all.

He raised one eyebrow and looked at me. "How did you know, anyway?"

"How did I know what?"

"That I was a Healer."

"Well, my knee was bleeding and you put your hands on it and regenerated my skin. I know many people might not have caught on, but I'm pretty observant like that."

"No. That night outside Mike Petty's house. You were in the tree. You jumped on me and told me you weren't worried because of my ability."

I swatted my hand through the air. "Oh. That. Yeah, I didn't know. I was hoping your reaction to my statement would give it away."

He gave a frustrated grunt. "I'm stupid."

"No. I'm just incredibly smart." I drummed my fingers on my arm. "So back to my fav—" Wait. I couldn't get past the fact that he was half Norm. "So your dad lives on the Outside then?"

"Yes, of course."

"Huh," I said in wonderment. I'd had no idea. "Were you worried you weren't going to Present?"

"Will you just ask your favor so you can go?" He took several more pictures of the bike, then pocketed his phone. A streak of grease ran down the left side of his nose, and I realized he must've been working on his bike before coming here.

"How old were you?"

"When I Presented?"

161

I nodded.

"Twelve."

My shoulders fell. Even a guy with half-Norm blood Presented at twelve.

"Your brother still not showing signs?"

"He'll get there."

"Is he using Face's track?"

"Yes."

His jaw tensed.

"Why?"

"No reason." He reached over the barrier that was supposed to prevent people from touching the antiques and grabbed a set of keys out of the bike. "I wonder if it still runs."

"They wouldn't have gas near the city, even if it is historical." I snatched the keys from him and climbed over the waist-high barrier.

"What are you doing?"

"Testing my theory." I slid the keys into the ancient starting device and turned. Nothing happened.

"That's not how you start a Norm motorcycle."

"Well, come over here and show me how you start a Norm motorcycle, oh Norm expert."

He jumped over the barrier and moved me aside by my hips. A chill shot up my back. He turned the key a notch, then used one foot to push down on a bar by his leg, then did something on the handle. There was a small purr of the motor, followed by silence. "Ha!" A smile lit up his face. "That was incredible."

162

I laughed. "It didn't start."

"But it turned over." He slid off the bike and gave it another appraising stare.

A smile looked good on Connor, and I couldn't decide if it was because it was such a rare occurrence or because it lit up his whole face. I realized I was staring and forced myself to look away. "I'm surprised we haven't been kicked out yet."

"You're kidding, right? This place is so understaffed it's laughable. Plus, it's sanctioned. They can't even bring Para security systems here. They want to keep it pure."

"But you've never tried to start the bike before?"

"No."

"Too sacred?"

Instead of hopping back over the barrier like I expected him to, he walked deeper into the relics. Toward the back was an Amtrak train sitting on some rusty tracks. He gave me a smirk and climbed up through the open door.

"So, what is it that you need, Laila?" he asked from inside.

"I need you to restore Addie's memories. If that's even possible. I mean, you kind of owe it to her, since you almost ran her over and everything."

His head reappeared in the doorway. "What?" But he didn't wait for my answer, just disappeared again.

Was he honestly going to make me climb into that rusty old thing? Would it even hold the both of us without falling apart? With a grunt I reached for the vertical bar on the side and hoisted myself inside. He stood just inside the door, and I almost swung myself into him. I stopped short. It was dim—only the light from an old light post glowed outside the single open door.

"I need you . . ." I stopped because he was staring at me intensely, and I didn't understand why. I looked down to make sure I wasn't subconsciously gripping his shirt again, but both my hands were at my sides like well-behaved children. My heart wasn't playing the well-behaved game, though, and decided to beat out of control. When I looked back up at him, I realized where I had stopped my sentence and quickly added, "To help me. To help Addie."

He took a step back and then seemed lost for a moment, like he didn't remember what he was doing. I bit back a smile. Did I actually have an effect on him?

He finally sat down on a bed that folded out from the wall. This must've been a sleeper car. "Is she hurt?"

"No. I Erased her memories and she wants them back. You can do that, can't you? You can reopen blocked memory paths, regenerate stagnant memories."

"No. I can't."

"I know you can, so are you saying you won't?" I actually didn't know he could, but confidence in a suspected truth had gotten many people to admit many things to me.

"That's exactly what I'm saying."

"You're kind of a jerk sometimes."

"Sometimes? I was going for all the time. What more do I have to do?" He stood and walked deeper into the train. My heel caught on some sort of bolt on the ground, and I almost tripped.

I got my phone out to light the way and followed him. When I caught up, I grabbed hold of his arm and used it as support while I took off my shoes. I tossed them onto a seat. "Don't let me forget those on the way back."

He glanced at me several times as we continued walking.

"What?"

"You're shorter than I thought."

"I am not short."

"I said shorter."

"I always wear heels." I sighed. He really wasn't going to help Addie. "I guess it's back to me advancing my ability."

"What makes you think that you advancing your ability will result in restoring memories?"

His arm accidentally brushed mine, and my heart raced. Stupid, traitorous heart.

"The note. It's a long story. It just will . . ." I stopped with a gasp. We had reached the front of the train, and the windows that surrounded us now looked out onto the river, across which shone the city lights. The tracks at one point must've gone across, but they were now a gnarled mess. The train rested on the last track, its progress halted by the water. We stood in the old, looking at the new. With Connor standing so close, the darkness surrounding us, and the lights streaking the water white in front of us, an energy began to build in the air. An energy that seemed to push against me.

"Have you ever tried to restore memories?" he asked.

"Nope." I sat in one of the big chairs behind tons of knobs

and buttons. "But there's no time like the present." The only problem was, Connor was no help. I couldn't Erase his memories and then try to bring them back. I looked around, then dug my phone out of my pocket.

I rested it on top of two knobs. "Addie's house." Immediately the directions to Addie's house appeared, a red line showing the way. I lifted my hands and concentrated. A computer was different from a brain, but I could still feel the most active components. I shut them off and opened my eyes. The directions were gone. Awesome.

Connor sat down on the other seat. "You can Erase a computer's memory." He said it with such a flat voice I wasn't sure whether he was impressed.

Now for the hard part. I tried to concentrate, force my mind to send out its power. A buzz started in my head, and I thought about how Addie was worried about me trying this. How she thought her ability had been damaged by pushing too hard. I shook off the thought. Other people advanced their ability all the time; it couldn't be that bad. But nothing was happening. I gritted my teeth and tried again.

"You're trying to restore its memory by advancing your ability?"

"Yes."

"And you need some strong emotion?"

I paused. Strong emotion? I didn't let the gasp that wanted to come out escape with the revelation, with the memory of just minutes before when I'd felt an energy building around me.

That was usable? So Connor knew more about advancing abilities than he let on. "Yes."

"You must be off the DAA program then. If you've been using that, it's not going to work."

A lot more. "I am." I swallowed hard. "Can you just . . ."

"Can I just what?" He turned toward me, his eyes meeting mine. They were electrified, like a lightning storm raged behind them. I needed to feel that energy. I swiveled my seat toward him, rested my hand on my knee and turned it palm up. That was as much risk as I could take. Now it was his turn.

CHAPTER 21

Addie: Need to purchase some protective face gear.

"Trevor, wait!" I called down the stairs. He was at least a floor below me. I could hear his footsteps but couldn't see him when I leaned over the rail. "Wait!"

The footsteps stopped, and I walked down the remaining space between us.

"Your grandfather's kind of different, yeah?"

"That's a nice word for it."

He smiled. "What was the thing that looked a lot like a toaster sitting on the coffee table?"

Possibly the reason he's been able to stay hidden all these years. "I think it was a modified toaster. Maybe he receives transmissions from Mars on it. I don't know."

"Maybe it tells him the future."

"Let's not get carried away."

"So . . ." He started walking again. "You came after me why?"

"You think there's another way out of this building? Besides the lobby?"

"I'm sure there's a back exit. I think there's a parking lot back there."

"So we have a choice?"

"My car's parked out front, so that makes my choice easy."

"Can you just . . ." I grabbed his arm and he stopped. "Can we just sit for one minute?" One minute should be enough to do a quick Search. "I'm feeling a little dizzy."

"Sure." He helped me sit on a step and then leaned against the wall. "It seemed like you hadn't seen your grandfather in a long time."

This wasn't going to work if he tried to talk to me. "Yeah, I hadn't. I didn't realize he lived here. I've been learning a lot of interesting things lately."

A discarded kid's tennis shoe sat on the step by Trevor's foot. He nudged it a few times with the toe of his shoe, flipping it, then flipping it again. I wondered how many times some mom had searched her apartment over for something that wasn't there. For a shoe that was sitting here in the stairwell. She might never find it, because she obviously had no memory of it falling here.

I put my forehead on my knees so it wouldn't look suspicious when I went catatonic for a minute during my Search. I braced myself for the headache that would follow, wondering if I should even be using my ability right now when I was worried about the lasting effects of these headaches. Of what caused them to begin with.

"Addison," he said, stopping my Search before it started.

I looked up and barely saw the flash of an object as it hit my face. "Ouch." The kid's shoe landed on the step below me with a thump, then rolled down a few more. "Did you just throw a shoe at me?"

"I'm so sorry." He rushed forward and sat on the step below me. "I thought you would move fast and catch it."

I rubbed my cheek, trying to hide a smile. He was relentless. And funny. Why did he have to be so easy to be around?

"I'm sorry. Are you okay?" One of his hands went to my elbow while he inspected my cheek. He cringed. "There's a red mark." He retrieved the shoe, then held it out for me. "You have my permission to throw this at my face as hard as you can."

I laughed. "I'm not going to hit you in the face with a shoe."

"It would make me feel like less of a jerk."

"It's fine. It doesn't even hurt."

He tossed the shoe aside, then ran his fingers lightly over my cheek, which, despite what I'd said, actually stung a little. He studied the new mark intently. "I don't know what's gotten into me. I don't do this. I don't follow people. And I don't throw things at girls."

"What do you do?"

"I . . ." He stopped, and I could tell I'd caught him off guard with the question.

"Tell me more about your comic. What's it about?"

"My attempt at a comic."

My eyes went to his hands, where I could see a callus along the inside of his middle finger along with lead smudges. I meant to just point at his finger, but instead my hand brushed along the smudge. "You don't earn a callus like that from just attempting."

He put his hands palms up and inspected them. "I've been trying to throw with my left hand."

I figured he was talking about a football. "And how is it?"

"As evidenced earlier, I'm a much better aim with my right."

I laughed.

His eyes traveled over my hair and then came to rest on my neck. "Your hair is starting to curl underneath. Is it naturally curly?"

I smoothed my hair. "Yes. I straighten it every day."

He pulled lightly at one of my curls. My heart stammered in my chest as a familiarity at his closeness washed over me again. Maybe I was just remembering the Search from the hospital. Or the way he'd looked at me in the mall.

The mall. With Stephanie.

I cleared my throat and crossed my arms, trying to provide a barrier between us. He was so close. And he smelled so good. And . . . I needed to stop. "Stephanie bought this really amazing dress for the formal. You really should ask her."

He laughed a little and backed away, leaning his head against the wall. "Are you and Rowan ganging up on me?"

"Rowan?"

"He keeps telling me to ask her, and like I told him the other night, I'm kind of tired of her drama. I know you're friends with her and everything, but she and I aren't good together."

A tingling worked its way over my arms. Despite my body thinking this was a good thing, it wasn't. Stephanie was my friend, and she really liked him. "You should give her one more chance. She's working on her drama."

"We'll see."

I buried my head in my arms again, remembering I still needed to Search. He seemed lost in his thoughts, so now was as good a time as any. I took a deep breath and concentrated.

"Are you okay? Does your face hurt?" Trevor asks.

"No. I'm fine." I lift my head, meeting his eyes. They are full of concern.

"Are you sure?"

I stand. "Yes. Can you give me a ride home after all?"

"Of course."

I glance over my shoulder, up the stairs toward my grandpa's apartment. I'll come back tomorrow. We walk down the remainder of the stairs and I peer out the lobby doors, still not sure whether my grandpa was being paranoid. I don't see anyone "waiting to intercept" Trevor, but it's probably better to be on the safe side.

"So you're going to think this sounds ridiculous, but can we circle around the back?" Then I'll be able to scope out the street.

"Why?"

"There were some guys on the street earlier who made me

172

uncomfortable. I don't feel like passing them again."

He stands a little taller. "We'll be fine." He takes a step toward the lobby, and just as he almost comes into view of the windows, I grab his hand.

"No. Please. Can we just go this way?" I pull him toward the red exit sign I see at the end of the hall. He doesn't argue, just lets me lead him out back. I wait for him to pull his hand out of mine, but he doesn't. His hand is warm and comfortable. It swallows mine in its grip. I should let go. I don't.

Once outside we sneak around the building, and I peer up the street. There are several parked cars, but none of them occupied. There doesn't seem to be anyone after Trevor. I relax with the thought.

Trevor lets go of my hand, then points. "I parked a couple blocks down."

Perfect. When we reach his car, he opens the door for me.

I start to get in but stop. "Thank you."

He has one hand on the open door, and he puts his other hand on the top of the car next to my head, boxing me in. "For what?"

I lift my hand, my first instinct to put it on his chest, but hesitate and grab a section of my hair instead. "For not making us go out the front."

He doesn't move away, just stares at me through his thick lashes. My heart flutters. He feels very close all of a sudden, even though neither of us has moved. His eyes drift to my cheek, probably checking on the red mark he made there, but then they flit to my lips. I take a breath in through my mouth, my lips parting slightly with the action.

My hand that grabbed a piece of my hair has frozen, and the hair slips slowly through my fingers, my hand now hovering in the air, empty. As if it has a mind of its own, it presses itself right over his heart, each fast beat now crashing against my palm. He leans closer and his breath washes over me, my eyes closing. He hesitates for a second too long, and I quickly drop my hand and back into the open car door, out of breath. He stares down at me for a moment and then shuts the door.

The memories of the first option flowed together with the memories of the second.

"Are you okay? Does your face hurt?" Trevor asks.

"No. I'm fine." I lift my head, meeting his eyes. They are full of concern.

"Are you sure?"

I stand. "Yes. Can you give me a ride home after all?"

"Of course."

I glance over my shoulder, up the stairs toward my grandpa's apartment. I'll come back tomorrow. We walk down the remainder of the stairs and I peer out the lobby doors, still not sure whether my grandpa was being paranoid. I don't see anyone out the wall of windows that line the front of the lobby. So the modified toaster doesn't work after all. My grandpa is just insane. Is that why my dad didn't want to tell me about him?

He didn't want me to see him like this? My stomach clenches. Whatever the reason, I'm still angry that my dad kept something this big a secret. Especially after he promised me he wasn't keeping any other secrets from me.

I don't stop Trevor when he heads for the lobby doors. I just follow him. Once outside, he points to the right. "I parked a few blocks down."

Despite feeling like Trevor is safe, I look up and down the street. There is no one waiting to intercept him.

We walk in silence for a few minutes, and then he says, "I still think something is going on. And as you've learned, I'm not a very good detective. So maybe you could just tell me."

"Trevor. Really. It's nothing." I've never liked having to be dishonest with him, but this is the first time my stomach turns with the lie.

We arrive at his car, and he sighs. He unlocks the door, then walks around to his own side.

"Sorry if you missed your workout for me," I say when we're inside.

He runs a hand down his face, his expression seeming to say, *And all for nothing.*

I snapped out of my Search, keeping my head on my knees, waiting for the sharp pain to radiate in my head, but only an uncomfortable pressure developed. That seemed like a good sign. Maybe resting my ability had helped.

"Addison?"

175

What had I missed? "Yeah?"

"Are you okay? Does your face hurt?"

"No. I'm fine." My heart raced and I lifted my head, meeting his eyes. They were full of concern.

"Are you sure?"

I stood. "Yes. Can you give me a ride home after all?"

"Of course."

I glanced over my shoulder, up the stairs toward my grandpa's apartment. I'd come back tomorrow. We walked down the remainder of the stairs, and when we got to the bottom I looked both ways—first to the lobby and then to the red exit sign at the end of the hall. Why did my entire being want to go the red exit sign way? I tried to tell myself it wasn't because Trevor almost kissed me when we went that way. It wasn't because I could change that part of the future and let him.

He took a few steps toward the lobby and then looked back at me. "Are you coming?"

My heart ached, but I forced myself to take a step in the direction of the lobby. "Yes."

I changed one little thing from how I had seen it play out. Instead of forcing myself to walk a foot away from him to the car like I had in this version of the Search, I let our arms brush all the way to the passenger-side door. It didn't change the fact that he still got upset when I wouldn't tell him anything. He drove me home in silence. As I watched him drive away, I stood wishing I would've taken the other path.

CHAPTER 22

Laila: Sitting in the dark is bad.

Connor looked at my upturned hand. "I thought the emotion you were channeling with my presence was hatred."

It took every ounce of self-control not to yank my hand away. It took all the coldheartedness I'd learned over the years to keep my face passive. "It is, but the closer you are, the more disgust I feel." I flexed my fingers. "Hurry."

I wasn't sure if he bought my well-delivered lie, but he grabbed my hand. The problem was that now I really was annoyed with him. Now my heart didn't speed up like it normally did when he so much as brushed my arm with his. Now I just wanted to leave.

He shifted his hold on my hand and one by one laced his fingers between mine. The glowing light of my phone clicked off with inactivity, and his face became shrouded in shadows.

"Your dad really stole your money, didn't he?"

It seemed easier to tell the truth in the dark. "Yes."

"Why?"

"He's addicted to suppressors. He's a Telepath."

I felt his body move as he nodded his head.

"Why are you doing this for Addie?"

The city lights across the river seemed to flicker. "Because she's my best friend."

He cleared his throat. "I don't buy that."

"I never asked you to. It's the truth."

"There's more."

"I screwed her over. Made out with her boyfriend while she was still with him. I owe her this."

"Duke."

"Yes."

He was quiet for a while, seeming to consider whether he wanted to tell me something. "I know you want me to restore her memory, but believe me, neither you or she would want that."

"But I do want that, and actually, she wrote a note to herself. . . . She wants it as well."

He sighed. "Does it get tiring?"

"What?"

"Always thinking you're right."

I smiled. "No, not really. It's other people not realizing I'm

178

right that gets tiring. Now talk. Why wouldn't we want you to?"

"If I Healed Addie's mind, anyone's mind, everything that had ever been Erased would come back."

"That's fine. The one she wants back is the only one I've ever Erased."

"The only one *you've* ever Erased. You're not the only Memory Eraser in the Compound."

"She doesn't know any other Memory Erasers."

"But I'm sure her parents do."

"You think her parents had some of her memories Erased?"

"I think most parents alter their children's life experience. They think they're doing us a favor. But it's not just Erased memories that my ability would restore, it's suppressed memories, forgotten memories, memories of every image she ever saw. There's a reason Healers are used in torture. Not even a strong mind would be able to handle it."

I had no idea, but it made sense. "Yeah, I guess I don't want to subject Addie to torture . . . do I?"

"Believe me, you don't."

For a minute I had forgotten about our clasped hands, but now, in the new silence, my entire being seemed to focus on them. I tried to use that energy, but I only felt scattered and flustered. I needed to concentrate, think about something else. And I didn't want to share any more personal items, so that left him.

"What about you? What's your story? Why do you sell illegal expansion programs?"

"Because they shouldn't be illegal. I think the DAA should allow for some competition. It makes for better products."

"You're doing this out of goodwill? Connor, the spokesperson for a free-market society? Nice try."

His hand twitched a little in mine. Just enough for me to know I'd correctly called his bluff.

"What's the real reason?"

My eyes had adjusted somewhat to the dark, and I saw the muscle in his jaw tighten with the question. "Maybe I want to be kicked out."

Now *that* I wasn't expecting. "What? Why?"

"Then I wouldn't have to make the choice."

"What choice?"

"The choice between going or staying."

Our breaths rose and fell together as I watched him, waiting for him to expound. He didn't, so I did for him. "You're hoping someone takes away your power to choose by forcing you to leave the Compound?"

"If I have no choice in the matter, then there's no guilt."

"So you want to leave. That's the issue. You want to be with your dad?"

"I don't know my dad. So no. I feel trapped here. Limited."

"Wouldn't you feel the same out there? You could tell nobody what you can do. You'd have to live in secret. That would be a nightmare."

Connor flipped our hands so that mine was on top and studied the back of it. "So if you feel terrible about what you did to

Addie with Duke, why did you do it? Why do you still hang out with him?"

Okay, apparently we were changing the subject back to me. "We don't hang out that . . ." I trailed off because Connor gave me a look that said I wasn't answering his question. So I told him the real reason. "He's a Mood Controller."

"I guessed as much."

"He's really good at his ability."

His hand tightened on mine. "He gives you false emotion."

"It doesn't feel false when I'm around him. When he's there, I feel pure happiness. A feeling I can't get anywhere else." Why was I telling him all this? I nudged my phone so the light would come back on. It was too dangerous to talk in the dark.

His voice went low. "But it's fake emotion."

I shrugged. "It feels the same to me."

"Then you've never felt the real thing, because forced happiness is not the same as real happiness."

I turned to face him head-on. "And forced choices aren't the same as real choices," I said, anger bursting in my chest.

We held each other's stare, and without meaning to, my body moved an inch closer to him. He reached over with his free hand, took me by the back of the head, and pulled me to him. Our lips collided roughly. As though years of pent-up emotions were waiting to come out, the kiss was hungry and raw. Our hands unclasped, and mine found his hair and entangled themselves there. His hands went to my waist, pulling me off my chair and onto his. My chest expanded, but at the same time, I couldn't get enough air. I didn't need air, though. I only needed him. In the midst of it all, a horrible fear struck me that I wouldn't be able to Erase this. That he'd remember my vulnerability. My desire. My need.

I pulled away.

"That should work," I said, and backed into my chair again to face my phone. My breath wanted to come rapidly, and I forced the movements of my chest to at least appear calm and even. I tried to ignore my lips, which stung from the kiss. I concentrated on channeling my emotion to reopen the paths I had blocked on the phone. I even closed my eyes to push out the distraction that was Connor. That's when I felt it, the buzz that hung around me. The energy seemed to vibrate against my body. I forced it all toward the phone. A monotone voice said, "Approximately twenty minutes with traffic." I opened my eyes again. The red line was back. The blinking dot that represented Addie's house flashed on and off.

I'd done it.

With Connor.

Whether I'd be able to do it without him was the question. When I went to Dallas in three days, could I give Addie her memories back?

I didn't want to look at Connor, too afraid of what I would . . . or wouldn't . . . see. So when his chair shifted as he stood, I didn't look over.

"If I could Erase that, I would," I said.

"Consider it forgotten." His footsteps echoed out of the small cabin.

182

I stared at the lights in the distance. The monotone voice on my phone reminded me that Addie's house was twenty minutes away, with traffic. I wished I really were going to Addie's house. She'd tell me I was an idiot. She'd tell me what I was supposed to do now.

I finally allowed myself one look over my shoulder, but there was only darkness.

CHAPTER 23

Addie: Liars suck.

As I walked into the house, I was so angry my eyes were hot. A note on the counter announced that my dad had gone out to pick up some dinner. Every minute he was gone, my anger intensified.

"Hey, baby," my dad said when he finally came home.

I wanted to scream, *Guess who I saw today?* I started to but stopped myself, my throat tightening. The only way I would ever be able to forgive my father was if he told me the truth without being cornered. I needed to hear from his mouth about my grandfather still being alive. So I'd give him a chance to come clean on his own.

"I brought us some food." He held up a bag of what smelled like Chinese food.

"I'm not hungry."

"Oh." He got down a plate and unloaded the boxes from the bag. "What have you been up to today?"

"Nothing."

"Nothing?" He had the nerve to sound irritated that I wasn't being completely honest with him.

"How's that whole 'getting Grandpa's grave moved here' working out?"

"Like I said, it might take a while."

"Really?" *Like, you're waiting for him to die?*

He stopped midway through scooping some rice onto his plate. My anger was seeping out, despite my intentions. "What's going on, Addie?"

"Nothing. I'm tired."

I left him with his Chinese food and went to my bedroom. My phone, which was sitting on the dresser, chimed. The text was from Stephanie.

Hey, Addie, guess who called me just now?? Trevor. He asked me to winter formal. Eeeeeh.

I stared at that message. My heart clenched. What was wrong with me? That's exactly what I wanted to happen when I opened my mouth and said, *You should ask Stephanie to winter formal.* So why had I hoped he wouldn't listen to me? Why did that text hurt so much? I typed: *Are you sure you're ready to give him another chance? Didn't you say he had issues?* My finger hovered over the Send button. With a sigh, I erased the text and instead wrote:

That's great, Steph. Call me tomorrow.

My room seemed extra cold that night, and I pulled the blankets up to my chin. Still, a shudder went through my body as I thought of that text from Stephanie; as I wished I had let the almost-kiss future play out so that Trevor had that memory too and not just me. He wouldn't have asked Stephanie to the formal if he had that memory. I rolled onto my side and groaned. I tried to think of something else, anything else, but I could almost feel his breath on my lips. I traced my lips with a finger. What was wrong with me? Why was I so drawn to Trevor?

I sat up suddenly, grabbed my phone off my dresser, and searched through the text messages. It took me a few minutes to realize Laila hadn't texted me the news about the letter I wrote myself after coming out of my Search. She had told me. What had she said? She said I wanted her to restore my memory. I had thought it was because I had found out some of the secrets my parents were keeping from me. But what if it was something different I wanted to remember? Or someone?

An overwhelming desire to have my memories restored so I could figure out why I wrote that note filled my entire being. How could I do that? My mind scrolled through options and then just as quickly dismissed them. Did I know any other Memory Erasers who were more advanced than Laila? Even if I did, they were hundreds of miles away. The only abilities that were here for immediate use was my own ability—useless.

And my dad's—even more useless. I threw myself back on my bed and closed my eyes. But then they popped open with a thought—my grandpa. He was a Healer. Could he Heal my mind? Reopen the paths?

My head whipped over to my digital clock. Two a.m. Way too early to go running to his house. This was going to be a long night.

After showering and dressing for the day, I strode with purpose to the living room. It was Saturday morning; my dad would let me use his car. I opened my mouth to ask him as much, when I saw he wasn't alone. Two men in jeans and polos sat on the couch. I thought they were new neighbors or something until they stood and I saw the scar down the side of one man's cheek. I froze.

"Addison," Scar-Face said. "Good to see you again."

"Why are you here?" I didn't mean to be so blunt, but I was worried. Last night I'd discovered my grandpa alive, and now the Containment Committee was in my living room. Had I done something wrong?

"Addie, this is Agent Farley and Agent Miller. They are just making a routine visit from the Compound. They're the agents assigned to the greater Dallas area."

Routine visit. Did my dad believe that or was he playing along? He would know if they were lying. "Oh. Hi. Good to see you."

"We wanted to stop by to see if you had any questions. If you were adjusting well."

"I'm fine." I hovered in the doorway, not wanting to commit to the room.

"We understand you've become friends with a Trevor Davis."

My heart skipped a beat. This wasn't about my grandpa. This was about Trevor. Great. He must have talked to the wrong people. Was he telling others about what he had overheard in the locker room? "Yes."

"It seems Trevor has learned some Compound secrets. Has he come to you with those?"

"No." I stopped myself in case one of them was a lie detector. "I mean, he said something about our football players deliberately injuring him, but I told him it wasn't true." There. Now nobody, not even my dad, could claim I'd lied.

"That's good. We wanted to make sure you were firm in your cover story and that you were upholding your contract."

"Yes, I am."

My dad moved to the door, almost as if he were as anxious to see them leave as I was.

Scar-Face nodded, then handed me a card. "If you have any questions, like your father mentioned, we're stationed in the area."

That seemed like a threat. "So there are a lot of Paranormals in Dallas?"

"There are a few in Dallas. But we cover a large area of Texas."

A few. As in three? My dad, my grandpa, and me? I looked at his card, then put it in my pocket. "Okay, thanks."

When they left, my father and I had a silent standoff. I wasn't letting him out of his lie. He still needed to come clean. I wondered if he would now. But all he said was, "Be careful."

"Did they come here because I messed up somehow?"

"Not necessarily. But watch yourself. Stay away from this Trevor character. They have a lot of power when it comes to protecting the Compound."

"Protecting it from me?"

He smiled. "Not from you. But from everyone else."

By that I knew he meant the Norms. As if Trevor had the power to single-handedly destroy the Compound. I sighed. I guess in a way he did. They all did. If they told people, if our secret could no longer be contained, we could be in danger. But Trevor would never do that. If he knew how important it was to keep it secret, he wouldn't talk about the Compound. My chest tightened. "They won't hurt him, will they?"

"Hurt who?"

"Trevor."

"Of course not. They'll do their best to keep him safe and us safe. It's their job."

I nodded. He was right. They'd dealt with Norms for hundreds of years. They knew what was best. "Can I borrow your car?"

"For what?"

"To drive."

"Where are you going?"

"To see a friend." *To get my memory back.* My dad handed me his car keys without further questions.

CHAPTER 24

Laila: Talked to your mom lately?

"Eli, be my guinea pig."

My brother looked up from his bowl of cereal. "That's not really a stellar sales pitch."

"Come on, I need your help."

"What exactly would I have to do?"

"Just let me Erase this conversation from your mind and then try to restore it." I'd tried to do it on my phone in my room for half the night, but it hadn't worked once since the train with Connor. I had tried to re-create the feelings I'd had when he was there, by thinking about him. I even forced myself to think about kissing him. It didn't work. Maybe I needed a human subject to try it on. And so here I was, asking Eli.

He took another bite. "Yeah, whatever. Just five minutes."

"Of course." I raised my hands and Erased five minutes of his memory.

I started to conjure up images of kissing Connor before Eli even came back to full awareness. The feel of his hands on my waist. My fingers in his hair. A slight buzz of energy pressed against me. But it didn't feel as present as it had the night before.

"What do you want?" Eli asked.

"I need you to be my guinea pig." Maybe I could try different emotions. Like the anger I had for my dad or the love I felt for my brother. This time went no different. I kicked the chair and made Eli jump.

"What's your problem?" he asked.

"Nothing. I'm ticked."

"Obviously."

"I'll be back later." Time for plan B. I grabbed my jacket off the back of the chair and left.

It was weird standing on Addie's front porch without the excuse of seeing Addie. I knocked on the door and looked up at the retina scanner so it would announce who I was to her mom inside. A few moments later, the door slid open.

"Laila." She seemed genuinely happy to see me.

"Hi, Mrs. Coleman." I paused. She probably wasn't going by Mrs. Coleman anymore, but I had no idea what her maiden name was. "I was hoping you could help me."

She stood aside, gesturing for me to come in. "How have you been?" She led me into the living room.

"Good, thanks." I wanted to straight-out ask Mrs. Coleman how to control my advanced ability better. She knew how. She worked for the Department of Ability Advancement. That's what they did—helped people advance their abilities. But I was almost certain she would say no. Because she also made sure people under eighteen didn't push too hard. And if I tried to beg, then she'd know what I was after and she might not fall for my other idea. My stupid idea. But I was desperate.

"What can I do for you?"

I put on my best pleading face. "I've been having nightmares."

"I can get you a program to help with that."

"No. I mean, I think that would just mask the problem, but I don't think it would solve it."

"What did you have in mind?"

"I want to see Bobby Baker."

There was a long pause. Not necessarily one borne out of shock or disbelief, but a silence that seemed to be filled with her trying to assess my motives. She was correct to assume I had them. Mr. Coleman's lie detecting made it hard for me to hide my scheming from them. But now, with him gone, I was pretty sure I could fool Addie's mom.

"If I see him, see that he's just an average guy, maybe he wouldn't haunt my dreams."

"Bobby's brain patterns are being studied right now to help create the best recovery track."

"They aren't wiping him?" I didn't mean to say that so loudly, but it surprised me.

"He's a minor. We've had great success with total brain reha-
bilitation."

How exactly did they qualify "great success" with a crime
rate so low? Most people like Bobby were cured long before they
reached that level of madness. So it had worked on one other
murderer, years ago? "He's at the DAA then?" Even better.
Here I thought I was going to have to ask her to use her Bureau
connections in order to see him, but she could get me into the
DAA any day.

She nodded. "Okay."

"Okay?" My disbelief was apparent in my voice. I thought it
would take a lot longer to talk her into that. Maybe even some
tears. *Okay?*

"Did you want to go now?"

Was I not the only one with an agenda here? I wasn't going
to question her willingness. I jumped up and made a beeline for
the garage.

"Just a word of warning," she said as we made our way through
the halls of the DAA. "He's being housed in a room that cuts off
access to all abilities. Yours will be unavailable as well."

We came to yet another security desk, and she palmed the
pad and directed me to do the same.

"Visitor for Bobby Baker," she said.

We went through a door flanked by two cameras, their lights
blinking.

"His room is also monitored twenty-four/seven." She gave me

a sideways glance with that statement, as if saying, *Watch what you say, because you will be heard.*

We stopped in front of a thick door, and she slid a panel aside, revealing a window. And there he was, sitting on a bed. My heart seemed to freeze for a moment. I hadn't prepared myself for this. I didn't think it would be a big deal. It was a big deal. He had almost killed me a few short weeks ago, and I guess I hadn't fully processed that. The completely Healed cut on my neck seemed to itch with his presence.

My breath was shallow, and I tried to suck in some air without letting it show how much he affected me. I threw my shoulders back. Bobby did not have control over me. I was stronger than him.

"You ready?" she asked.

"Yes."

She pressed a button on the keypad next to the door. "Bobby. You have a visitor."

He looked up and met my eyes through the glass. I held his gaze, refusing to look away. He wore a T-shirt and jeans, no shoes. Small circular devices were attached to his temples. He swung his feet to the ground but didn't stand.

Mrs. Coleman entered a code on the keypad, and a glass partition lowered from the ceiling, effectively cutting his room in half. Then the door in front of us slid open. I didn't move. I had to remind myself why I'd come. I needed to control my advanced ability. Bobby knew how to do that. Or at least he had known. Mrs. Coleman had said they didn't do a complete wipe on him, but did they do a partial one?

"Do you want me to go in with you?" she asked, reminding

me I hadn't taken a single step forward.

"No, that's okay. I got this."

"This door will remain open. I'll be right here." She pointed to a workstation at the end of the hall, fewer than ten feet away.

"Sounds good." I took my first step forward.

Bobby still sat perched on the side of his bed with a semi-amused expression on his face. "Laila." His voice was perfectly audible on this side of the partition. Clear, precise, confident. Just like it always had been. He still had his memories fully intact. "Welcome to my home."

A metal chair sat in the corner on my side, and I hooked it with my foot and dragged it as close to the barrier as possible to prove to him he didn't scare me. "Hey there, Bobby. How've you been?"

"What do you want?"

"I needed to see you here. Helpless." My head started to hum a little, and I remembered what Mrs. Coleman said about the blockers in this room.

"You've seen me. You're free to go."

I reached forward and ran a finger down the glass. "It must kill you to know that if only you could use your ability, you'd be out of this room in less than a second."

One of his eyelids twitched. "I hear Addie might be my neighbor soon."

That sentence stopped my finger midway down the glass. "What?"

He just smiled his creepy smile, showing me his statement had hit the mark.

Just then I heard voices in the hall. Unable to advance my hearing, I could barely make them out.

"This is getting awfully close to warning her, Marissa."

"Laila sought me out. I haven't said a word to her."

"Good, because this has to happen without interference for the deal to be valid. One word from you and we'll enact the Threat to the Compound clause and bring her in here."

Bobby raised his eyebrows at me. "Like I said."

"What did you say to them?"

"Why do you assume it was me?"

"Because you're a lying psychopath." Mrs. Coleman said I was being listened to, so I made sure not to say anything that would indicate I'd heard the conversation in the hall. "How did you do it?"

"Do what?"

I so didn't want to say this, but I hoped it would be vague enough for anyone listening and specific enough for Bobby. "Become the master."

The smile that took over his face reminded me why I hadn't wanted to say it. But he got the reference. "If only you had been a better student before"—he knocked on the glass—"this. Now it's too late." He lay back on his bed, dismissing me.

"Bobby. Be a good citizen."

He just laughed. His laugh was very unnerving.

Mrs. Coleman poked her head into the room. "Everything okay in here?"

I stood. It was obvious Bobby wasn't going to help me. "Yes. I'm ready to leave."

After he was locked up and we were leaving the building, I said, "I thought you were going to fix him. He's still completely deranged."

"Right now we are just gathering the data. Then we fashion the program. It's an enlightening study for us. We can pinpoint brain patterns and hope to be able to prevent this in other children in the future. It may be against his will, but Bobby is being a good citizen." Her use of the word made me realize she had heard everything we had said. Did she know I had heard her as well?

"Where are we going?" I asked as she turned right instead of left on Main Street. "Isn't home the other way?"

"I just had a small errand to run on this side of town. Is that okay? It shouldn't take long."

"Sure."

We came to the large tunnel that ran beneath the river separating old town from new. I hated this tunnel. Avoided it at all costs. Not just because it went under the river, but because it marked the beginning of Founders Park—our preserved piece of history. So I always expected this tunnel, its engineering centuries old, to collapse at any moment. I watched the mounted lights go by, noting how different they were from the updated part of the city. Suddenly, Mrs. Coleman stopped the car and instructed its flashers on. Then she turned toward me.

"I need you to warn Addie when you see her. Not over the phone."

"Of what, exactly?"

"Just tell her to be careful. Not to show her hand. They can't know Bobby affected her in any way or they will lock her up. They think she has a piece of Bobby's ability now. He said it went both ways when he tried to take a part of her ability." She was talking fast, and I found myself watching her mouth so I wouldn't miss a word. "They fear him. The first serial killer the Compound has had in over a hundred years. We thought the programs had cured that mind abnormality long ago."

"Addie is nothing like Bobby." It was apparent she'd wanted me to hear that conversation in the hall.

"I know." She glanced at the clock on her dash. "Tell her to get back on the program I sent with her. It's suppressing any advancement in her ability. Keeping her safe." Mrs. Coleman stepped on the gas and peeled through the tunnel fast, obviously trying to make up the few minutes we had been at a standstill. "I'm glad you came today. It would've been too obvious if I had sought you out," she said right before we exited. The sun blasted the window as we came out of the tunnel. She laughed. "And that is why I will never own a dog."

I blinked. Oh. Right. She was making up a story for the tunnel. "I'm glad you didn't hit it," I said, doing my part. I swallowed and looked out the side window. Addie's mom was hard-core. I had no idea.

CHAPTER 25

Addie: I figured out a solution.

"Addie, hello again." He put on the headphones and ran the imaginary metal detector stick over me again before he let me in. "It's good to see you."

After the agents showed up at my house that morning, I could sort of understand his paranoia. "Are you sure the Compound doesn't know you live here?"

He shut the closet door and turned around. His smiling eyes went serious for a moment. "The only way to truly be free from the Compound is to disappear."

"What do you mean? Do they think you're dead or something?"

"It's the only way."

That wasn't a direct answer to my question, but I guessed it meant yes. At least in his mind. And if he was happy, I wasn't going to try to change it.

The agents had sidetracked me, but there was a reason I was in my grandpa's apartment again. I wanted my memories back. The desperate urge to have them back had been coursing through me all night. I had hardly slept. "Can you restore memories?" I blurted out.

His eyes went wide, but then he slowly nodded.

"Will you restore mine?"

He picked up a mug full of steaming liquid off the coffee table and brought it to his lips. Then he set it back down next to his odd devices—the devices that reminded me he wasn't quite sane. "Let's go to the box."

My eyes lingered on the toaster, and I hesitated. Should I really let him do this? He slid open the back door. He was a Healer. The worst thing that could happen was he wouldn't be able to Heal. I followed him to his back patio. The box took up most of the patio, but the other half, I now noticed, was covered by a vegetable garden growing in big pots. The smell of the fertilized dirt made my stomach turn.

He held open the flimsy cardboard door for me. The phone in my pocket chimed with a text message. I stepped into the box.

"What exactly are you hoping to restore?" he asked.

"I'm not sure, actually. My best friend is a Memory Eraser, so . . ."

"You think she stole some of your memories? You don't trust her?"

It took me way too long to say, "I trust her. And no, she didn't steal any." Laila left all the memories of her betraying me with Duke perfectly intact, and she could've Erased them. She didn't.

"I used to do this for the Bureau all the time," my grandfather said.

"Do what?"

"Restore memories."

"Is that why my dad wanted to work there? Because you did?"

"Yes."

If he did this for the Bureau, he must've been a very capable Healer. I had nothing to worry about. And we were having a normal conversation about it. That meant he wasn't completely insane, didn't it?

"I'll never forget the haunted screams."

"What?"

"Why don't you sit down while I do this?"

"No. Wait. Is this safe?"

"Of course. I'm an expert."

I sat down, and for the first time realized the box didn't have a floor either. The cold cement seeped through my pants, numbing my legs. My grandfather's hands touched my head. I wondered what memories I was going to get back. Laila had said she had only ever Erased me once, but maybe I was about to find out otherwise.

My grandpa smoothed my hair and settled his hands more firmly on my head. I took a deep breath, and my phone chimed again.

My nerves and the persistent texter caused me to yank my head out of his reach and pull my phone out of my pocket. "Hold on. Just let me see what they need."

I read the text from Laila: *I did it. I learned how to restore memories . . . sort of. Just in time for my trip out there. Oh, and I talked to Bobby.*

"What?" I pushed myself to standing. "Sorry, hold on, Grandpa. I need to talk to my friend."

"I have all day."

I smiled. "Okay, just hold on." I exited the box and dialed Laila's number.

She answered after half a ring. "I thought that might get you to call me."

I went inside, shutting the glass door behind me. "Oh, good. So that means you didn't talk to Bobby?"

"No, I did. I just needed you to call me. Things are happening here. So aren't you excited? I can restore your memory. I don't need a lot of praise, but a little wouldn't hurt."

I glanced to the sliding door, where my grandfather stood with a watering can, dumping water on his plants out of the top instead of using the spout. "I might not need you to restore my memory."

"Well, someone better need me to restore their memory, because I went to a lot of work figuring out how. It involved kissing guys I didn't want to kiss and the whole works."

"There's a guy in the world you don't want to kiss? This is big news. He must be over fifty."

"Funny. He's actually our age. So there."

"Do I know him?"

She hummed a little and tried to say casually, "I think so. Connor Bradshaw."

"Wait. Connor? The guy who almost hit me with his motorcycle?"

"Yes."

"Why wouldn't you want to kiss him? He's gorgeous."

"Because he's a cocky, uncontrollable, frustrating idiot. He never listens to me. It's annoying. Plus, he thinks he's so smart. And he kind of is, which bugs me so much."

I didn't know why it took me so long, but the realization exploded in my chest. "OH!"

"What? Why are you yelling?"

Laila had never felt that strongly about anyone. If someone annoyed her, she moved on. "You love him. You love Connor Bradshaw!"

"Stop yelling. I do not. I'm annoyed with him because I can't Erase his memories, not because I like him."

"Love him. This is crazy. I never thought I'd see the day. My closed-off little Laila has finally opened her heart to love."

"You know, if you were here you'd be seconds away from being punched."

"So sweet."

203

"Moving on. Why don't you want me to restore your memory?"

"Long story, but I found my grandpa. He's alive. And he's a Healer. So, I guess he can do it."

"Whoa! There are so many things you just said right now that I need to comment on, but first and most important, do not let your grandpa touch your brain."

"Why not?"

"Because Connor said it's like pure torture to have a Healer give you your memories back. I guess more than the memories come, and it's really intense and horrible. They use it in interrogations and stuff."

Suddenly, the "haunted screams" comment my grandfather said made a lot more sense. It was hard to believe he was willing to do that to me. I whirled around to look at him. He was staring into his obviously empty watering can and shaking it. My initial anger softened. He wasn't exactly all there. I guess I couldn't blame him for that. "It's a good thing you don't know how to leave me alone when you want to talk, because I was literally seconds away from him restoring me."

"Once again my selfishness is rewarded. I'm never going to learn my lesson."

"Let me call you back and you can fill me in on the Bobby stuff. And I'll fill you in on all the back-to-life Grandpa and Trevor stuff. I better leave before he tries to feed me again."

"Okay. Call me when you get home."

I hung up and looked to see my grandpa standing inside,

staring at me. I jumped. He was so quiet.

"Are you ready?"

"I changed my mind. My friend is going to help me."

"You don't trust me?"

"No. It's not that. It's just . . ." My vision blurred for a second, and I rubbed my eyes. My brain was tired. I was angry that my dad had kept something this big from me. I was tired of the lies, and I was tired of worrying about my ability.

"It's just what?"

"I don't know you very well anymore."

He looked down at the coffee table, and I followed his gaze to where the modified toaster sat. Metal wires were wrapped around knobs and then extended like antennae straight up.

"What is it?" I asked.

"It tells me if their devices are anywhere near."

I didn't believe I'd almost let him Heal my brain. "And are they? Near?"

"Not today."

"Good. Then I better head home."

He hugged me tight, and I felt guilty for leaving. Guilty that he seemed so lonely. I wondered if my dad visited him often.

CHAPTER 26

Laila: Brace yourself. I'm coming.

The line of people was moving fast, but for once I didn't want a line to move fast. At least it wasn't moving as fast as the twelve-hour pass line. Those people just had to list a reason for leaving and get a palm scan. They were probably mostly commuters. My weekend pass line was a little more paperwork.

I looked down at my phone again. No new messages. I quickly typed *So? Are you coming or what?*

"I'm here," Connor said from behind me. The way my entire body reacted to that single statement reaffirmed why I needed him to come with me. He was the only one who could bring the emotional power I needed to restore Addie's memory. I tried to get those emotions under control. The last time I'd seen him on

206

the train swirled through my mind, and my weakness unnerved me. I bit the inside of my cheek hard, then whirled around.

He stood, arms crossed, bag slung over his shoulder. His hair was a bit messy, but his face was free of the normal grease stains, which drew my attention to his muddy green eyes.

"So you're coming?"

He held up his phone, my text on the screen. "'Bring your ancient truck and meet me at the Tower at nine. Pack for the weekend.'"

Huh. When he read it out loud like that, it made me realize how little explanation I'd given him. "I actually just need your truck, but I figured you wouldn't loan it to me, so I guess you'll have to tag along."

He reached into his pocket and held a set of keys out to me. I took them, and he started to walk away. Why did he have to call my bluff? Stupid boy.

"Wait. No."

He stopped.

"I . . ." *Need you too.* " . . . don't know how to drive it." A lie. I was sure I could easily figure it out. It was probably automatic, but I had even practiced a stick shift in one of the simulators at school when I was bored one day.

"Where exactly are we going?"

"To see Addie. There's a football game tomorrow. The holiday bowl."

He seemed to be waiting for me to explain why this was important.

"I haven't seen her in weeks."

He got an amused smirk on his face, then. "You can't do it without me."

"Do what?"

"Restore her memory."

"Because no one frustrates me quite as much as you do." Totally true. "Soon, the thought of your face will do it, but now, it seems I need your annoying presence as well."

He held out his hand, and I dropped his car keys onto his open palm. "This trip will be good for my research," he said, his smirk still in place.

Why couldn't I get him angry? He was always so calm. "I'm only doing this for Addie."

His eyes searched mine, and then he gave a small nod.

We were silent while the line inched forward. He stared off to the side, and I followed his gaze to the sign that said LONG-TERM AND PERMANENT PASSES, THIRD FLOOR, BY APPOINTMENT ONLY. Did he wish he were on the third floor instead?

He drove with one hand on top of the steering wheel and the other arm resting on the open window. The wind whistled through the cab and made it almost impossible to talk when we reached high speeds. I was not looking forward to four hours of this.

When we were almost to Addie's, I came to a realization. "You've never been on the Outside before." The way he'd been taking everything in, as though he was seeing it for the first time, made me think this.

His knuckles went white on the steering wheel, but he didn't say anything to deny or confirm my observation.

"Look at me, making one of your dreams come true. You and your Norm truck driving around Normville."

"You're practically a god."

I shoved his shoulder, producing a smile on his face. "Half god, but whatever."

We pulled up to Addie's, and Connor unloaded the bags from the truck bed. I knocked on the door, and she answered. A little piece of me fell back into place. She gave me a big hug, clinging to me for a bit longer than normal. Maybe she actually needed me in her life as well.

"Hi, Connor."

"Hey, it's good to see you when I'm not about to run you over."

She laughed. "I know, right? Come in. Let me show you where you can stay." She led Connor to a room on one end of the hall, then the two of us went to her room while he settled in.

She turned to me. "So you have a letter for me?"

I retrieved it out of my purse and handed it to her. A huge burden lifted from my shoulders as I did. Her eyes took in the writing on the front. She even ran her hand along the numbers. Then she opened it. I already knew what it said, so I watched her face for her reaction. She gnawed on her lip.

"I promised a person, someone I cared about, that I wouldn't Erase my Norm path. You didn't tell me that part." She also didn't seem surprised by that part.

"I figured it didn't matter. You didn't remember anyone. Do you think you know who you made that promise to?"

There was a hopeful look in Addie's eyes, like she had someone in mind.

I shook out my hands. "Okay, so when do you want to do this?"

"The memory restoration?"

"Yes. I've been practicing on the way over here. I'm not going to lie, I'm pretty awesome." I left out the part that I had been practicing on my phone and that Connor had to be there for me to do it.

Addie laughed. "I guess the sooner the better." She took a breath and looked around the room, like she was going to sit down somewhere that instant.

"We can wait until tomorrow after the game. Whenever you want."

"I think now would be good."

"Okay. Now." I rubbed my hands together. "I need to go get Connor."

"Why?"

"He helps."

She raised her eyebrows. "Oh, really?"

I picked up a pillow off her bed and threw it at her.

She laughed and pulled it against her chest. "How do you extend your ability, anyway? I want to try. I told you about the whole slowing-down-time thing, right? But I have absolutely no control over when and where it happens."

I raised one eyebrow. That girl must've had some strong emotions swirling around for her to trigger it without trying. Or did it have nothing to do with advanced ability at all? Had Bobby really unintentionally given her a piece of his ability? "I need to tell you something I found out. Something your mom wanted me to warn you about." I filled her in on what I'd learned the day I visited her mom.

"So, wait. That flash drive, the one my dad stole—it's been suppressing my abilities?"

"Attempting to, I guess. If something Bobby did affected you, she was hoping to smother it."

Addie took a deep breath of relief. "So it's the program that's been giving me headaches. My mom was trying to block my ability. No wonder they've been tapering off since my dad stole it from me."

"She wants you to get back on it."

"Not a chance," Addie said, her fists clenched. "I am nothing like Bobby."

"I know that." I grabbed her hand. "Your mom knows it too. But the stupid DAA and CC don't know that."

"This advanced ability is mine. He didn't give it to me. He did not alter my mind. Let the CC watch me. They'll see I'm nothing like him."

Her conviction surprised me a little, but then I smiled. "Go, Addie."

"I guess my dad stealing my program helped."

"So maybe you should thank your dad after all."

211

She gave a short laugh. "It'll be awhile before I'm ready to thank him for anything."

I'd never heard Addie talk that way about her dad. I needed to change the subject. If she wanted to keep extending this extra ability she'd inherited, regardless of where she got it, then I would help her learn how to control it. "The key to advancing your ability is to channel strong emotions. Think of something that will get your pulse racing."

"Does it have to be a good thing?"

"No. Why? What's making your pulse race in a bad way?"

"My dad not admitting that my dead grandpa is really alive."

"That sucks. The lie detector lying seems so wrong."

It really did suck because unlike me and my father, Addie and her dad actually shared a really good relationship. The kind where finding out he was lying to her might actually be surprising instead of just an everyday occurrence. By the looks of her, though, it didn't seem that memory was going to make her pulse race, but instead throw her into a deep depression coma.

"That's not going to work." I pulled her by one arm off her bed. "No lying dads on the agenda tonight. Something different. What else makes you mad?"

"I don't know."

"Or happy?"

She smiled. "So what exactly will I feel?"

"Almost as if something is physically surrounding you. Then you let it gather and push it."

There was a knock on the door, and my heart jumped. Addie

opened it. Connor pushed his hair off his forehead and met my eyes over Addie's shoulder. Yes. This would work just fine.

"I heard we needed you," Addie said with a smile, standing aside so he could come in.

He walked into the room. "Apparently, Laila doesn't know how to channel anger without me."

"Oh, is that what you bring out in her?"

I shot Addie a look, and she laughed. I pulled out her desk chair and gestured for her to sit. She did.

Connor went to the window and inspected the string hanging down by the drapes. Addie started to say something, but he grabbed hold of the string and pulled. The curtains parted and light filled the room.

How did he know how to open those? He was a quick study. I positioned myself behind Addie. It had been about ten weeks since the memory wipe. I easily found the path of memories I had closed. Now, to open it. I concentrated hard, but nothing happened. Connor was ten feet away, staring out the window. I thought for a moment that I was going to have to ask him to come closer. He turned, as if sensing I needed him. His fiery eyes triggered an image of the night in the train, and the energy pressed against me. I gathered it and, with one burst of mental force, pushed to open the path. Her entire body went tense.

I dropped my hands from her head, but she sat there, catatonic, like someone had just killed her dog. Like *I* had just killed her dog. Addie had never had a dog, so maybe that was a bad analogy. That's when it hit me. I had been so focused on learning

213

how to do this that I'd almost forgotten my main fear: that she'd learn something about me that would make her hate me. The look in her eyes made me realize this was probably true. My hands twitched, dying to shut off the path I had just opened. I needed her in my life. She made it easier to breathe.

She stood but then leaned against her desk as if she might fall. Connor took her by the elbow. "Addie. You need to sit down before you pass out. You're overwhelmed."

She lowered herself back into the chair and started laughing. The laugh was creepy. Like someone had just killed her dog and then brought it back to life. The laugh of a person on the verge of insanity.

"I'm going to get her something to drink," Connor said to me, and left the room.

"Wow," she finally said.

I had never seen Addie this way, and quite frankly it was terrifying. "You hate me."

Her glazed eyes met mine, and then she popped back up and grabbed me by the shoulders, crushing me against her. "No. You're alive."

"I'm alive."

"It felt so real."

"I . . ." My mind reeled. "I died in your other life?"

She nodded, her cheek rubbing against my hair as she did. And then she whispered it so quietly I almost didn't hear her. "I love Trevor."

"What?" Then I clarified her statement. "You mean that you

214

loved him in your other future."

Addie sat back, her eyes so glassy I knew she was seconds from crying. "I can't separate the two. Don't you understand? These memories, it's like they really happened. They feel as real as you sitting in front of me."

I didn't understand. At all. It was weird for me to think that a vision essentially could feel as solid as reality, but the look on her face was unmistakable—her feelings were real. "So you love Trevor . . . that has to feel awkward."

She shook her head almost violently. "It doesn't. He is . . ." And then the tears came, pooling in her eyes and spilling down her cheeks. "It doesn't matter. I thought I wanted these memories, but now I realize that he hardly knows me."

CHAPTER 27

Addie: Not knowing seemed easier.

He hardly knows me. The words broke me. Because I knew him. Everything about him. From his easy smile to the way his hand glided across paper when he drew. The timbre of his voice, the shade of his eyes, the feel of his breath on my face. And the memories were as real as he was. Meeting him at the football game, talking in the classics section of the library, being trapped in the principal's car together, our first kiss. What had I done? It wasn't too late. I could have Laila Erase it again, take him away completely, because this was beyond torture.

And Stephanie. She was so awful to me in the other version of my life that I had a hard time reconciling the two sides of her.

I had pushed Trevor back to her. She did not deserve Trevor. She was a drama queen. A huge, big, fat, ugly drama queen. I sighed. Only she wasn't. She was gorgeous and nice. I had seen a different side of her, the one where she didn't feel threatened by me, and I liked that side. That side was vulnerable and happy and kind. This sucked.

I dropped my forehead to the desk and moaned.

"You want this Norm boy?" Laila still sounded confused over this fact.

If I were selfless, I'd say no. I'd say, *Let's see how this plays out. Let's see if Stephanie and Trevor can figure this out.* But she'd already had chances with Trevor, and when it came to him, I was very selfish. "Yes. I want him back."

"Then we're going to get you this Norm boy."

"Oh." I sat up, wiping at my eyes with the back of my hand and turning to Laila. "I have Trevor's phone number now. Should I call him?"

"Absolutely not. You must play coy."

"I told him in the other version. I told him about the Compound and abilities and nothing happened. Nobody came after me . . . or him."

"Okay. That's a good thing. So wait, you want to tell him about the Compound and abilities?"

I had to. He was hurt so badly when I kept it from him last time. And I wanted to. I wanted him to know me. "Yes. He's practically figured it out on his own anyway."

"Well, that's good that no one came after you. . . . Did you

217

have the whole slowing-down-time thing in the other version?"

I bit my lip. I didn't. My grandmother had never even hinted at having this advancement. Did that mean Bobby really had given it to me? "No. My ability hadn't advanced that far yet. Will that make a difference?"

"Maybe. If they think that has to do with the whole Bobby thing."

I thought back to the Tower. "But they don't know. I didn't claim that ability."

She gave me a smile like she was proud of me for not informing the Tower. "That's awesome, but you're an awful liar. I'm sure their computers picked up that you were hiding something. And because of Bobby, they're watching you closer this time."

She bit her bottom lip. "So you told Trevor when? Like right away?"

"No. I told him a couple days before the Search was over."

"So in other words, if you had stayed in the Search, it's possible that the Containment Committee would've shown up at Trevor's door."

I pushed my fingertips to my closed eyes. "Yes. I guess that's possible. Why didn't I think of that?"

"Because you always hope for the best, and I always plan for the worst. It's okay, though. We'll figure this out. The best time to approach Trevor is going to be at the football game tomorrow. It's loud. It's distracting. If the CC happens to have people tracking you or him, it would be really hard to do it with so many bodies and so much noise."

I nodded, then looked around. "Do you think they can hear us now?"

"No. I'm sure your dad sweeps his house. He used to work for the Bureau, after all. It's probably why your mom wanted me to tell you here instead of over the phone."

Even though I wanted to see Trevor right this second, she was right. We had to be careful about this. If the CC was watching, it might be suspicious to invite him over right after Laila showed up. But I knew the giant hole that now existed in my chest would not be filled until Trevor was a part of me again.

"Operation Win Trevor Back begins now." She sat down on the bed across from me. "So what do you know about him that we can use in our quest?"

"Everything. I know him."

"Then this should be easy."

The door creaked open, and Connor came back in carrying a glass of water, which he handed to me. "Everything good?"

"It will be," Laila said.

He nodded. "Perfect. Then I'm off."

"What do you mean *off*?" Laila asked.

"I'm staying out of your way." He backed out of the room. "We're leaving Sunday, right?"

Laila nodded, and then he was gone.

I took a sip of water and looked at Laila, whose gaze still lingered on the door. "So why haven't you told him you're in love with him?"

She rolled her eyes. "Oh, please. When have I ever been in love? Now, back to Trevor. Tell me everything you know."

The cement was cold on my bare feet as I leaned against the porch railing, but I didn't want to go inside. I twisted the bottom of my long-sleeved nightshirt over and over again around my finger and stared up at the moon. It was a crescent, just like it had been the night I met Trevor. I had marveled at it that night, having only seen a lifetime of full moons. But now I had a memory full of the moon at different stages. I liked the changes. There were so many things about the Outside that I liked.

The sliding glass door opened and I turned, expecting to see Laila, who I had left asleep in my room, but it was Connor.

"Hey, Addie, can I borrow your computer?"

"Yes, of course."

He didn't step back into the house but instead closed the door behind him and asked, "Are you okay?"

I shrugged. "I will be. I think. It's weird getting all these memories back that no one else has. I wish there was a way I could give them to Trevor. But it's not like he lived them and had them Erased. He never lived them at all." I stopped myself abruptly before I started crying again. I didn't need to cry in front of this almost stranger, no matter how much Laila loved him.

He crossed his arms and walked over to join me at the railing. Then, like I had been doing, he stared up at the moon. I waited for him to say something about how odd it was to see a moon so small, but he didn't. It didn't seem odd to him at all. He must've spent some time outside the Compound before.

He was quiet for a while, and I was glad he wasn't trying to give me false assurances or made-up solutions to my problem. He seemed to know there was nothing he could say to change the reality of it. This silent understanding made me feel better. It also made me realize why he was so good for Laila. She hated it when people tried to solve her problems. He was just a calming presence.

I let out a little gasp as I realized how much better I felt and thought about what he might be doing. He turned toward me.

"You're not a Mood Controller, are you?" I asked.

"No." Confusion passed over his face. "Didn't Laila tell you my ability?"

"No. She didn't." I relaxed, glad he wasn't manipulating me. I'd had enough of that with Duke. "Laila is really good at keeping secrets. If you asked her not to tell, she wouldn't even tell me."

"I didn't ask her not to tell."

I smiled. *Well, you're different,* I wanted to say, *She loves you.* If she thought it was important to him that people didn't know, I could see why she wouldn't tell me. This only validated my knowledge of her feelings even more. "She must've thought you didn't want anyone to know."

His eyes moved to the sliding glass door, as if he expected to see her on the other side.

"She's asleep," I answered his unasked question. "Come on,

I'll show you where the computer is."

He followed me inside. The computer sat on a desk in the corner of the living room. I powered it on, then pulled out the chair for Connor. He sat down and waited for it to come up.

"Did you need help with anything? They don't have all the sites here that we have in the Compound." There were so many things I knew now with my memories.

"I know." He clicked on the internet icon and then hovered his hands over the keyboard. "Thanks."

I thought he might be waiting for me to leave, but just as I turned to go, he typed a map service into the address bar. "Did you need the printer too?" I asked, thinking he might be printing up directions.

"No, just refreshing my memory."

I looked at the screen, where he had typed in "Bowie, Texas." It informed him that it was approximately one hour and forty-two minutes from Dallas. What was in Bowie, Texas, that Connor was so interested in? I took a deep breath and swallowed the question. It was none of my business. If Connor wanted to tell me, he would. He'd probably already told Laila. "Okay, well, good night."

"Good night."

I paused. "I take it we won't be seeing you tomorrow?" I nodded toward the computer.

"Probably not."

I didn't care how good Laila was at keeping secrets. I'd ask her what that was all about tomorrow.

CHAPTER 28

Laila: Is there a mind pattern to take away my sense of smell?

I added a layer of lip gloss to my lips and let out a sigh. "Bowie, Texas?"

"Yes."

"I have no idea why he'd go there. And I don't really care. He can do what he wants." That was what I needed to keep telling myself when it came to Connor. That I didn't care. Otherwise I had to admit that he had way more control over me than I wanted him to.

Addie put some gel in her hair. For the first time since we added the blue streak two months ago, she was wearing it curly. "So what's the plan?" The football game wasn't until tonight; I wondered if we needed to do anything to prepare for it.

"I'm trying to remember anything Trevor mentioned he liked." She pointed to her curls. "There was this zombie note. I don't think I can really duplicate that, but maybe I can find some other scenarios to duplicate."

"A zombie note?"

"Yeah. It had to do with books and Charles Dickens."

I laughed. "Of course it did. So what? You want to do some role-playing right now?"

"No, let's go somewhere and get my mind off things, so I won't have a mental breakdown."

"Okay. Let me just call home real fast."

"I'll meet you in the kitchen. I'm going to get some breakfast."

She left, and I grabbed my phone and shut myself in her bedroom. Eli answered on the third ring. "Were you sleeping?" I asked.

"No, but I'm eating," he said around an obviously huge mouthful of food.

"Everything going good?"

"Yeah. You know. Same as normal." He continued to crunch his food, making his voice come out muffled.

"Is Mom at work?"

"Yes."

"And Dad?"

He hummed the "I don't know" noise.

"Well, you're no help."

He cleared his throat, and his voice, now clear, said, "I started it last night."

My face seemed to lose all feeling, and even though I'd heard him perfectly, I asked, "What?"

"I started it last night. The program you gave me."

"Eli. I wish you would've waited until I got home."

"Why? Besides, it didn't work. Nothing happened."

"It probably takes a few sessions. But just wait until I'm home to do more."

"You really don't trust it, do you? Why would you give it to me at all if you didn't trust it?"

Guilt twisted my insides. He was right. I may have used Eli as my guinea pig sometimes, but I shouldn't have turned him into Face's. "Just wait."

"All right, fine. Can I finish eating now? My cereal is getting soggy."

I stood and headed for the door to join Addie in the kitchen. "I'll be home tomorrow night."

"Thanks for checking in, young lady. I hope you're staying out of trouble," he said in his attempt at an adult's deep voice.

"Ha-ha." I opened the door and walked into the hall.

"Oh. Hold up. Derek wants to say hi."

I listened as the phone got passed between my brothers. "Hey, Laila. It's supposed to snow again tonight, and we're going to build a snow house."

I smiled. "You think you'll get enough snow for that?"

"Yes. And then when you come home, we're going to ambush you with snowballs."

"You gave your plan away. Now I'll be prepared."

"We'll see about that. Well, bye. See you tomorrow."

"Bye, kid." I hung up the phone and turned to continue down the hall when Connor stepped out of the bathroom, straight into my path. We nearly collided. He smelled fresh out of the shower, like soap, toothpaste, and deodorant. He wore jeans and a tee, his feet were bare, and a towel hung over his shoulder. He used the end of it to run over his wet hair a few times.

"Hi," I said from where I had just barely stopped myself from running into him.

"Hey." He studied my face. Then his eyes dropped to the phone still clutched in my hand. "You look happy. Good phone call?"

"Something like that. Are you going somewhere today?" I asked, wondering if he'd tell me about the trip he had planned.

"Yep." That's all he said.

A drop of water clinging to the end of his hair distracted me for a moment. I wondered if he would blow it dry or if his hair air-dried to the perfect combination of messy and styled that normally existed on his head. This thought irritated me more than it should've, so I asked, "Need a blow-dryer?"

He ran the towel over it again. "No, I'm good."

I took a step back, needing to be out of the bubble where all his scents were making me dizzy.

"Why didn't you tell her?" he asked.

"Tell who what?"

"Why didn't you tell Addie my ability?" He stared at me with those intense eyes of his. As if the answer to this question would answer more than just this question.

I didn't tell her because I knew how much effort he had put into keeping it a secret. Not that I thought Addie would tell everyone. But it wasn't my place to tell people. I thought about that answer, what it would imply. Then I thought about how little he was telling me and what that implied. So I answered, "Because you never crossed my mind when I was talking to her."

He held my stare for one more moment, then turned to walk away.

"What's in Bowie?" I called after him.

He stopped at the entrance to his room, his back to me.

"Your Norm roots? Are you discovering yourself?"

"Something like that." He went inside and shut the door behind him.

I was angry at myself for providing an answer for him, no matter how snarky it was supposed to be. It gave him an out for having to provide an answer himself. Even a made-up one could've given me some sort of clue. I let out a low growl and went to join Addie.

CHAPTER 29

Addie: I need to practice my hiding skills.

Right away I saw Trevor in the stands. He sat the way he always did when watching football, his hands buried in his jacket pockets, his booted feet on the bench in front of him. If I didn't know how torturous it was for him to watch the game, it would've seemed like he was the most relaxed person on earth. I wanted to sit next to Trevor, grab his hand, feel his arms around me, but I resisted. Thank goodness Stephanie was cheering tonight, because I was sure I wouldn't have been able to handle the two of them together without losing it.

"Oh no," Laila said.

"What?" I followed her gaze but only saw a group of people

standing at the front railing, cheering.

"I was hoping they wouldn't come."

I studied the group closer, their broad backs and purple sweatshirts. Carter High's colors were blue and silver. Lincoln's colors were purple and gold. My eyes shot back and forth down the line until I saw his familiar hair. Duke. No.

"Why are they here?"

"It's a football game."

I ducked down a little and positioned myself behind Laila. "Just don't let him see me."

"I'll do my best."

As though he could feel me staring, Trevor glanced to where we walked down the aisle a few rows away from him. I gave him a small wave. He looked behind him and then back to me. I smiled, and he gave me a head nod.

We really shouldn't have sat a couple of rows in front of Trevor, because then it was so obvious when I turned around to look at him.

"How are you going to do this?" Laila whispered at halftime. "You can't just stare at him every minute like a creeper."

"I should go and talk to him?"

"Yes. Like I said, you should be good at the stadium. There are so many people here."

"Okay. I'm going to talk to him." I'd sit next to him and say, *You're not crazy. I have so much to tell you.*

"Good."

"Right now."

She laughed and gave me a push. "You know him, remember? You'll know what to say."

She was right. I knew him. I stood and made my way down the aisle. Just as I turned to walk up the steps, a hand on my shoulder stopped me. I turned and was eye-to-eye with Duke. His smile blasted me. I backed up a step.

"Addie. Hi."

"Hi. What are you doing here?"

He jerked his head toward the field. "Our competition. We're studying their weaknesses."

Anger flared through me. "What?"

The anger must've shown on my face, because he quickly added, "No. Not so we can injure them. Just their football weaknesses."

"Oh. Okay. Have fun." I started to leave.

"But I was hoping to see you too."

His words stopped me, and a familiar warmth crept through my shoulders and neck. "Don't. Just. I—I have to go."

I whirled around, but Trevor wasn't there. I scanned the stands, then raced up the cement steps to the exit and back down them to get to ground level behind the stadium. My entire body relaxed when I saw him at the snack hut, buying a soda. This was very familiar. Maybe I could do a little reenactment of the night we talked behind the stadium in my other future—the night he told me he felt out of place. A chill went through me as I remembered how he had lifted me into his arms. There was so much electrical charge between us that night it was insane. I walked toward the snack hut, anticipating him turning to the darkened baseball field in the back, but he turned toward me and the stadium instead.

He saw me right away.

"Hi," I said when we were within talking distance.

"Hi."

As he got closer, I smelled his familiar scent and couldn't believe I had forgotten it. "I . . ." My mind went blank.

He tilted his head.

I pointed to the field. "Will you walk with me for a minute?"

"Um . . ." A soft mist hung over the empty field, and he seemed to take in the scene. It did look like the perfect place for an assault. Was he worried that my ability and I were going to steal his wallet or something? That's when I remembered how we had left things the last time I saw him outside my grandpa's apartment. He was mad that I wouldn't talk. He was obviously still mad.

"Please."

"Sure." He followed me as we headed into the darkness, the lights and sounds of the stadium becoming more distant. When we were between the stadium and the back fence of the baseball diamond, I stopped and faced him. Time to make some magic.

I looked up at him, and my heart danced. I had to restrain myself from hugging him. Everything about him was familiar and comfortable, from his easy smile to his relaxed stance. He made me happy. "Is it hard watching them play?"

"Not really."

Hmm. Okay, that didn't work. "Do you ever think about would've beens?"

"Not usually."

Work with me, Trevor. He finished off his soda.

"Have you ever read *Ninja Wars II*?"

"Yes . . . ," he said warily. "Have you?"

"Yes." I held out my hand for his soda can. "Remember how Naoto smashed the can between his hands all crazy-like?"

He laughed a little. "And you think you can do that?"

"Hello. Know."

"All right. Let's see it."

I turned the can sideways and pushed. Nothing happened. Holy cow, that took a lot more strength than I gave Trevor credit for. No wonder Naoto's eyes were bugging out of his head when he did it.

"Any day now," Trevor said.

"Shut up," I said, laughing. "I'm trying."

"You want to know a secret?"

I stopped laughing and met his eyes. "Yes."

His smile dropped. "Um . . . I mean about the soda can."

"Oh. Right. Of course about the soda can." *What other secret could you possibly tell me, Trevor?*

He put his hands over mine on either side of the can. "You have to twist a little as you push." He twisted the can and then easily crushed it between our hands. "See."

He let go, and the can slipped from my grip and onto the ground between us. We both stared at it.

But my eyes couldn't stay off him for long, and my body inched a little closer. It wanted to be near him. "I miss you."

"What?"

"I missed it." I pointed to the can. "Dropped it."

He reached down and picked it up. He spun the can on the tip of his finger. It did a couple of rotations before wobbling off balance and starting to fall. He caught it.

"So, I know you were kind of mad last time we talked because I couldn't tell you about . . ." I glanced around. This wasn't exactly the noise and commotion Laila said would be ideal to talk about the Compound. "Well, you know. But I want to tell you tonight. Answer your questions."

"I'm sorry. I'm lost. Last time we talked? At the graveyard?" Was he trying to be funny?

"No. Outside my grandpa's apartment."

"Your grandpa?"

His bewilderment caught me so off guard that I stuttered for a moment before saying, "What?"

"Did you ever figure out why your grandmother's grave was there?"

I opened my mouth, then shut it again. He thought the last time we talked was at the cemetery? And then it hit me like a punch to my gut. "Did you—? Did they—?" The Containment Committee Erased him? When? After my grandpa's house? It was the last logical place I could think of. "Crap."

CHAPTER 30

Laila: I should charge you for this.

When Addie came back, she looked defeated. She slid into her seat. "They Selectively Erased him. I should've known they were going to do that. Those agents at my house told me they knew he suspected something. They took the memories of going to my grandfather's apartment. He knows me even less than before."

"So I guess that means you didn't tell him about the Compound."

"Yeah, and have him think I'm a complete wacko?" Addie looked over her shoulder to where Trevor sat again, watching the game.

"You're screwed. The CC is not going to let your future

boyfriend know anything about the Compound."

She twisted her hands together. "I'm scared."

"Why?"

"They messed with Trevor, but this also means they not only know about my grandpa but now think he's a threat. It's all my fault. I need to go check on him. Warn him. You have to help me." She met my eyes. "Do you think you can give Trevor back his memories?"

"I don't know if I can without Connor here."

"Can you try? If it works, tell Trevor to meet us at the box. If my grandpa is okay, then I can talk to Trevor there. My grandfather's toaster device really did detect the Committee the other day. So maybe the box works too. Maybe he can tell us how to keep Trevor safe."

"The box?"

"It's at my grandpa's apartment. He'll get it."

How had I gotten myself into this mess? I was in the business of stealing people's memories, not putting them back. I forced my way down the aisle behind Trevor. When I was directly behind him, I squatted down and said real close to his ear, "Hi, doll, you don't know me, but I need you not to freak out for a minute."

To his credit, he didn't jerk his head away or jump or anything. He just turned slightly to look at me. "You're Addison's friend."

"Yes. Laila. Hi. Now, I'm about to return something that belongs to you. There are certain people who don't want you to have this. It is imperative that you don't overreact. It might be shocking. When the game is over, meet us at the box." I felt like some sort of criminal. *Bring the money to the box and you can have your life back.* I really hoped my theory that the noise of the game would mask our conversation was true, because if the Committee was tracking him, they might be listening in right now.

"The box?"

"Addie says you'll know what that means in a minute."

By now I could tell Trevor thought I was weird, so better to stop talking and just return his memories. I took a breath. I hoped this would work. I was getting better. Connor had been ten feet away in the room. I didn't even need to touch him—just think of kissing him. Stupid Connor, why did I have to think of stupid Connor to make this work? But it did. I felt the energy and opened Trevor's paths. He drew a breath of air.

"Relax," I whispered. "Don't draw attention to yourself. After the game. At the box." Even I didn't know what the box was, but he seemed to, because he nodded. Good. My work here was done. I made my way back to my seat, unable to contain the smile on my face. I'd done it without Connor. Well, without Connor's presence.

"Did it work?" Addie asked the second I sat down.

"Do you doubt me?"

"No."

Addie spent the remainder of the game the same way she'd spent the first half—looking over her shoulder every other minute. Only this time, Trevor was returning the glances.

• • •

As we hurried through the parking lot, Addie looked nervous. I was starting to get nervous. Maybe the Compound was tailing her. I looked over my shoulder and screamed when I saw a shadowy figure.

"It's just me," Duke said, stepping closer.

"Duke. You're an idiot. You scared me half to death."

"I was just going to tell you that a bunch of us are going out right now to grab some food. You ladies want to join us?" He was looking at Addie when he asked, but I answered for us.

"No. We don't. We're in a hurry." I shouldn't have used those words, because they seemed to pique his interest.

"Why? What's the rush? Does this have to do with that Norm guy I saw you talking to? Trevor?"

"It's none of your business." I hooked my arm through Addie's, and we continued our walk to the car.

"So the CC doesn't need to hear about it, then?"

We stopped, and Addie took a sharp breath next to me.

"Listen, just tell me what's going on and I'll leave you alone."

"Why do you care, Duke?"

"Because I don't want to see you get into trouble."

"Why would talking with a Norm get us in trouble?"

"Because . . ." He grunted. "Because that particular Norm has been talking and got me and the whole football team questioned last week."

Addie turned to face him, venom in her voice. "And you didn't get into trouble for the things you've done to him and other players?"

237

"It's football, Addie. What Trevor is doing is exposure."

"And what you did wasn't?"

"Wherever you're going right now, I'm coming with you, or I can call the CC. They gave me their phone number in case I thought of anything else I needed to tell them."

Addie took one angry step forward and practically spit out her sentence. "I kept your stupid secret, Duke. I didn't tell the coach about your real ability. And now you're trying to blackmail me?"

"I'm trying to protect you."

"Go. Away."

He held up his hands and backed away. "Fine. I'm leaving."

"He's going to follow us," I told her as we got into the car.

"I know," she growled.

The hall was deserted when we made it to her grandfather's floor on the third level of the apartment building. We stopped in front of his door, and I toed the peeling edge of the carpet with my shoe. She knocked, but nobody answered. The next to arrive was Trevor. When Addie saw him, she let out a relieved breath but then looked nervously over his shoulder.

"Did anyone follow you?" she asked.

"I don't think so."

But then a mocking voice from down the hall said, "You're not very observant, dude," and Duke stepped around the corner. I thought about punching him again, like I had at the hospital after the Bobby incident, but remembered how bad my hand hurt afterward and decided against it.

"Well, I guess it's a party then," I said.

Footsteps drew my attention down the hall again, and a woman too old to be wearing such a short skirt walked into view. She stopped at the apartment next door to where we stood and inserted her key in the lock.

"Have you seen the man who lives here recently?" Addie asked. "He has white hair, kind of tall."

She furrowed her brow. "The only person I ever see coming out of that apartment has dark hair. He's in his forties maybe."

"My dad," Addie whispered to me. "Okay, thanks. We'll keep trying." She knocked again while the lady opened and shut her door.

"I don't think he's there, Addison," Trevor said.

"Why do you call her that?" Duke asked. "She goes by Addie."

"He can call me whatever he wants," Addie said.

"Really? He can call you whatever he wants? What if he wants to call you Amber or Lori or Stephanie or the names of all the other girls he's been with?"

I took one step back because I saw it coming. Trevor's fist clenched for one brief second before he let it connect with Duke's jaw with a sickening smack. It was very satisfying. Not so satisfying was Duke's answering blow or Addie's horrified expression. She stepped between them before another fist could connect.

"You are a jerk," she said to Duke.

"Are you sure you want to do this right now?" I asked.

"Yes. I have to make sure he's okay." She walked to the neighbor's door and knocked. The lady in the short skirt answered.

"Hi. I don't mean to bother you, but can we use your phone? My grandfather was supposed to be here tonight, and he's not."

"And none of you teenagers have cell phones?"

I wasn't sure what Addie's plan was, but I stepped forward to help her lie her way out of this one. I could tell she wasn't going to answer right. I pointed to all of us in turn, starting with Addie. "She got grounded from hers." Then to Duke. "His fell in the toilet yesterday." Then to Trevor. "His got stolen at a football game." And then pulled mine out. "And mine is out of batteries."

"Wow, that's an awful lot of bad cell phone luck." She nodded. Duke must've been helping her with feelings of trust, because she held the door open and led us to the kitchen, where she handed Addie a phone. She took it, then nodded to me. The words *back door* came into my mind, and I realized she'd used Thought Placement on me. Wow, my little Addie was turning into a hardened criminal.

"Distract her, Duke," I whispered.

While Duke started asking Short-Skirt questions, I took Trevor's arm and pulled him to the back door.

"What's going on?" he asked.

"You think you can boost me from this balcony to that one?" I pointed over to the balcony that was attached to Addie's grandfather's apartment. He looked over and then at the gap between them and the three-story drop.

240

"I don't think it's the smartest idea."

I started to climb up. He grabbed my arm and pulled me back. "If anyone is going to go, it will be me."

I didn't argue and made way.

He climbed onto the railing and assessed his surroundings. There was the smallest ledge against the building, and I could practically see his brain working.

"I would just jump if I were you," I told him.

"It's too far," he said. "I'll miss by about half a foot." Only an athlete would know exactly how far he would miss a jump by.

With one hand holding the ceiling above, he stretched his foot to about the halfway mark between the two balconies. Only the side of his foot fit on the ledge, and my heart began beating in my throat. "Don't die or Addie will kill me."

He grunted and, with one push off that precariously balanced foot, shoved himself toward the other balcony. My breath caught because he was going to miss. I could see that his body wasn't quite long enough to reach the top of the railing. A squeal escaped my lips as his fingertips just missed it. But they caught on the bottom rail, and I closed my eyes and breathed a sigh of relief. He wasn't out of the woods, but he wasn't splattered on the pavement.

I looked around for a stick or broom handle or something I could extend out to him. There was only a table and chairs. I didn't think a plastic patio chair would go very far. When I looked back up, he was pulling himself over the railing. Oh. I had forgotten he was strong. He glanced back at me, and if I didn't

241

feel as much relief as I saw on his face, I might've laughed at his expression. I decided right then, with that unguarded expression on his face, that he was the perfect match for Addie.

He walked to the slider and held up crossed fingers. The door slid open. Addie must've Searched this and knew the back door would be open. She could've told me Trevor's brains weren't going to splatter on the sidewalk.

I headed back into the apartment and met Trevor at the front door.

"Thank you so much for the phone," Addie said.

Short-Skirt was giving Duke dreamy eyes, and he was blasting her with his perfect smile.

"Let's go."

Even though Trevor had just walked through the apartment to unlock the door, we all entered at a snail's pace, like something was going to jump out at us. After we were inside, Addie walked to the back rooms.

A stack of newspapers sat in the corner by a computer. I expected them to be dusty with age, but they were clean and crisp. That's right, people actually read newspapers here. A few articles were pinned to the wall as well. "Man Swims 150 Miles Solo"; "Woman Wins Eating Contest"; "Teen Survives Shooting." Did he think they were Paranormals? And why was he so interested in them?

"He's not here," Addie said when she returned.

Duke studied a picture on the wall. "Why are *we* here?"

Addie shot him a look.

"He probably just went out. I'm sure he's fine," I said. "Is that the box of secrets?"

"That's it. Do you think it's possible that it really does have some sort of soundproof material or maybe a scrambling device in it?"

Between the oversize box and the large pots, the back patio could not hold all four of us comfortably, and yet we all went back there to check out the box. Duke made his declaration first. "It doesn't even have a roof. I'm guessing it's just a box."

Addie sighed. "He claims the box keeps conversations private. And the CC didn't seem to know what my grandfather and I talked about in the box, only what Trevor and I talked about in the living room. And that locator device seemed to work as well. I'm guessing all this stuff might actually work." She pointed to the table inside, where I saw a sad attempt at electronics.

"Well." I held open the door to the cardboard box. "Then perhaps you two should give it a whirl."

Addie gave Trevor a sideways glance. "You still want to talk, right?"

He nodded.

I hooked my arm through Duke's and dragged him into the apartment, leaving them alone. I knew Duke wasn't going to let me get away with not telling him what was going on. But I didn't need a box to keep a conversation secret. It was time for some Thought Placement.

CHAPTER 31

Addie: Should I feel bad about forcing a hot guy
into a small box with me?

If possible, the box was smaller than it seemed when my grand-father and I were in here. Then again, Trevor was thicker than my grandpa.

"Too bad there aren't chairs in here," I said.

"I don't think two chairs would fit in here."

"True."

A bruise was forming on the side of his face where Duke had hit him. I reached out and ran a finger softly over it. "Are you okay? Do you want some ice for that?"

"I'm fine."

"I thought you said you didn't punch someone unless you said something nice first."

"I figured I owed him one." He stretched out the fingers on his right hand. "I'm sorry I did that in front of you."

"He deserved it." Being this close to him was hard. It made me miss him. My heart wouldn't give me a break as it fluttered away. "Do you want to sit?"

"If you do."

I did. I had a feeling this might take a while, because I was willing to stay in the box until he loved me again. He joined me on the floor, and our knees touched. "Tell me what you think you know, and we'll go from there."

"What I think I know is crazy."

"Try me."

"I think Duke and his teammates have some sort of powers and they purposely injured my shoulder."

I nodded.

"So are you saying that's true?"

"Yes."

He took a short breath through his nose. "And you. You have powers too?"

It probably took about an hour to explain to Trevor about the Compound and what I could do. Unlike when I'd revealed myself last time, this time Trevor had pieced clues together on his own over time, so it wasn't as shocking.

"So you can move really fast."

"No. I can manipulate time. Slow it down and move through it. That's why it looks like I'm moving fast. I can also see forward in time."

"See the future?"

"Kind of. If I'm given a choice, I can see the outcome of both possibilities. And that's how I know you. You were part of a path I wasn't able to take. So I have memories of you. Very vivid and real memories of a life with you. I still have them because you made me promise I wouldn't Erase you."

"So you were given a choice, and in one version of that choice, you ended up with me. And the other was the one you picked . . . the one where you ended up with him?" He gestured toward the apartment with his head.

"No. I mean, yes, but it wasn't about him. If I had stayed here in this life with you, Laila would've died. I had to choose the other path."

"So you know me."

I closed my eyes and drew in a breath. "I know you." I opened my eyes and met his. He seemed skeptical. I needed to prove it. "You draw amazingly well, but you don't think so. You're hard on yourself. You have a trash can and car full of just how hard on yourself you are. Your mom's name is DeAnn, and whenever she meets a new person she has them tell her about themselves. It embarrasses you, but you love her, so you let her get away with it. Your brother, Brody, idolizes you. He wants to be you when he grows up."

"I don't know about that."

"He does. Believe me. And you are so good with him. If anything were to happen to him, your world would end."

His jaw tightened, and I knew I'd gotten that one right.

"Up until last year all you wanted to do was play football, and now you're not sure what you want to do." I wondered if this part was still right. Maybe without me here he had figured out what he wanted to do. "You're a little lost, searching for a path you want to take and hoping beyond anything that one exists that feels as right as football did."

He intently studied his palms. "You know me." His voice was smoky, like it always was when he tried to hold back emotion.

I reached out and touched his bruised cheek again. This time he put his hand over mine. "Are you sure you don't want ice for that?"

"Addison."

"Yes?"

"But I don't know you that well."

I choked back a sob. "I know." It was so ironic. Last time he only saw me and not my ability. This time, he only knew me for my ability.

"Please don't cry. I want—"

The sliding glass door banged shut, interrupting him mid-sentence. "We have company," Laila said. "Make room."

Suddenly, both she and Duke were in the box with us. We stood to make room, but it was cramped.

I swiped at my eyes to make sure they were dry. "Who's here?"

"I don't know. We heard the door being unlocked and came out here."

"It's probably just my grandfather."

"Yeah, but since your grandfather doesn't know me or Duke,

I figured it was best that we come out here. Considering he's the one who made that weird toaster on the coffee table, I didn't know what he'd do when he walked into a room full of strangers."

"Good point."

I opened the box a crack and looked through it. The apartment was lit up, so I could see inside perfectly as a man who was most definitely not my grandfather searched the place. But I did recognize the man. It was Agent Miller—one of the CC agents who had come to my house last week. "It's not him."

"It's not?" Duke asked. "Great."

"I wonder what he's looking for."

"Us?" Laila said. "Just a wild guess."

"Let's hope not, because we've packaged ourselves handily," Duke said.

Panic gripped my chest. "Do you think they've done something to my grandpa, then? They seemed to ignore him for ten years, but now this. Do you think he's in trouble for talking to me? Telling me all his theories about the Compound?" I'd just gotten him back in my life. I wasn't ready to lose him again.

A warm hand grabbed mine, and I looked down to see it was Trevor's. My heart exploded.

"Your grandfather is probably fine. Like you said, they've ignored him for ten years," Duke said. "We'll just hang out here until that guy gets what he wants and leaves."

We were too cramped for Duke to notice my hand in Trevor's, and I was glad because I didn't want him to ruin it.

"So how does it feel?" Duke asked, looking at Trevor.

His hand tightened on mine, as if that was what Duke was asking about and he wasn't going to let go. "How does what feel?"

"To know there are advanced minds in the world and that you aren't one of them."

I forgot what a jerk Duke could be. "Duke."

"I'm just wondering. I always wondered how Norms would feel if they knew about us. Does it make you feel like less of a person?"

"Not at all. What about you? How does it feel to know that even though you have an advanced mind, the girl you love wants me?"

My eyes widened, and I almost laughed. Trevor wasn't known for being rude, but that was a pretty low blow.

Laila raised her hand. "Could I request a no-fist-fighting-in-the-box rule? It's too crowded. As soon as we're free, please, carry on."

Outside the box, the agent sat on my grandpa's couch and picked up some of his handmade devices on the table.

"Maybe if you had kept your mouth shut," Duke said to Trevor, "the CC wouldn't be so interested in you."

Trevor had angled himself slightly between Duke and me. "I actually started suspecting because you and your teammates couldn't keep your mouths shut in the locker room."

"No, seriously," Laila said. "If someone ends up hitting me by mistake, I will wipe them clean and won't even care."

"He's getting on the phone," I said. All of us fell silent, and I knew Duke and Laila were advancing their hearing along with me.

"Yes, he's taken care of." He paused, and I took a small sip of air. "No. I have it under control. No, I'm not monitoring the apartment. No one is here." He listened.

I looked up and around at the mention of the monitors. Had I missed them before? I waited for some sort of light to come on indicating we were now being monitored. Nothing changed.

"I thought we'd decided she's all but passed. Her compassion indicators are high. She has respect for authority." He paused. "No, she didn't tell the boy." The agent turned in a big deliberate circle. "I'm standing in the apartment right now. No one is here."

"Can you read his lips?" Trevor asked.

"Shut up," Duke said. "We're trying to listen."

"Don't tell him to shut up," I said.

"Shh," Laila hissed. "I think he's leaving."

I concentrated.

"I'll fill out a report. I'll send it on Monday." He put the small black box he had picked up back on the table. "No. I don't know." Suddenly, his eyes darted to the sliding glass door, to the box. I let out a small gasp.

"What's the plan if he comes back here?" Duke asked.

"Addison can slow down time and we can run," Trevor said.

"Duke can soothe him, I can Erase him, and yes, Addie slows down time and we run," Laila said as we all prepared to be discovered.

250

Agent Miller walked slowly to the door. His hand gripped the handle, but instead of opening it, he locked it. "Yes. We're good. Email me any questions." He headed for the front door, opened it, and flipped off the lights. The apartment went black.

We were all silent for a while. Then Duke said, "We're locked out here."

I exited the box, needing some air, and everyone followed. "They took care of him? What does that mean? Did they hurt him? What should we do?"

"First we should get off this balcony," Duke said.

Trevor took me gently by the arms. "Do you have your grandpa's cell phone number? Maybe we can start there."

"No . . . ," I started to say, but then remembered that I did have his info from when I took it off my dad's phone. I scrolled through my contacts and found it listed under Brett. Was that my dad's code name for him or something? I dialed.

On the fourth ring he picked up. "Hello?"

I let out a huge breath of air. "Grandpa? It's Addie."

"Hi, Addie. How are you?"

"I'm fine. Are you?"

"Yes. I'm fine."

"I think I messed up. The CC was at your apartment tonight, and it was my fault. They must've followed me there last time."

"Or me," Trevor said from next to me.

My grandpa sighed. "It's okay. I'm fine."

"I'm sorry. This is my fault." It couldn't be a coincidence that my grandpa had managed to avoid them for years and the moment I found him, they're suddenly interested too.

"It's fine. I'm just in their system now. They check up on me."

"You gave them free access to your apartment?"

"Were they inside?"

"Yes."

"How do you know?"

"I saw them."

"Where are you?"

I started to say, *On your back patio*, but thought better of it. If the CC was monitoring my grandpa's apartment, I needed to be careful here. "With some friends. I'll come see you in a few days, okay?"

"Perfect."

"Be careful, Grandpa, okay? Don't trust them."

He chuckled. "You don't have to tell me that."

"Okay, I'll see you soon, then. Bye."

We hung up.

"Now that we know Grandpa is okay, can we get out of here?" Duke asked, trying the door and proving it was still locked. He looked like a caged animal, pacing the small balcony.

"So if my grandpa is okay, then what did 'he's taken care of' mean?"

Laila nodded her head to Trevor. "Maybe they meant him."

"Oh. Right." I had almost forgotten Trevor's memories had been Erased.

"Can we discuss this when we are off this tiny balcony?" Duke asked.

"We have two options out of here," Trevor spoke up. "Down two balconies . . ." He pointed over the edge to the balcony below us. "Or over one." He nodded to the balcony of the lady we had lied to earlier.

"I don't think Short-Skirt is going to let us in again," Laila said. "Well, she'd let Duke in, but that won't help us. Plus, I saw the way Trevor got over here, and I don't think I'd make it."

"Addison," Trevor said. "Which way will work?"

"Oh." A choice. Why didn't I think of that? I quickly Searched the two options. "Down. Duke first. Trevor last. One balcony at a time."

"Perfect," Trevor said, trusting my answer completely.

Duke walked to the rail and Laila followed, directing him where to place his feet. As he climbed over, he looked directly at me. "I still don't believe you told him. Not smart." Then he dropped down.

"Can you get in trouble?" Trevor asked me.

"Yes."

He nodded, then stepped up to the railing. Duke was already on the balcony below us, and Laila was climbing over. Trevor took her hands and helped lower her down. Then he looked at me. "You ready?"

I stepped up to the railing, and he put his hands on my waist to help me over. An energy buzzed through my body, and I had to stop myself from hugging him. I had to remind myself he didn't remember our other life. I climbed over the railing, stand-ing on the small ledge on the outside of the metal bars. Below me Duke held his hands up, waiting to grab onto my legs. In front of me, Trevor placed his hands between mine on the metal rail.

"I want to know you," he said, finishing the sentence that was interrupted in the box. "I need to."

CHAPTER 32

Laila: Everyone is falling apart.

I knocked on Connor's door. We had about six hours to make it home before we risked a citation. We had only applied for a weekend pass. Why wasn't he ready?

He opened his door, sleepy eyed. His hair stuck out at odd angles, and the room behind him was dark.

"You were asleep? It's almost noon."

"Is it?" He ran a hand down his face.

"We need to go."

His eyes were bloodshot, and he rubbed at them. "I'll be ready in five."

I took a step back, ready to walk away, but forced myself

to ask, "Are you okay?"

He offered a fake smile. "Perfect."

The car ride home was quiet—tense, even. His silence was so loud it made me want to scream just to make noise. I caught him glancing over at me and used it as an excuse to talk.

"What happened yesterday?"

"Absolutely nothing," he said softly.

I was trying to understand what he meant by that when I saw his bloodshot eyes again. "Are you hungover?" That would explain a lot.

"No. I'm not."

I wondered if Connor ever told me the truth. "I won't judge you if you are," I mumbled.

"I'm not."

"Fine. Whatever. I mean, you left all day yesterday. You weren't around when we got home. If you were out partying or something, that would at least explain what you were doing."

He sounded tired when he said, "I didn't realize I was under investigation, but it sounds like you gave me an alibi."

I curled my hands into fists. "Connor. I was just asking a question. I didn't know your life was top secret. Excuse me for being curious."

We were both quiet for a while when he finally said, "That's the problem, isn't it?"

I sighed. Now I was tired. "What's the problem?"

"The only reason you want to know is to satisfy your curiosity.

You can't stand not knowing something."

"Well, I'm glad you know me so well." I crossed my arms and stared out the window for the rest of the trip, my throat tight. I didn't need to know anything about him. That was fine with me. When he stopped in front of my house, I slammed the door to his truck. If I never saw him again, I'd be happy. Not thinking about him ever again would make me even happier but seemed impossible. He constantly circled through my mind. Between thoughts of him and worrying about Addie, my mind was constantly occupied.

On my third day home from Addie's, my brain wouldn't shut up about what the CC would do to Addie if they found out we'd told Trevor. Would they, like the stupid DAA, think it was because she was unstable like Bobby? Did they think that meant she'd blab to the world about the Compound? The thought made me angry. Addie was the opposite of Bobby in all ways. I tried to calm myself. We had all made a pact not to talk about it. The CC thought Trevor was Erased, and they said Addie had all but passed whatever lame test of loyalty they were administering. Sure, they were monitoring her grandfather now, but he seemed extremely careful. It would be fine. My preoccupied mind didn't register how eerily quiet my house was when I first stepped inside, arms full of groceries. It wasn't until I put the milk away and shut the refrigerator door that it hit me.

"Hello?" I called out. "Where is everyone?"

I checked my dad's room. He wasn't there. Then I went to

my brothers' room. It was empty. Just as I was about to walk out, though, I heard whimpering in the closet.

I slid open the door to find Eli, cowering in the corner. I cursed under my breath. "What's wrong?" I dropped to my knees and crawled into the closet with him. "What is it, Eli? Talk to me."

"Stop. Go away."

"No. I'm here now. You're going to be fine. Did he hurt you? Look at me, let me see your face. Do you need ice?"

"Stop."

I tried to pull his hands away from his face. I was going to kill my dad.

"Stop it! Stop thinking! Don't think anymore!"

"What?"

"I don't want to be in your head. I don't want to be in his head. I want to be alone. Leave me alone." He took a pillow from the floor and pushed it over his face and ears. "Please," he whimpered. "Stop thinking."

I tried to make my mind go blank like I often did when my dad was around. Nothing. A blank canvas. An empty screen. A gray night.

"I can hear that. Go away." He started rocking back and forth, whimpering again.

"You didn't get off the new program?" I asked, pulling the pillow away and forcing him to look at me. His eyes were haunted. "Eli. Look at me."

He blinked and focused on my eyes.

"Have you been doing the new program? The one I gave you?"

He nodded over and over.

"Where is it? Where is your card?"

He pointed to his dresser. I backed out of the closet and saw his tablet sitting on the dresser. I took the card out of the slot and unclipped the small chip, sliding it into my pocket. "I'll be back in a while." I started to leave but then went back to the closet, pulled him into a tight hug, and whispered, "I'm going to fix this. You're going to be okay."

I stood and walked out. Was this why everyone had left? To give him space? I stumbled back to my truck, rolling my ankle when my heel sank in the grass. I tripped forward, grabbing the door handle to keep me from falling. A sob escaped from my tight-pressed lips. How could I have done this to my little brother? I was supposed to look out for him. Another sob came, and I pressed my forehead to the truck window.

No. I couldn't lose it now. I had to help him. I clenched my teeth and climbed into my truck.

It took me ten minutes to get to Face's house, ignoring the traffic signs that seemed more like suggestions today and stopping only when it was absolutely necessary. I pounded on his door until a teenage boy answered. His dark hair was spiked, he wore a white tank with holey jeans, and he held a lidded Styrofoam cup with a chewed-up straw sticking out the top. When he saw me, he raised an eyebrow and put one hand high on the door frame.

I almost asked for Face, because I didn't see the blurry spot on his neck, but then he said, "Laila."

So this was his real face. He was so young. "What is this?" I asked through my teeth, holding up the chip.

"It's everything you asked for and more," he said in the same voice all his faces used.

"I didn't ask for the more. My brother is sick. Very sick."

"Sick how?"

"He's overwhelmed. His ability came on too fast. He doesn't know how to deal with it. And he's getting more than he should. Everything."

Face smiled. His real face was distracting. Too young. Too attractive. Too something. "You're welcome. I just gave your brother his full ability."

"He shouldn't have his full ability yet. That's something he should grow into."

"Not true. The DAA tries to administer an ability slowly with blocks and suppressors. I gave it to him all at once. The natural way is somewhere in the middle. Now your brother is at his full power and can learn how to deal with that with his young mind. The DAA thinks their way is better. I would argue my way is better."

"Right now all I care about is making my brother better. So give me something to help him."

"You have cash?"

"Face. Seriously. Help him."

He sucked air between his teeth. "Yeah. Not gonna happen."

260

He took a drink from his chewed-up straw and then let the door slide shut between us.

I punched it, immediately regretting that action. My hand throbbed. "Please, Face," I begged. "Please just help me." I sank to the step and dropped my head to my knees.

Standing outside Connor's door, I had to swallow my pride. He was the last person I wanted to ask for help but the only person I knew who might be able to. I knocked. A big man answered who looked nothing like Connor. Probably his stepdad.

"Is Connor in?"

"No. Connor is not in. He has not been in for three days. If you find him, tell him to get his sorry butt home and apologize to his mother for causing her this much worry."

Three days? He'd left right after we got back?

It wasn't like I knew Connor's habits or hangouts, but if he wasn't at Face's and he wasn't in his garage, there was only one other place I could think of that he might be.

It was closing in on dusk when I got there. Founders Square looked even more antiquated in the dark. I walked by the statues, passed by the motorcycles, then headed for the train.

The metal door to the train that had been opened last time was shut. I pulled myself up by the vertical rail next to the door and stood on a small metal step. Then I knocked. No answer. No sound. Nothing.

I knocked again and tried to open the door, but it must've

been locked from the inside, because it wouldn't budge. I started banging with the side of my fist, calling his name. The sound echoed through the night.

I stopped and listened after a few minutes. Just when I was ready to start my pounding again, I heard the sound of footsteps and the scrape of metal against metal. The door slid open half a foot and Connor stood inside, hair a mess, pajama bottoms resting just below his hips, chest bare. My heart raced to life at the sight of him. It felt like I hadn't seen him in forever.

He sighed. "You must need something."

I held back a curse. I did need something. More than I'd needed anything else before this moment.

"That's what I thought." He moved to shut the door, and I stuck my leg inside.

"I don't know who else to go to."

"Anyone else."

"It's my brother. He needs someone to help him. Maybe you can Heal him or something."

"I'm not your personal Healer, Laila."

"What's your problem? Someone break your bike or force you to make a decision?"

His knuckles whitened from where they gripped the frame of the door, but his face remained calm, tired. "The only decision I need to make is how to most effectively get you to leave me alone."

I knew I was being mean, but I needed to see some emotion from him. Get a rise out of him. Anything. It was like the life had been drained out of him. And tired Connor wasn't going to be motivated to help me at all. "Maybe if you weren't half Norm, these decisions would come easier to you."

He leaned forward a couple of inches so that his upper body breached the doorway and said in a low voice, "You've now used the three whole things you know about me to insult me. Do you feel better?"

I knew more things about him. Didn't I? I racked my brain. He liked old things, which was because he was half Norm. He wanted someone to force him to leave the Compound, which was why he sold illegal mind expansion programs. Crap. I only knew three things about him. Two, really. He was generous in his summary. "You don't tell me anything."

I wanted to know him. He wouldn't let me. But if I were being honest, I never tried very hard either. I was trying to keep him at a distance. If that was my goal, I knew way more than I should. I knew that he worked on his motorcycle more than anyone should want to. And I could tell now by the lack of grease marks on his face that he hadn't worked on it in days, and that was probably driving him crazy.

I knew that despite his obsession with the past, he knew as much as any Bureau agent about technology. And I knew he cared about people, no matter how much he tried to hide it. That if he did leave this place he would miss it. And I knew he was exactly like me in that he wouldn't let anyone in unless they showed some vulnerability. If I took down my guard and took him off the defense, he'd let me in. And that was the problem—we both needed the other to act first.

He looked at my leg still in the door and then my hand still gripping the metal bar. I should've realized that meant he knew he could push my leg out without throwing me to the ground. But I didn't realize that until he grabbed hold of my leg. Just as he almost successfully cleared it from the train, I threw my arms around his shoulders. This was a big mistake. He was using his weight to push me out, and without me supporting my own weight on the handle, he stumbled forward. I fell backward, out the open door.

My foot caught in the slat of the metal step and got lodged there while the rest of my body continued to fall. When I hit the ground I heard my ankle snap. Then I felt the pain, hot at first and then so intense I thought I might pass out. Connor landed on top of me but was off faster than I could register that he'd fallen too.

He freed my foot and scooped me up, saying something under his breath that sounded suspiciously like he was cursing me to a fiery death or at least an unsaved one. But then it changed to calling himself an idiot, which I completely agreed with.

He carried me into the train and onto one of the beds that folded out from the wall. The one he'd obviously been using, because there was a pillow and blanket on it that smelled just like him—a combination of soap, hair product, and musky deodorant.

He threw off my shoe and wrapped both his hands around my ankle. For a moment the pain was even more intense, and as my eyes stung, I gripped the bed until the ache was replaced with a tingling warmth. Next he moved to my head and put one hand on the back of it.

"I'm good now. It's fine," I said, trying to sit up.

He pushed me back down by the shoulders. "Stay down for a minute; you're bleeding."

I felt it then—liquid seeping through my hair. But as soon as I felt the pain, it was soothed.

"Where else?" he asked, his eyes more alive than I'd seen them all night.

"Nowhere."

His gaze traveled my entire body. "Will you just stop and feel for a second before you answer? Where else?"

A trail of blood ran down a cut from his temple that he must've received on the way out of the train. "You're bleeding."

He wiped it with the back side of his wrist and then looked at me like I still needed to tell him where to Heal me. The cut on his head slowly closed. He hovered above me, close, too close.

"I'm fine." I sat up and swung my feet to the ground, then rotated my ankle around. It felt perfect.

He sat on the floor, leaned back against the wall, and grabbed a fistful of hair. "I swear, Laila."

"Yeah, you do. A lot."

He let out a small groan. "I need you out of my head."

I gasped, thinking of my brother in that closet, whimpering. "I know I've asked you for a dozen favors."

"It's the only thing you *ever* ask me for."

"I know."

He sighed. "What's wrong with your brother?"

"He's having a breakdown. His ability fully Presented and is driving him insane."

"Telepath."

I nodded.

"He used Face's program?"

I nodded again.

He pushed his palms to his eyes. "Doesn't your dad have any suppressors he can use?"

I opened my mouth, then shut it. I hadn't thought to ask my dad. "My dad uses them as fast as he gets them."

"I don't sell suppressors, but I have a program that might help." He stood and pulled his case out from under the opposite bed. He opened it and threw me a chip. Wasn't a stupid chip what got me into this mess?

"Is this even going to work?" I held it up. "Can't you do something . . . with your ability? Lessen the effects or something?"

His jaw tightened. "No."

I thought of the fact that he was failing all his Para classes, how he hated that I knew his ability, and it hit me—he didn't like to use it. Maybe he was hoping that if he never used it, he'd be more willing to leave the Compound. Live on the Outside. The cold air and the metal walls of the ancient train seemed to push against my lungs. "You can't or you won't?"

"I'm offering that." He pointed at the chip I still held up.

I wanted to throw it on the ground and stomp on his offering.

Why wouldn't he just help me? I grabbed my heel, which had ended up by the wall, and slipped it on. I paused by the door, wondering if begging would help. Then I felt the tears gather at the back of my eyes, so I gritted my teeth against the sting and left. My brother needed me.

CHAPTER 33

Addie: I'm getting the word *welcome*
tattooed on my forehead.

Now that he knew the truth about the Compound, I thought Trevor would be at my house every second, needing to be around me as much as I needed to be near him. Yet here I sat, in my room, staring at the very black screen of my phone. He was weirded out. I knew it. There was a knock on my bedroom door, followed by my dad's voice, "You decent?"

"No."

Obviously knowing that was a lie, he walked in. "We need to talk."

"What?"

"For starters, that. What's going on with this new bad

attitude you have toward me?"

"I'm angry, Dad."

"I can tell. Would you care to expound?"

"Would you?"

"I'm lost. I need you to help me."

"Oh, you want me to tell you what lies I know about so that you can know which ones to confess to? No thanks."

"Is this about the new mind pattern again?"

"I know about Grandpa." I blurted it out before I changed my mind.

"What about him? They've delayed the transfer of his grave."

I squeezed my eyes shut.

"Your mom wants you to go home for Christmas, and I think it's a good idea."

My eyes popped open. "What? No."

"You're obviously not happy here. Your mother said since I got Thanksgiving, it's only fair that she get Christmas."

"No. I want to stay here."

"Your mother—"

"You left her and you still let her control you?"

My statement took all the fight out of his face. "You have never talked to me like this before. When did that change?"

"When you became a liar."

"You're going home for Christmas." His voice was soft. "I'm going for a drive." He shut the door when he was finished. He'd always gone for a drive after he and my mom fought. My eyes stung, and I blinked away the pain.

My phone rang. I answered before the screen even had time to register the caller. "Hello."

"Addie. This is Rowan."

I sighed.

"That disappointed, huh?"

"No, sorry. Hi."

"I would like to propose an idea."

"Okay."

"So I found out that Trevor asked Stephanie to winter formal."

"Oh yeah." Suck. Who else wanted to come stomp on my mood today? Apparently, I was open for business.

"I was thinking it would be fun to go as a group. You and me, Steph and Trevor. What do you say?"

I walked to my window and watched my dad's car drive away. "Your winter formal? I don't even go to your school. Besides, would Stephanie even go for that?"

"So are you telling me you don't want to go to the dance with me?" Rowan asked.

"I would just feel a little weird going to your school's dance." The doorbell rang, and I rolled off my bed to go answer it.

"Trevor thinks it's a good idea."

Trevor was in on this plan? Suddenly, everything was different. "He does?"

"He said I should ask you."

Maybe Trevor didn't understand that when I told him I had ended up with him in the other version of my life, that meant I wanted to end up with him in this version. Or maybe he wanted me to be there. "Okay?"

"Was that a question?"

"No, it was an answer. Yes, I'll go."

"Awesome. I'll pick you up at six on Friday."

I hung up my phone and answered the door. Trevor stood there, and I almost burst into tears from happiness and relief. I stepped forward and wrapped my arms around him. "I just had the worst fight ever with my dad."

When his whole body went still, I realized I didn't have these privileges anymore. I let go and backed up with a mumbled apology.

"No." He tentatively ran a hand down my arm. "It just took me·by surprise."

"Come in."

He stepped inside and took everything in. I reminded myself, again, that he didn't have the same memories I did. So he'd never been inside my house before.

"Um." My eyes stung, and I pressed my fingers to them. "I'm sorry. This is just so hard for me." I squared my shoulders and took a deep breath. "Can I get you anything?"

"No. I'm good." He followed me to the couch, where we both sat down. "Has Rowan called you yet?"

"Yes, just barely. Like right before you got here."

"Good. You said yes, right?"

"Only because he said it was your idea."

"I wish I could ask you. I asked Stephanie after they"—he

271

paused, then lowered his voice—"messed with my memories. I thought it was easier than having her hate me."

I smiled. "You don't have to explain yourself to me."

"I want to, though. If I could un-ask Stephanie I would, but I think that would be very rude at this point."

"It would." My stomach twisted when I realized that at some point Stephanie was going to find out that Trevor and I were . . . were what? Getting to know each other? I was in love with him and he was in I-might-one-day-want-to-date-you with me? This was so complicated.

It was quiet for a few minutes, and Trevor broke the silence with a small chuckle. "This is weird. I'm being weird. Talk to me. Tell me about you."

An image of him telling his mother all about me in our other life flashed through my mind, and I burst into tears. He looked like a deer caught in headlights for a second, then pulled me toward him, wrapping his arms around me.

"Shh." He petted my hair. "Addison, it's going to be fine. We'll figure it out. Listen, even before this, before you told me about . . ." He trailed off. We had agreed not to talk about it out loud. "I was interested in you. I threw a shoe at your face and nearly kissed you. Don't you remember?"

I nodded against his chest. "I swear I'm not a baby."

He laughed.

"I just miss you." My heart ached as I said it.

He hugged me tighter. "We'll figure it out."

The garage door swung shut, and a set of keys hit the counter.

Trevor stood, almost whacking me in the head when he did. "Hello, sir," he said.

My dad finished his brisk walk into the living room and stopped in front of Trevor. "Hi. Who are you?"

Ugh. My dad was not trying to get off my bad list at all. "This is Trevor."

My dad's jaw tightened. He probably remembered that he had asked me to stay away from Trevor because the CC agents had mentioned him.

"Good to meet you, sir." He extended his hand, and my dad shook it. Trevor knew my dad's ability. I wondered if that was intimidating.

"We were just leaving," I said.

"Where are you going?"

"Downtown." I looked at him, waiting for that to register. For him to realize that was where my grandfather's apartment was.

He didn't. "Be home by curfew."

Outside, we stopped by Trevor's car. "I wanted to check on my grandpa. I've been worried about him. Did you have plans before I kind of threw you into mine?"

"As long as I don't have to eat anything there, I'm good. Let's go see your grandfather."

When my grandpa answered the door, I realized just how worried I'd been. Even though I had talked to him, with that guy lurking in his apartment, I thought maybe they had done something to him. But there he was, stick and headphones in place, just as crazy as ever. I was getting used to his craziness, though. It made me smile.

"Hi. I brought you seeds." I held out a pack of squash seeds I had bought on a whim the other day when I saw them in the checkout line at the store.

He looked at the pack and then offered me a big smile. "Addie. That's so nice. Come in, come in."

I scanned his living room. Everything looked just as it had last time we were here. "Is everything okay?"

"Of course."

I eyed the toaster. It wasn't beeping or flashing warnings at me, so supposedly that meant there were no foreign devices around. They may have been monitoring him more closely now, but I hoped they still thought he was fairly harmless. Because he was.

Trevor seemed to follow my cue and leafed through the stack of newspapers he'd been so interested in before. "Any unexpected visitors?"

"Yes. You're here."

"What have you been up to?"

He flicked the pack of seeds. "Growing things. And making things."

He brought me the black box from his table.

"What is it exactly?"

"Talk into it."

I put the box up to my mouth. "Hello."

It repeated my word back to me. If my grandpa wanted a recorder, couldn't he just buy one? They did have that kind of stuff here, didn't they? Maybe they didn't. "Cool."

"Let Trevor try," he said. When he handed it to Trevor, he said, "Say a few sentences."

Trevor looked at me. I just shrugged, my sign that meant, *Humor him. We both know he's on the crazy side.*

"Hi," Trevor said into the box and then, like me, must've run out of words to say to an inanimate object, because he tried to hand the box back after it said hi back.

My grandpa was too busy looking at the top of Trevor's head to be bothered to take the box. "You're tall, young man."

"Yes, I am."

"How long have you been that tall?"

"Um . . ." He smiled, and I could tell he was trying not to laugh. "A while now."

I laughed and grabbed the box from Trevor, putting it on the table. "We better go. It was fun to see your stuff." I had just wanted to check on him. Now that I knew he was fine, I wanted to spend some time with Trevor away from reminders of the Compound.

My grandfather pulled me into another hug, and for the first time since I'd met him again, my body relaxed. It was nice having my grandpa back in my life, especially because my father and I weren't exactly getting along. I hugged him back. It was hard to believe my father had robbed me of this relationship for the last ten years.

275

On the way down in the elevator, Trevor said, "Tell me three things."

I looked up at him. "What?"

"From our other life. Three things."

Thoughts and feelings raced through my body. I wanted to tell him everything in that moment, but I loved the way he limited it. Three things. Slow steps. So much like Trevor. Which three things, though? Maybe I should just start with the first three things.

"We met at a football game."

He smiled. "Very appropriate."

"My dad forced me to go sit in the student section, and there you were, an open seat next to you. It was fate."

The elevator dinged as we reached ground level. We stepped out and started walking to his car.

"Okay, thing two. The following Monday at school we ran into each other in the library, where I found out you hate classics."

"Classic what?"

I sighed and shook my head. "Classic books."

"Oh yeah. Yuck. You like them?"

I laughed. "And thing number three. Because of this very attitude about classics, I wrote you a note about being attacked by the decaying, awoken-from-the-grave body of Charles Dickens."

He laughed. "You threatened me with zombie Dickens? Nice."

"And that's when I decided we were going to be best friends."

"Best friends?"

"I was delusional."

We reached his car, and he opened the door for me. I took in the littered mess that coated the floor and smiled. It was so nice to have my memory back.

CHAPTER 34

Laila: When wrong, is it absolutely necessary to admit it?

Eli slept, and for the first time that night my anxiety eased. The chip seemed to help. I had watched the mind patterns for a moment, but they only made me dizzy. For him they seemed to take the knots out of his neck.

"Is he going to be okay?" Derek asked. I hadn't realized he was awake.

"He'll be fine. Where were you earlier?"

"Dad said we had to leave. Said Eli needed some quiet."

"Dad took you somewhere?"

"We went to the field by the school and threw around a football." He took off his socks, folded them together, and threw them at my head. "I know, shocking, right?"

"Yes. Good night, Derek." I picked up the socks and, when I reached the door, pelted him with them. He laughed and then lifted his blanket up in front of him, probably worried I'd find more ammo.

My dad watched television in the living room, and I waited for a while, trying to collect my thoughts, not sure exactly what I wanted to say.

"What?" he asked from where he sat. "Spit it out. Your thoughts are so loud I can't watch my game."

"I'm worried about Eli."

"He'll be fine."

"Fine like you? Because you're far from fine."

"I don't know, Laila. He'll learn to deal with it in his own way. Whatever way that is."

That wasn't exactly the reassurance I was hoping for, but when could I ever count on comfort from my father? The memory of my brother in the closet, pillow clamped over his head, seized me. Maybe for the first time in my life, I could understand why my dad would want to suppress that. I grabbed my keys off the counter. "I'm going out. Don't wait up." Not that he ever did.

He grunted and turned up the volume on the television.

Now that Eli was better, I realized how ungrateful I had been to Connor. I knocked on the train door. It didn't take as long for him to slide it open this time, but he still opened it only half a foot.

"Hi," I said.

"Hey. Is he okay?"

"Better." I cleared my throat. "Thank you."

"How'd those words taste in your mouth?"

"Awful."

He smiled. We stood there in silence. He didn't offer to let me in, and I knew it was because he wanted me to ask. He liked to make things hard on me.

"Can I come in?"

"Why?"

"Because I want to talk."

"Why?"

"Because you're here, and I want to know why."

He rolled his eyes and started to shut the door. I put my hand on the edge. "Because you need me, and I've never needed anyone more than I need you."

He pulled me inside and against him before I even finished the sentence. I clung to him, letting down the defenses I'd tried so hard to keep in place. I felt exhausted without them. Maybe he was tired too, because his hand shook a little against my back. I met his eyes. This close I could see the brown that seemed to surface from the center of a pool of green.

"Why are you here?" I asked him.

"I figured this was the closest place we had to live like I would on the Outside."

"You like it there?" I wasn't sure, because he'd seemed so upset on the way home. "You should've shown me your favorite places."

"You were too busy hanging out with Duke."

"Forced necessity."

He shrugged.

"Were you jealous?"

"Insanely," he said in a low voice.

I laughed.

"You find that amusing?" His hand, still pressed against my back, pulled me closer. Energy shot up my spine.

"Yes, I do." But I wasn't going to reassure him that I thought of Duke next to never and him all the time. A little fear in a guy was healthy.

But then he said, "Do I have reason to be?"

And I couldn't help but say, "Never."

His lips moved to mine and pressed softly against them, teasing me. I didn't like to be teased. I put my arms around his neck and pulled his face to me. "Don't make me regret this," I said against his mouth.

"I'm surprised you don't already."

I smiled. He knew me well. Maybe better than I wanted him to, but maybe just as much as I needed him to. The cold air surrounded us, but I felt warm against him. His breath on my mouth, his hands on my back, his chest against mine. Unlike our first kiss, this one was soft and thoughtful. It made me ache inside with more joy than I had ever felt. Now I knew what he meant when he said there was a difference between real and manufactured happiness.

I wanted to stay this way, lost in him, but I knew we needed to talk. "Go sit over there so we can talk."

He looked behind him to the bed I was pointing to, and I sat down on the opposite bed.

"And you're going to sit there? We have to be separated to talk?"

"Yes, actually."

"Why?"

"Just go sit."

He laughed the kind of laugh that meant he knew his nearness would prevent any talking and plopped onto his back on the bed across from me. The first thing he said was, "I wasn't supposed to meet you."

"What?"

"You threw off my list. I had it figured out. The reasons for going, the ones for staying."

I tucked my feet underneath me. "Going was winning?"

"Yes."

"And now?"

"And now you." He stared at the ceiling. "You wouldn't want to leave, would you?"

"No." Not even if Addie stayed with her dad. My brothers were here. As at home as Addie felt out there, I felt like a foreigner. "I won't ask you to stay for me, Connor. There's no way I want you to wake up one day full of bitterness and realize I'm to blame." Good thing he was ten feet away or I might not have been able to say that. I might have begged him to stay.

"He wasn't a Norm."

It took my brain a little while to place the words. "Your dad?"

"He was Telepathic."

"Was?" I moved onto my back, mirroring his position of staring at the metal ceiling of the train.

"He begged me day and night. My mom begged me not to. . . ."

"Begged you for what?"

"To Heal him."

Those words hung in the air above us, clinging to the cold, waiting for me to figure them out.

"I was twelve," he finally said. "I didn't understand. He just told me that there was a part of his brain that was overdeveloped. That he wanted it to be made whole." He sounded so anguished. "I Healed him of his ability."

"Healed him of it . . ." It took a long moment for that to click. The words and the cold rained down on me, numbing my cheeks. "Made him Normal?"

"Yes."

"Is that what he wanted?"

"No. He had this theory that if a Healer could make a section of his brain a little closer to Normal, it would make him more in control of when and what he heard. But he could never get a Healer to do it."

I could hear my breaths. Is this what you did for people you cared about? Listened to their horrible pasts? I didn't know what to say. That was a memory that should be kept deep down inside him and never brought out. Like the time my father gave

283

me a black eye and split open my lip. Not even my dad got to remember that one.

Now was the time I was supposed to say something. Anything. "Wow. That sucks. Too bad you can't have your memories Erased."

He started laughing. Low and quiet at first and then deep and full.

"What's so funny?" I couldn't help but smile at the sound.

"My mom made me go to a therapist for about a year after my dad left the Compound."

"A therapist? As in someone you talk to? I didn't even know we had those in the Compound. Why didn't they just give you some programs to ease the guilt?"

"Not a lot of stuff works on a Healer. But anyway, the therapist told me over and over again that I was only twelve, I didn't know any better. My dad shouldn't have made me do that. And you, after five years of guilt, confirm that my guilt is justified and my life sucks."

"Yeah, well, I'm probably just projecting. I would've found a sick pleasure in wiping my dad of his ability. I'm sure you felt genuinely horrified."

He didn't argue the point.

"And so if you deny yourself the opportunities to use your ability by living on the Outside, somehow you've righted a wrong? You've taken your punishment?"

He drew a breath and let it out slowly. "You're the only person I've used my ability on in years."

"You suppressing your ability is not going to return his. Especially your ability, Connor. One that can help so many. That therapist was right. It wasn't your fault. You are only going to make bad worse." I rolled on my side to face him. "Look at me being all motivational and crap. Did you hear that? That was some good stuff. I don't think Addie could've said it better."

He smiled a ghost of a smile at the ceiling. His hands rested on his chest, and he let the arm closest to me fall open to the side and then gave a slight beckoning movement with his fingers.

"Are you wanting me to come over there? Because that was the lamest effort ever after my amazing display of advice-giving skills."

"Get over here."

"I'm only coming over there because I'm freezing and you have a blanket." I crawled across the metal floor to him, and he pulled me into a tight hug.

"You're the first person, outside of my family and the therapist, of course, that I've told."

I ran my hand along his chest. "So do you ever talk to your mom about it?"

"Initially. But she's moved on."

"And what about your dad? You said before that you don't know him now."

"He hasn't talked to me since he left." His hand went to my arm, and he seemed to absentmindedly run his fingers along it, his thoughts far off. "I tried to see him."

"When?"

As his fingers brushed my arm, small tingles of energy moved along my skin, leaving a trail of goose bumps. Was he doing that on purpose? Did he even realize that his touch was almost electric? It must have been related to his ability, and it was driving me crazy.

"I saw him once a few years ago and once a few days ago."

My breath seeped slowly into the air and created a tiny puff of fog in the coldness. "That's who you went to see when we were in Dallas? That's what was in Bowie, Texas?"

"Yes. But I couldn't do it. I drove a hundred and fifty miles and couldn't force myself to walk the last twenty steps to his door."

No wonder he'd looked so torn up the next day.

"When he was sentenced to leave the Compound, I couldn't look him in the eyes. And I still can't."

"What?" I propped myself up on my elbow, taking my arm back so I could concentrate. "They forced him to leave? I didn't know they did that."

He met my eyes. "They do, and I'm pretty sure he still blames me."

"He should blame himself."

He took a few deep breaths in and out. "It's easier to blame someone else."

"You don't seem to have a problem blaming yourself." I searched his eyes, needing him to release the pain I saw there. "Why don't you blame me for a while? Give yourself a break?"

He gave a single laugh. "Because you had nothing to do with it."

"Only slightly less than you did."

He squeezed his eyes shut and then pulled me back into his arms. "Thank you," he whispered against my hair.

"How did that taste in your mouth?"

He laughed. "Awful."

CHAPTER 35

Addie: Apparently, I have no self-control.

I wasn't sure what to say to Stephanie. I had wanted to talk to Trevor about it. Ask him what I should tell her, but it seemed weird to ask him how I should talk to his ex about my feelings. I knew that no matter how I told Stephanie I liked Trevor, I was going to sound like the biggest jerk. More than a jerk.

Whatever I decided to tell her, the time to do it was not as we got ready for winter formal in her bedroom. Not with the huge football poster plastered on the wall behind her, Trevor's face circled with a heart. Not with pictures I hadn't seen last time of her and Trevor taped all around her mirror. No, tonight was most definitely not a good time to tell her.

"How are you doing your hair?" Stephanie asked as she

applied another layer of mascara.

"I was thinking just down. Is that not good?"

"You should put it up in a loose twist and let some curls hang around your face and down your neck. It would look really hot. You want me to do it?"

"Sure."

I faced the mirror, and she positioned herself behind me. As I tried to stare at anything but the pictures of her and Trevor together, my mind wandered to the last time Stephanie had lost Trevor to me. She was not very happy. She set out to ruin me. Expose me and my lies to him. A woman scorned was not to be messed with.

"I can't believe you and Trevor talked me into sharing my winter formal with Rowan," Stephanie said.

"He's not as bad as you think."

"Well, nothing, not even him, is going to ruin tonight for me."

She didn't say anything about tomorrow. Tomorrow was available for ruining.

The boys showed up, and I tried my hardest to keep my eyes to myself. I did not need to ogle Trevor, but man, did he look amazing.

"Addie," Rowan said, "you look hot. And Steph, you look beautiful tonight as well."

You look gorgeous, I pushed into Trevor's mind.

"No fair," he said out loud.

"What's not fair?" Stephanie asked.

"Yeah, Trevor, what's not fair?" I added.

He smiled his amazing smile. "The amount of beauty in this room. We better get going."

Stephanie beamed as though that was a compliment for her and her alone, then hooked her arm through Trevor's. I wasn't sure if this was a good idea after all. If I had just let Trevor go to this dance without me, I wouldn't have to be a witness. Rowan held out his elbow for me, and I took it. Might as well get this torturous night over with.

We had formal dances at the Compound twice a year. They were awesome. Illusions filled the venue in whatever theme was decided on. One year the theme was Ocean Sunset, and an entire wall of the building looked like an ocean, lapping onto the dance floor with an always-setting sun.

This was nothing like that. This was cheesy decorations and a halfway decent band. But this was all real and represented a committee's hard work. I appreciated it, but as I watched Stephanie and Trevor dance their third slow song, I was ready to personally pop all the balloons that made up a fake archway.

"So," Rowan said. "Do I have to ask the question for a third time or did you hear me?"

I turned my attention back to Rowan, who was doing a really good job of making sure our swaying back and forth matched the beat of the song. "I'm sorry, what?"

"That's what I thought. Would it help to know that he likes you too?"

"Who?"

"Who?" He laughed. "I don't know, maybe the guy you've

290

been staring at for the last thirty minutes."

"I'm sorry."

"It's okay. I've already been told that at approximately seven o'clock I am supposed to steal Stephanie for a dance so he can ask you." He glanced at his watch. "That's the next song."

"Really?" I hugged him. "Thank you."

"How are you two going to tell her? You know her wrath is like no other."

"I know. And I have no idea how I'm going to do it. Any suggestions?"

He laughed again. "Run?" The song ended, and we separated. Trevor and Stephanie rejoined us.

"If I were in charge of the decorations this year, I would not have gone all nineties with the balloons. So tacky."

"I kind of like them," I said.

"Decorations?" Rowan asked, then looked around as if noticing them for the first time.

"Oblivious," Stephanie said. We walked over to the food table because the next song was a stupid fast one. That song felt like it lasted an eternity. When the first chord of the new song was strummed, my heart sped up. I hoped Rowan could make this happen.

Stephanie turned to Trevor, and Rowan cleared his throat. "Let's mix it up this song. You want to dance, Steph?"

"What? No." She grabbed Trevor's hand.

"That would actually be really fun," I said. "Just for one song."

Trevor added, "I'm up for it."

"Fine," Stephanie said with a sigh. "One song."

Trevor led me to the middle of the dance floor. "Hi."

I smiled. His hand against my back felt so familiar and amazing. His shoulder was broad and strong beneath my grip. "Hi."

"Tell me three things."

I smiled. I liked this game. It made me happy. "One time we got trapped in the principal's car after losing a bet. We had to steal his bobblehead. Only Rowan, who was supposed to distract the principal, didn't do a very good job and the alarm got set."

"What did we do?"

"We talked until Rowan got the keys and freed us."

"Sounds interesting," Trevor said.

"Oh, then there was this time you were trying to prove how strong you were and you picked me up. This was way before we were together, by the way," I said.

"When you still thought I was supposed to be your best friend?"

"Yes."

"And I picked you up. How?"

"It was fast. You pulled me forward and then had me in the air, holding me around the thighs."

"And you still thought I wanted to be friends?"

I laughed. "I told you. I wasn't the greatest with your signals."

He moved my hand, clasped in his, up to his shoulder. The action closed the space between us. "Have you learned my signals yet?"

I was hyperaware of every inch of his body—his hands, now

on my waist, one foot between mine, his chest against my own. Warmth spread from his hands all the way up my back. My heart raced. My chest expanded. "I think so," I whispered. I felt the energy gathering around me before I realized what I'd done.

He noticed first. "What's wrong with the music?"

It had changed to a distorted moan. I looked around, and the entire dance floor was at a near standstill.

"Are you doing this?" he asked.

I tried to make my heart settle, hoping normal speed would return faster. "Just stay still. If we move, it will be obvious."

"Addison?"

I looked up at him. He moved his hand as slowly as possible to my cheek. I leaned my face into his palm. So much happiness burst inside me that the music came to a complete stop.

"Nobody is moving," Trevor said. "Does that mean they can't see us?"

"I don't know. I've never stopped it all the way before." If I had to guess, I'd say no.

"So then I can probably do this." Ever so slowly he brought his lips to mine. Even though I saw it coming, it still took my breath away when our lips touched.

"I think I love you," I said against his mouth.

"I think I can get used to that," he said back. I knew he couldn't love me yet. He was just now getting to know me. So that was the best thing he could've said in return. A new surge of happiness welled up inside me. Time wasn't returning to normal anytime soon. I wove my fingers into his hair and kissed

293

him again. Even our kiss we kept slow and calm, which only intensified each movement and heightened my senses each time he released a breath.

The music started moaning again, and I pulled away. I let just my eyes take in our surroundings and saw two people looking straight at us. Their expressions were distorted because they were hardly moving. One was Stephanie. Her face twisted into half shock, half hurt, and all the way angry. The other person, standing just inside the doors, was Duke Rivers.

CHAPTER 36

Laila: Guys don't think.

I walked the familiar path to Connor's garage. He was working on his bike. Again. How much stuff could a person possibly do on one motorcycle? Especially at seven o'clock at night. Did he ever stop? Maybe he was making up for the three lost days on the train.

He looked up as I entered, then back down to his bike, the smallest of smiles forming on his mouth. This tiny indication that he was happy to see me radiated joy through my entire body.

"Did you find an inch of the handlebar that didn't look Norm enough for you?" I slid onto the bar stool next to the high counter.

"Just messing with the calibration."

"Sounds important . . . and boring."

"It's so much less boring now that you're here."

I grunted. "You better say that after weeks and weeks of ignoring me every time I came into this garage."

"Ignoring you?"

"Yes, your bike had all your attention. I've never been more jealous of an inanimate object."

He chuckled a little. "You're impossible to ignore, Laila. I was acutely aware of exactly where you stood, what you looked at, when you took a breath."

"Wow. Look at you. You know how to say romantic things." I walked over to his bike and threw my leg over the seat. "What about when I sit on your bike? Does that bother you?"

"If you weren't blocking what I was trying to work on, then it might not bother me as much." He kissed my neck and then wrapped his arm around my waist and lifted me off his bike.

"Ha! See. I should be jealous of this piece of metal."

"I should be jealous," he muttered under his breath, returning to his task.

"No, I'm pretty sure I hate your motorcycle, so no need to be jealous there."

"I thought you and Duke were done scheming," he said, his back to me, tightening a screw.

"I don't know that Duke and I have ever schemed. And I have no idea what you're talking about."

"What does he want with a listening device?"

"What?"

"This morning he came in wanting a body chip." He must've noted my confused look, because he added, "A listening device you can attach to your body. Usually used to spy on people."

Spy on people. "And did you sell it to him?"

"He said you sent him. Plus he had cash, unlike some of my customers."

"My looks are my currency, baby."

"So true."

"I did not send him." I sighed, thinking about what Duke might want with a listening device. "Oh no." I pulled out my phone and dialed his number. He didn't answer.

"How about you take me for a ride on your little bike?" I grabbed the extra helmet off the shelf.

"Where are we going?"

"Duke's house."

"You really don't care at all about my jealous rages, do you?" he asked in an even voice, a little smirk letting me know he was at least partially kidding.

"Not right now."

He returned the tool he held to its place and put his helmet on. "Let's go."

I climbed on behind him and at first tried to get away with just grabbing his waist with my hands, but as he sped through the night, streetlights flying by in a blur, I wrapped my arms around him tightly.

"While driving, it's nice to be able to breathe," his voice said in the helmet speaker.

"Yeah, well, I'd like to be able to live, so I'm good."

We pulled up in front of Duke's house, and I slid off the bike as fast as possible. And I thought I'd hated his motorcycle before. Was definitely not a fan now. I didn't wait for him to do whatever pampering he did to his bike at the end of a ride and walked up the steps to the front door. Before I could knock, a robotic voice inside announced my arrival. I hadn't even realized I'd been scanned.

Mrs. Rivers answered. "Hi, Laila. Welcome," she said just as Connor stepped up behind me. "He's not here. He left this afternoon."

"To where? Do you know?"

"He went to check out the college campus in Dallas. His trip there for the football game made him realize how much he liked Dallas."

Right. A trip to check out the college campus. I'd believe that when I saw it. "Okay, well, thanks. Do you know when he might be home?"

"I'm not sure. Do you want me to tell him you stopped by?"

"No, I'm good."

"So what's the plan?" Connor asked as we walked away.

"What exactly can he do with a listening device? I'm assuming he can record. If he let the Containment Committee know his plans before he left, is there a way he can patch what he records directly to them?"

He didn't need to answer. The look on his face said my assessment was correct.

"He's going to ruin Addie's life."

"He'd do that?"

"He and his teammates permanently injured Trevor's throwing shoulder using their abilities. He's capable of anything." I dialed Addie's number. She didn't answer. She'd told me she was going to be at that stupid winter formal tonight. So did that mean she didn't have her phone on her? I tried again. When she didn't answer, I looked at Connor. "She's not answering."

"Come on, I have an idea."

We climbed onto his bike again, and when we pulled up in front of Face's house I asked, "Why are we here?"

"Face has these birds he uses to watch Paras in the Norm world. He likes to monitor suspicious activity out there. Mainly the children of Paras who were kicked out or left."

I raised my eyebrows. "Why?"

"He likes to study abilities diluted by Norm DNA. Or uninhibited by DAA programming."

"He's been spying on her? Why didn't you tell me?"

"I'm not sure if he's been spying on her. I'm just hoping he has been so we can see what's going on with her now." He knocked on the door. "Don't look at me like that. I don't spy on her. He does."

I growled and turned my dirty look on the door. It slid open.

A blond, middle-aged man stood before us. Now that I knew he was really a teenager, I was less intimidated. "You should try on a girl's face. It would look nice on you."

"Ah, it's the lovebirds. What do you want?"

Connor smiled. "Addison Coleman. Have you been watching her? We need some info."

He must've respected Connor, because he stood aside and let us in. We followed him back to the room I had been in before with all the computers. He sat behind the desk and clicked through some screens on the computer.

"How did you even know to start watching her?" I asked.

"I may or may not be patched into the Tower system that tells me who leaves the Compound and who the CC takes a special interest in."

In the middle of the wall in front of us, six projected screens turned black and then became one large picture of a parking lot, dissected into equal parts by the white wall between the screens. "Addison has an interesting ability. Time manipulation. She can use it in a variety of ways too."

We all stared at the parking lot on the wall for a while.

"It looks like she's unavailable."

The metal bird on the desk flapped its wings once. It looked so real. "So how do you hack into the Containment Committee's birds?" I asked, still staring at it.

"These aren't Containment Committee," Face said as though offended. "These are my design. The CC is all about keeping this place a secret. Do you think they'd risk exposure by sending something like this into the world?" He patted the bird's head. "They generally have people stationed in Normville, not things."

Like the agents Addie had already met. I shook my head. "You two are so blatant. How have you both not been caught already?"

Face laughed, and his blond hair changed to jet-black. "People see what they want to see."

"More like what *you* want them to see." Connor stood in front of me, and I ran a finger down his back. It still felt weird touching Connor and knowing he wouldn't get irritated. That he actually wanted me to. "Are you up for a trip to Dallas?"

He nodded. "Sure."

He and Face headed out the door, but I paused as the screens changed back to individual pictures. Realization struck me as the real reason Connor sold programs for Face came into my mind. It was his excuse to come here. I scanned the screens and wondered which one was Connor's dad. How many hours he spent here watching his life. Seeing his father live without him.

"I'm not as pathetic as it seems." Connor leaned against the door frame.

"There's nothing pathetic about wanting to see your own father. He raised you for twelve years of your life."

He looked over my shoulder, and I turned to follow his gaze. On the screen in the corner a man had just pulled into the driveway of a tan house and was helping a toddler out of the car.

"If we leave now, we can probably be to Addie's by midnight," Connor said.

I watched the small girl run up to the house, and my chest tightened in anger. He'd started over. Forgotten about Connor. I got my emotions under control before I turned to face him. He looked down with a sigh, and I walked forward and rested my arms on his shoulders, forcing him to look at me.

"I can handle this," he assured me. "I'll stop coming here. I'm going to stop."

I dropped my forehead to his shoulder. "I'm sorry." I gave a laugh I didn't mean. "We're both so screwed up. Are you sure we're good for each other?"

To answer my question he pulled me closer, breathed me in. Then he turned on his heel and said, "Let's go."

I gave one last lingering look at the screen, which now showed only the outside of a house. If that man didn't want Connor in his life, it was his loss.

Eli sat in the backseat. If Duke had gotten the Containment Committee involved in all this, I wanted all the abilities I could get. A pair of headphones, with music so loud I could almost sing along, was shoved on his head. I wondered if that helped block people's thoughts.

"Not really!" he yelled. "So keep talking."

I put my fingers to my lips and tugged out one of the earbuds. "No need to yell."

He pointed between Connor and me. "You told me you two would talk." Before the trip started, Eli said that talking people thought less. We had agreed to do our best. But an hour into the trip, Connor, who wasn't a big talker to begin with, was talked out.

Eli took out his other earbud. "Connor. You either think a lot less than my sister or you're really good at blocking."

"I can guarantee I think a lot less than your sister."

That was a load of crap. Connor lived in his head.

"My sister thinks that's a load of crap."

"Ha!" Connor said. "I can get used to having this kid around."

I grabbed Connor's knee and squeezed. "You're holding out

302

on me. Do you have a blocking secret?"

"I thought I sold you a block enhancer a while back."

"You did. I guess I should practice more."

"Start now," Eli said. "Please. I don't need any more thoughts about how hot Connor is. And if you want to know what he uses on his hair, just ask him."

Connor laughed, and I rolled my eyes. "Eli, you will now hear only thoughts of your imminent death." Then I punched Connor in the shoulder. "And stop smirking. Your hair isn't that great."

He ran a hand through it. "I have amazing hair."

If Eli weren't here, I'd be running my hands through Connor's hair right now. My mind went back to the train and the way it felt to be in his arms, my fingers tangled in his hair. Then I stopped my memory short and looked at Eli. "Keep that thought to yourself."

"Believe me. I wish I didn't hear it. There's no way I'm going to repeat it." He stuck his headphones back on. "Talk."

I could tell he was disgusted from having intercepted that last thought. I felt bad. "So can you teach me?" I asked Connor.

"I wish I could. I think it's another perk of my ability. My mind is not open. This is totally my own theory, but I think part of a Telepath's power must have something to do with opening channels into your thoughts. And because my mind heals itself fast, they are only able to pick up on an occasional thought. I'm grateful for that right now, because your brother does not need to hear the thoughts I have about you." He grabbed my hand and stuck it back on his knee.

I grumbled. "So unfair. I bet your ability somehow makes your hair shiny too."

He laughed.

"Wait. So if people can't penetrate your mind, then that time Duke and I came over to your house, he didn't do a thing? Why did you give me Face's address then?"

Connor just smirked.

"Tell me."

"You were asking for trouble. I knew you'd find it one way or another. Maybe I wanted to keep an eye on you."

I grabbed his hand and squeezed. As much as I liked to take care of myself, it felt nice to be looked after now and then.

"Have you tried Addie again?"

I lifted my phone. The screen didn't show any missed calls. I dialed anyway. Her voice mail told me she'd call back. "Still not there."

"So what's the plan if the CC found out she's been intentionally telling people about the Compound?"

"I don't know. Any ideas?"

"Let's just hope they haven't, because there are certain procedures that are irreversible."

"Like being Healed of an ability?"

He nodded once.

"They wouldn't do that . . . would they?"

"I wouldn't put it past them. Especially because you already reversed the procedure they did on Trevor. If Duke told them that and can get proof, she's in trouble."

"Drive faster."

CHAPTER 37

Addie: My hot ex-boyfriend is annoying.

"We need to stay perfectly still. Stephanie is looking at us. If we move, it will seem like we're moving superfast." I said this while trying to move my lips as little as possible. "Stephanie cannot suspect anything." If she somehow figured out my ability, my life was over.

"She saw us kiss?"

"Yes."

"She needs to know anyway."

"I know, but I didn't want it to happen like this. I just ruined her night."

"*We* just ruined her night."

The music and people slowly picked up speed. With every increase in beat, Stephanie was that much closer to us. She arrived at our sides as soon as time returned to normal.

I wasn't sure what to expect, but what I didn't expect was for her to slap me across the face. All my breath rushed out of me in a gush of air, and I cradled my cheek with my hand.

Trevor grabbed her by the wrist. "Stop."

"I'm sorry," I said, trying to catch my breath. "This wasn't how I wanted you to find out."

"Oh, so is that why you kissed my boyfriend in the middle of the dance floor? Because you didn't want me to find out?"

"Stephanie, I am not your boyfriend. You know that."

"You might as well have been. I hate you both."

About this time, Duke sauntered up to our threesome. *Soothe her,* I pushed into Duke's mind.

"I thought you didn't like false emotion," he said to me.

Stephanie turned on her heel and marched away.

"You should go after her. Talk to her," I told Trevor.

"Are you sure?" He eyed Duke.

"Yes."

"Okay. I'll be right back." That message seemed to be more for Duke than me. And the kiss before he left was definitely more for Duke, but it still made my heart flutter.

"Why are you here?" I asked, when Trevor was gone.

"I'm not the type to just step aside. I still have feelings for you."

"Duke, I've made my choice. Please don't make this any harder than it has to be."

"So you want me to make it easy?"

"You should go," I said. "How did you even get in here? You're not a student."

He raised his eyebrows, like he was surprised I had to ask the question. Oh yeah, he probably charmed his way in. He had no problem getting whatever he wanted with his ability.

"We need to talk. I'm worried about you. I don't believe you told Trevor everything."

I looked around and then put my finger to my lips, telling him to shut his mouth. "I don't know what you're talking about," I said. "Trevor is clueless." We had worked too hard to keep this a secret for Duke to come in and ruin it all.

"Well, I know that, but I'm talking about the Compound. Why did you tell him?"

I grabbed his hand and pulled him onto the dance floor. If he insisted on saying things like that out loud, with Norms around, we should at least be in the middle of a crowd, where the music and voices could mask our conversation.

"You want to dance?" he asked, pulling me into his arms. It irritated me that when his hands touched my back, warmth spread through my body. I hated his ability so much.

"Listen, you can't just say stuff like that here." If the CC heard us talking about the Compound with Norms around, I'd be back to square one.

"Where then? Where can we talk? Because this is serious, Addie. You shouldn't have told him. He's not one of us."

"It's none of your business."

"Maybe I've made it my business."

"What does that even mean?"

"Just tell me what you told him."

"I told him nothing."

He gave a frustrated growl and leveled his gaze on me. His blue eyes were intense with emotion. "Just come outside with me. We can talk in my car."

"No."

"Where then?"

"Nowhere, Duke. This is over."

"If you don't talk to me, I'm going to report you to the Containment Committee."

My mouth dropped open, and I pushed out of his hold. "Why would you do that?"

"Because maybe I want them to wipe him from your memory."

"So it sounds like you're going to talk to them either way."

"No. If you explain to me why, what's going on in your head, I won't do it."

Did he really think he was endearing himself to me with this awful display of jealousy and control? "Fine. But I'm waiting for Trevor, so meet me outside in an hour."

"An hour?"

"I'm sure you can find something to do for an hour. Dance with some girls or something."

He sighed and wandered over to the food table. I went looking for Rowan.

• • •

Over an hour later, Trevor still hadn't reappeared. Duke caught my eye across the dance floor and nodded toward the exit. I shrugged and mouthed, *Meet me outside.* Then I walked out the door Trevor had left through earlier, hoping to find him. Searching the halls, I came up empty. The four of us had driven in one car, and that car—Stephanie's dad's Jaguar—was missing from the parking lot. Great. Trevor had gone home with her? What was *I'll be right back* about that? I reached for my phone and remembered, as my hand brushed over the silky material of my dress, that I had left it in the glove box of Stephanie's car.

Back inside, I found Rowan. "Steph and Trevor left."

"What? Why? My stuff is in her car."

"It might have something to do with Trevor and me kissing."

"Ouch."

"Yeah." A sense of panic welled up inside me. "Hey, I have to run." I gave him a hug. "Sorry to ditch you. I had fun tonight."

I ran back out to the parking lot. I wasn't sure what car Duke was driving, considering he couldn't bring a Compound car here. I scanned the lot for the biggest, flashiest one and saw a yellow Hummer parked on the edge.

I walked to the passenger side and knocked on the window. The doors unlocked with a clunk. I slid inside.

"Can I borrow your phone?" I asked.

Duke pulled it out of his pocket. I dialed Trevor, but no one answered. Either Stephanie was yelling so loud he couldn't hear, or he didn't want to be rude by answering the phone in the middle of a serious talk. I left a message. "Hey, Trevor. I'm still here.

Will you call me when you're . . . uh . . . done?" I hung up the phone.

I stared at the lifeless screen, then handed it back to Duke. It would be really weird to show up at Stephanie's at this point. Trevor would remember to grab my phone for me.

"So?" he said. "Let's talk."

I ran my hands along the interior of his car. Even though the CC couldn't have possibly known Duke would come talk to me today, I still wanted to make sure his car was clean. Maybe they bugged all the rental cars.

"What are you doing?"

"Checking for bugs." I crawled into the backseat, my knees slipping along the material of my dress while I did. Once in the back, I continued searching.

"Addie, you're being paranoid."

"I am not." When I didn't find anything, I settled against the bench seat in the back.

He looked over his shoulder. "Aren't you going to come up here?"

"I'm good."

He tilted his head a little and then climbed into the back-seat next to me with a smirk on his face. Like he thought this was romantic or something. I just wanted to slap him. He sent a surge of happiness through my body and I backed up, the arm-rest digging into my back.

"Sorry," he said. "Sometimes how I'm feeling just comes out."

310

"Why are you so happy? I'm here to convince you that you need to leave me alone."

"So why did you tell Trevor, and why do you think I should keep this to myself?"

"Because I love him. I knew him from a life I Searched, and if you care about me at all, you will respect that."

"So you admit that you told him?"

"Why is it so important to you that I admit that? Of course I told him. He knows everything. He doesn't care about powers and the Compound. He cares about me."

He got this really satisfied smile then. Like me telling him Trevor liked me was the best thing I had ever told him. "And Laila restored his memories after the Containment Committee had Erased them."

"You know the answer to that."

"But I had no idea what you guys were doing."

"Okay. What's your point?"

"My point is you did it."

"So?"

He nodded. "Good."

I was confused. "So are we good then? Will you leave me alone?"

"Yes. I'll leave."

I gripped the door handle, ready to exit, but then stopped myself. I didn't want to go back inside alone. "Will you take me home?" I'd call Trevor from there.

Duke nodded, and we drove the whole way in silence.

311

I wondered if that was a record for him. When I got out, he pulled me into a hug. "Addie, it doesn't have to be this way. We're right for each other. Trevor will never be what you need. He's a Norm."

"Duke. Stop. Please." I pushed away from him.

He sighed, then ran his hand down his sleeve. "Well, thanks for telling me. This will make everything how it's supposed to be."

CHAPTER 38

Laila: How do you say "screwed" in Norm?

The sound of tires bumping over rough road startled me awake. My eyes popped open, and for a moment I forgot where I was. But then I remembered trying not to fall asleep, my head doing the embarrassing fall-forward-then-jerk-back-to-upright motion. No matter how many Alert mind patterns I scanned through, I could not stay awake. My lack of sleep over the last few days had caught up with me. So Connor had patted his leg and I'd gladly lain down, falling asleep immediately.

"It's just a section of the road. I'm good." Connor ran his hand along my cheek.

I sat up and stretched. "You sure you're not tired? I can drive." I stifled a yawn. "What time is it?"

"Not even eleven." He pointed at a road sign as we passed. It said twelve miles to Dallas. I glanced in the backseat. Eli was out, his music still blaring.

"You drove fast." I pulled my cell phone out of my pocket. "Did my phone ring?" I asked, even though I could see no new missed calls on the screen.

"No. She probably just didn't take it to the dance. We'll be fine." He obviously knew I was worried and was trying to pretend like her not answering the phone didn't mean that Duke succeeded in his mission and the Containment Committee was now wiping her of everything that mattered to her; or worse, hauling her back to the Compound to take her place as Bobby's neighbor. Duke was such an idiot.

Duke. I dialed his number again. It shocked me when he actually picked up.

"Hey. What?"

"Hey what, yourself. You better not be doing what I think you're doing."

"I have no idea what you're talking about."

"You're in Dallas. Have you seen Addie?"

"As a matter of fact, I took her home a while ago." Why did he sound so happy about that?

"What did you do to her?"

I could hear the smile in his voice when he said, "I'm doing my duty as a citizen of the Compound."

"I'm about to do my duty to your face. What did you do?"

"Don't worry. She'll be happier this way."

"She will or you will?"

"Both."

"You have no idea what you just did. This is more serious than you can possibly imagine. Not only do they know that she blatantly disregarded the laws of the Compound, they also know that she had Trevor's memories restored." They really were going to do exactly what Addie's mom feared—wipe a section of her mind to ensure her mental stability.

He went silent. "What? It's not a big deal. They didn't do anything when Trevor found out the first time."

"That's because he found out on his own, idiot. It was an accident. This was intentional."

"But they didn't even believe me. Said they'd been monitoring her and had no proof of any breaches. So I told them I'd get them proof."

"This is worse than you think. Beyond just a normal breach. They've been monitoring her because of Bobby." I let out a frustrated sigh. "She's basically on probation because Bobby said that she stole a piece of his ability."

He cussed. "He's lying."

I wasn't sure whether Bobby was lying. Addie did have an advanced ability that was beyond anything she'd ever had before. Maybe it was the result of Bobby. But unlike the DAA, I didn't think it was a bad thing. "Well, they're not going to think Bobby is lying at all. They're going to think Addie knows exactly what she's doing. How are you going to fix this?"

"I'm not. It's done. But I'm very persuasive. I'll make sure they don't do anything drastic."

"Well, that's not good enough for me, Duke. You are not

315

going to do this to Addie again. You are not going to use her and manipulate her just to make yourself happy. So you will either help us fix this or I will Erase every memory you have of her from your head the next time I see you."

He was quiet for at least ten long seconds. Then he said, "I'll meet you back at her house."

I pointed to the exit sign that showed her exit, and Connor nodded and pulled off. I hung up on Duke. "We could be in for some trouble."

He pulled to a stop at a crossroads.

"Three lights, then make a right."

"I remember."

Oh right. We'd just done this. I reached to the backseat and smacked my brother. "You ready for some action?"

He popped up like he always did, muttering nonsense. "I told him to stay in the cart."

Connor raised one eyebrow at me.

"Yeah, his body wakes up before his brain. It's very entertaining."

Eli unbuckled his seat belt and started to get out of the car.

I pushed the auto door locks. "Whoa there, kid. We haven't stopped yet."

Connor pulled over. I unlocked the doors, and Eli got out.

"Am I in an alternate universe?" he asked.

"You could say that." I hooked my arm in his elbow. "Come on, little bro. I have a best friend to save."

He gave a happy sigh. "Addie." My brother had the biggest crush on her.

"I do not," he objected to my thoughts.

We walked up the pathway to the front door. I raised my hand to knock, when I realized how late it was and how hard it was going to be to explain our arrival to her dad.

"Window?" Connor asked, one step ahead of me. Eli was finally up and alert, and he followed us around the back to Addie's window. I knocked softly. Nobody came.

"Do you think she's okay? What if the CC has her?"

Connor didn't answer, just knocked again, harder.

Addie parted the curtains. She was wearing a fancy dress and looked like she expected us to be someone else. Her eyes went wide, then she opened the window. "What are you doing here?"

I summarized how Duke had screwed us all over.

"What are we going to do?" she asked.

"Maybe your dad can help us."

She gave a laugh. "My dad? I don't think he'll look kindly on all the rules I've broken." She bit her lip. "Maybe my grandpa can help us. He doesn't trust the Compound at all. He'll probably know what to do."

"Can you sneak out?"

She opened the window wider and popped out the screen. "Yes. My dad doesn't even know I'm home yet."

I called Duke as we walked back to the car. "Change of plans. Meet us at her grandpa's house.

Duke was in the hall when we arrived, his elbows on his knees, looking like he actually felt bad. Maybe I wouldn't have to kick him too hard. He stood up as we walked toward him.

I crossed my arms. "Ah, here's the charming ex-boyfriend who recorded you and let the CC listen in."

"Well, technically, I didn't let them listen in, I forwarded the recording to them after we . . ." He trailed off when he obviously realized by the look on Addie's face that technicalities weren't important to her. "I'm sorry."

She took a deep breath. "That was over an hour ago. Why aren't they looking for me yet?"

He shrugged. "Who knows?"

I was proud of the cold look she gave him when she knocked on the door.

Her grandfather answered, his eyes weary. I recognized him from a few pictures I'd seen around Addie's house.

"Sorry for waking you up. We have an emergency we were hoping you could help us with."

"Of course. Anything." He held the door open wider, and we walked inside. "Let me get you all something to drink, then you can tell me about it. Have a seat."

"Addie's grandpa is young," Connor whispered.

"I guess," I said, as I watched the white hair on the back of his head disappear out of the room. He seemed grandpa age to me. Maybe Connor's grandpa was ancient.

Connor moved to the coffee table to look at some of the ridiculous modified devices. Just when I was about to tell him they were the handiwork of a crazy man, he pulled out his pocket knife and started unscrewing the back of a little black box with one of the tool attachments. Whatever. He could play.

318

"Can I borrow your phone? I need to try Trevor again."

I handed her my phone. "Yes, he should be here."

"Do you think . . ." She got a panicked look on her face. "You think the CC is taking care of him first?" She didn't even wait for my answer, just dialed.

Connor settled in at my side, pulled me close by the front pocket of my jeans, and said under his breath, "Something's not right here." He held up his hand, and resting on his palm was a small chip.

"What is that?"

"A high-tech listening device. Compound-made. I got it out of that black box on the table." He looked around. "Where did Grandpa go again?"

Right at that moment, her grandpa walked back in, carrying a few glasses of ice water. My vision blurred, and I blinked a few times until he came back into focus.

He smiled. "Here's the first round. Let me go grab two more." He set the waters on the coffee table and left.

Connor was right. Something wasn't right here, and I couldn't figure out what. I just knew that I had never felt a stronger desire to leave a place. So strong, I thought maybe Duke was projecting his feelings. A quick glance confirmed my suspicions—he looked uneasy as well.

"I thought you said he was a Healer," Eli whispered.

"He is," I said.

"I could hear his thoughts loud and clear."

"And what was he thinking?" I asked.

Addie and Duke must've overheard our conversation, because

319

they took a few steps closer for the answer.

"He thought, 'My backup better get here soon. I can't contain all of them.'"

My eyes darted to Connor. "Does that mean he's not a Healer after all?"

"I think that's the least of our worries. We better go."

Almost as if on cue, we all headed for the front door. Addie's grandfather stepped in front of it from a side hall.

"Where are you going?"

"My dad is expecting me," Addie said. "It's late." It wasn't even eleven-thirty, but the late excuse was a good one.

"I'll call him and tell him where you are."

"Okay," she said, obviously trying to buy us time.

I watched for his reaction to that, and my tired vision went blurry again. No. It wasn't my vision that was going blurry at all. I remembered Face and the little patch on his cheek that was always fuzzy no matter what face he wore. This was a different presentation of that same weakness. "You're a Perceptive."

I hadn't meant to say it out loud, but it came to me like a lightning strike and I couldn't hold it in. The face of Addie's grandfather faded away to the dark-haired man we had seen in his apartment last time we were here.

Addie threw her hand over her mouth with a gasp.

Oh. That's why Connor thought he looked young. He was. I hadn't realized that a Perceptive couldn't alter Connor's vision. No wonder Face had to trust him.

The man locked the door and entered a code into a keypad next to it. "Sit down," he said. "All of you."

CHAPTER 39

Addie: On the count of three, run.

The dark-haired man we had seen the other night and who had come to my house with Scar-Face stood before us.

"What have you done with my grandpa?"

"I've done nothing with your grandpa. I believe your father is still trying to get clearance to move his grave here."

My heart felt like it wanted to stop. That or burst out of my chest. I remembered the name in my father's phone attached to this address. And the name my father had introduced him as in my own living room. Why hadn't I made the connection before? "Brett Miller."

He only smirked. I felt so stupid. Of course my dad had the CC contacts for this area in his cell phone.

"Why would you do that to me? You gave me my grandfather back only to take him away again?"

"We're going to Erase these memories of your grandfather. He was part of your test. We needed to make sure you were loyal to the Compound. He offered you a safe place to divulge secrets, so we could tell if you were averse to authority. It's a shame. You were so close to passing. But then something changed." He looked at Duke.

"I thought my father was lying to me."

"We are going to Erase it," he said again, as if that made everything okay.

"Do you have no conscience?" Laila asked. "You made her think her grandfather was still alive."

Considering how awful I felt, I was tempted to tell Agent Miller to get it over with. Erase the reincarnation of my grandfather from my mind. Erase this whole experience from my mind. But I knew I couldn't. I needed to remember this. Remember what awful lengths the Compound was willing to go to. Taking away the memory of pain didn't keep a person from having to suffer through it.

"Your whole plan would've blown up in your face if I had told my dad."

"But you didn't, did you?" He smiled, like his statement meant more than he was saying. "My partner helps people make good decisions."

Connor gave a disgusted grunt. "She was Persuaded not to."

"I was Persuaded not to?" I had to repeat the statement

because I couldn't believe it. Scar-Face was a Persuasive. "But then why did you warn Trevor and me that the CC was waiting for us then, that one day we were here?"

"I wanted to test you to see if you'd tell Trevor anything. I was kind of rooting for you, kid. I thought for sure if you knew the Containment Committee was monitoring you that you'd be more careful."

I pointed my finger at the agent, anger ripping through my chest. "My grandpa wasn't crazy."

He shrugged as though he didn't care. "I didn't know enough of his real personality to pull it off. I thought it would be safer if you wouldn't question my answers too much."

"And what would have happened if I never showed up at your door?" I asked, thinking I'd found the flaw in their horrid plan. "Then how would you have tested me?"

"Like I said, my partner is very persuasive. He pretended to slip about there being two relatives on the Outside. We knew you couldn't resist investigating that. We had to make sure you weren't hiding any unclaimed advanced abilities after what happened with Mr. Baker."

This all came back to Bobby. And I'd fallen for every one of their tricks. I felt like an idiot. My heart ached. I couldn't believe everything they had put me through just for their stupid tests—conjuring up a dead relative, making me distrust my own father. It all made me so sick inside. I took the awful pain I felt and turned it into energy. Soon the room was crawling. I touched each person to bring them into the moment with me, tempted for half a second to leave Duke here to fend for himself. I didn't. "We have about two minutes. How do we get out of here?"

"I'll wipe the memory of the alarm on the door," Laila said, already walking toward it.

"What's wrong with Connor?" I walked around him, the only one who hadn't returned to normal speed. I touched him again and he only jolted for a moment, then returned to slow motion.

Laila stopped in her tracks and faced him. "Crap. It probably doesn't work on him because he's a Healer. Your ability can't get through to him. Duke, grab Connor. We have to go."

Duke shook his head and crossed his arms. "I've seen his temper. Got a pen stuck in my shoulder to prove it. I'm not touching him."

I grabbed the sleeve of Duke's shirt. "Please." That was all it took. He threw Connor over his shoulder, and we all waited while Laila disarmed the door.

"What about him?" Eli asked, pointing to Agent Miller, whose facial expression was just now starting to indicate that he realized what was going on. At least when I was in the Tower, I hadn't divulged my ability to slow down time. I had caught him off guard.

"I'll wipe him. I'm taking two months. Let him see how that feels." Laila muttered "jerk" a few times while she stood over him. We filed out the door while she finished.

We ran to the stairs, heading for the back exit. As we came to the long hall on the first floor, I thought I heard car doors shut out front. When the others looked over their shoulders as well, I knew the Containment Committee had arrived. The man upstairs might not remember the last two months for now, but I was sure that a memory restoration would be performed before we were even up the block. If we were going to wipe my breach from existence, we had a lot more than one person's memories to alter. We had an entire team and an entire computer/surveillance system. How could we possibly do this?

While the others rushed to the rear exit, I pressed my back against the wall and inched toward the front. I arrived at the corner and peered around it just as the group came through the lobby doors—three men and Trevor. And there was Scar-Face, a Persuasive, right at the back of the group. He must've been working on Trevor, because he wasn't even putting up a fight, just walking along with them like it was his idea.

My heart jumped to my throat and my hand to my mouth to prevent myself from making a sound. As they headed my way, I collected some energy with my heightened emotions. I was trying to decide if I could squeeze through the men and to Trevor without touching any of them. It seemed highly unlikely. Duke grabbed my arm and pulled me away. "Are you trying to get caught?" he asked once we were outside.

As if he had a right to ask me that question, when he was the one who had gotten me caught. "They have Trevor," I said to the group. "We have to go back."

Laila nodded. "And we will. But first let's see if they left anyone at the car or if we can do some snooping. We need to be prepared."

A navy van was parked on the street, and we stayed in the alley to determine if it was empty.

"I don't hear any thoughts coming from inside," Eli said.

I stared at him in awe. "You can read minds, Eli. That's so amazing."

He smiled and looked at the ground. "I'm still kind of new."

"You could've fooled me." I turned to the others. "Should we go check it out then?" I was worried about Trevor and what they might do to him. We had revealed our hand. If they could restore Fake Grandpa's memory, we'd be screwed. They'd know Laila could restore memories. They'd know I could slow down time. We would no longer have the advantage. I just had to hope that someone on their team couldn't manipulate memories because we needed a solid plan before we went back up there. If Trevor had an ability, I would be so much more confident, knowing he might be able to defend himself right now. Although, even with my ability I hadn't been able to protect myself against Fake Grandpa.

Laila pressed her face up against the tinted back window of the van. "No fair," she said. "They get to bring Para-tech here and we don't?"

I tried the doors, but they were locked. "Anyone know how to break into a locked car?"

She studied the numerical keypad beneath the door handle. "I can disable the alarm, but I don't think wiping the keypad's memory would result in unlocking the car."

Connor reached into his pocket and pulled out his cell.

"You going to call a locksmith?" Laila asked.

He bent over and grabbed a handful of dirt from the ring around a tree and sprinkled it over the keypad, then shined the light from his phone onto the numbers. I could vaguely make out smudges on the buttons. The first button seemed to have the most smudges, the third had none. "The combo has two ones, a two, and a four in it. Laila, disable the alarm, and I'll start going through some patterns."

After at least twenty attempts, I pushed on my temples. This wasn't going to work. My gaze kept drifting back to the apartment building. How much time did we have? Then, suddenly, I heard the clunk of locks opening.

"Nice," Duke said. Connor climbed inside and then opened the back doors for the rest of us.

"It's too cramped in there," Duke said. "I'll keep a lookout."

I wasn't sure if I trusted Duke as our warning bell. With us all crammed in the van, this could be the easiest capture ever. Eli, probably reading my mind, said, "That many thoughts in one place will make me vomit. I'll stay out here with Duke."

I squeezed his arm. "Thanks."

So Connor, Laila, and I sat in the back of the van, surrounded by Para-tech. Connor powered up the nearest screen, and what lit up in front of us caused my stomach to drop to my feet: a picture of Trevor and all his statistics—height, weight, build, hair color, etc. But much more too. His entire history—people,

327

places, tastes. Then in a column next to it was new info that I didn't recognize as his. Almost like the fake history the Tower had given me to study when I'd moved here in my other life.

"It's a Reassignment," Connor whispered. "They're giving him a new life. One on the other side of the country."

"But why? Why wouldn't they just Erase what he knows?"

They both looked at me as though I should know the answer to this question. But I didn't. Or maybe I needed it spelled out for me, because I didn't want to believe it.

"Because of you," Laila said. "They obviously know you won't give him up otherwise."

It felt like Duke's big yellow Hummer had run me over. My chest hurt, my eyes hurt, every inch of my body hurt.

Laila cracked her knuckles. "It's time to crash some computers. If they don't have this"—she waved her hand in front of the screen—"maybe they won't be able to complete the Reassignment. In fact, how about a total system failure?" She closed her eyes and held up her hands.

"No. Wait." Connor pulled one of her hands down, and she focused on him.

"What? Why not?"

"You heard what Addie's grandfather said."

"You mean her fake grandfather."

"Fake Grandpa. Whatever. He said that before Duke's information tonight, she had passed the test. She had been changed over to a non-threat. And considering that before tonight they thought Trevor had been Selectively Erased, I'm sure he

328

would've been safe too. So we don't need to take away the last month and their potential plans. That would be a huge red flag of empty memory. We just need to take away tonight without them suspecting."

"How are we going to do that?" I asked.

"Very carefully," he said.

CHAPTER 40

Laila: Add the definition of stupid to your list:
trusting the person who got us into this.

I watched Connor work at the computer. Addie had stepped out of the van and joined the others. She looked like she was in shock or going to be sick. Connor found the recorded conversation Duke had picked up on his body chip. He pushed a button, and it echoed through a pair of headphones resting on the floor. I slid them on. Duke's voice rang out, asking Addie if she'd told Trevor. She confirmed his suspicions, and I took off the headphones, disgusted.

Connor glanced my way. "Can you Erase it?"

"The conversation?"

"Yes. It's about five minutes long. It's stored on the computer as code." He pointed to the screen.

"Of course I can Erase it."

He lifted one side of his mouth in a half smile. "What was it you said again that you had to think of to advance your ability?"

I laughed. "I didn't say."

He grabbed me by the waist and pulled me onto his lap. "A certain night in a certain train?"

"Stop. I need to concentrate."

"You need to concentrate on a certain night in a certain train?"

"That's only for restoring. You're not responsible for all my awesome abilities."

"No, only ninety percent of your awesomeness." He kissed the back of my neck. "Work your magic."

I turned around and kissed him. He tasted like mint gum and Connor.

"I meant on the computer. Not on me."

"I already took care of the computer."

He looked around me and clicked a few buttons. "Nice."

"What next?" I asked.

"We need to figure out how to get three grown men with abilities from up there"—he pointed toward the apartment—"to down here." He patted the seat next to him.

"Sounds easy."

"I wonder if they have any supplies we can borrow." He slid me off his lap and started rooting through the cupboards. I tried to help, but had no idea what we were looking for. "Jackpot."

He held up a metal device—two half circles connected by an iridescent square.

"What does it do?"

"It's a demobilizer." He slid my wrist into one end and then nodded for me to put my other wrist on the other end. I did, and he pressed the square in the center. The circles slid shut, binding my wrists. "Like handcuffs."

The cold metal pressed against my wrists, and a sharp pain shot through my skull and then settled into an annoying buzz. I sucked air through my teeth.

"What's wrong?"

"My head."

His eyebrows shot up. "Even better."

"You're happy that my head hurts?"

"It means it's a blocker as well. It would be nearly impossible for you to access your ability with those on."

I tried to pull my wrists apart, and the metal dug into my skin. Pain bounced in my skull again. "I bet the Norms just love it when the CC has to use these."

"They can't use these on Norms."

"Why?"

Connor made a popping sound with his mouth. "Their brains wouldn't be able to handle it."

My brain wasn't dealing well with it either. It was like a con-centrated version of being inside Bobby's room. "Good thing it's a bunch of Paras we're rounding up tonight then." I pulled at the cuffs again. "Tell me you know how to get these off."

He pressed his finger on the square and they slid open. "The one who shuts them is the only one who can open them."

My head immediately settled when I removed my wrists. I grabbed the demobilizer from him, and he pulled out a few more. "This should be easy, then."

"Sure, we'll just ask them to stick their hands out so we can slide them on. Simple," he said evenly.

"It will be with Addie." I smiled big.

"And what about the other part of the night? Is Duke going to help?"

"He'd better."

I couldn't believe our fate rested in Duke's horribly slimy hands. But we needed his cooperation. I had to trust him. I jumped out of the back of the van and clapped Duke on the shoulder. "Thank goodness you are a good liar, because it's showtime."

"What does that mean?"

"It means, we are going to reset the night. First, we have to arrange all the players." I pointed to the apartment in front of us and handed everyone a pair of demobilizers. "Then you and Addie have to reenact the conversation you promised the CC."

Connor shut the van doors, wiped the smudges off the key-pad, and nodded. "Let's go."

On the way up the stairs, we discussed different ways of getting inside the apartment. In the end, we decided knocking on the door was as good a way as any, seeing as how we weren't trying to keep our presence a secret.

"Do you think you'll be able to slow time for longer than a couple minutes?" I asked Addie.

"I'll try."

"We need all the time we can get."

We arrived at the third floor and opened the door to the hall. A man was there to greet us. "We've been expecting you."

Duke punched him in the face, and he dropped like a rock.

I let out a heavy sigh. "*Duke*. Why did you do that? We have to reset the night. Now he's going to wake up with a sore jaw and a headache and wonder how he got them."

Duke toed him, and he rolled onto his back. A long scar ran the length of his left cheek. "Sorry. He came out of nowhere. We didn't discuss the potential for hallway people."

"I know him," Addie said.

"You do? What's his ability?"

"This is the Persuader from the Tower who debriefed me. He's also the one who came by my house with Fake Grandpa."

I elbowed Duke. "Put some cuffs on him and get him down to the van. We'll be down there with the others in a few minutes."

"I'm the muscle," Duke said. "You really want me to wait at the van with this guy?"

"Who assigned you as the muscle?" I asked.

"My biceps did. And considering you keep asking me to carry people, I'm pretty sure you agree."

"Well, Connor and Trevor can carry the other two down."

334

"No, I can't," Connor said. "But thanks for the confidence, babe. Duke is definitely the muscle. I'll follow him down and wait at the van. Don't do anything until he's back."

"Fine. Hurry."

Too bad that guy wasn't the Memory Eraser. I was certain there was a Memory Eraser here. It was the only ability that would be able to Reassign Trevor a new life. It was the main ability that scared me here tonight. If we all lost our memories, we'd be worthless. At least Connor couldn't be affected by it.

We waited just outside the door to the stairs, the apartment around the corner to our left. "So that was the Persuader?" I said to Addie.

"Yes. And Fake Grandpa is a Perceptive. That leaves two unknowns."

"One has to be a Memory Eraser," I said, and she nodded as if she had thought of that as well.

Eli cleared his throat. "The other one is a Mass Manipulator."

"Did you hear his thoughts?" I asked.

"No. He just walked through that wall." He pointed over my shoulder, and we all turned around to face the man walking toward us. He wore jeans and a collared shirt, his biceps straining the material. His head was shaved. He smiled, his white teeth bright against his black skin.

"Listen, kids," he said. "You've had your fun. It's time to come willingly into the apartment, fill out a report, and receive the consequences of your actions."

I shrugged at Addie. We had planned to knock on the door

335

anyway. We'd walk inside, Addie would slow down time, we'd cuff them and wait for Duke. Why not? "Okay."

He didn't seem at all shocked that we agreed so easily. He also seemed to find the demobilizers we held very amusing. Did that mean they knew our plans and had ways to counteract them? I glanced once back over my shoulder to see if Duke had arrived yet.

"He really thinks we're filling out reports," Eli whispered as we followed the Mass Manipulator to the apartment.

I held in a laugh. He opened the door, and we walked in. Trevor sat on the couch and looked up in relief at our arrival, as if he thought we could not only save him, but the entire world, with the snap of our fingers. I was relieved to see him alert and appearing to be in possession of all his memories. That is, until Addie gasped from beside me. I followed her gaze and saw, sitting in a chair by the sliding door, looking equally relieved, another Trevor. *Crap.*

CHAPTER 41

Addie: I can't tell the difference.
Does that make me a bad girlfriend?

I looked back and forth between the identical Trevors. One was obviously the Perceptive. As if I didn't want to kill him enough already with his fake grandpa act, now he had to throw in the fake boyfriend act. They must've known our plan.

"They're both going fuzzy," Laila said from beside me.

"They're both Perceptives?" I asked.

"No. The real Perceptive is projecting his weakness on the real Trevor."

I held up the cuffs. It didn't matter. We could still use the cuffs. Then, when Fake Grandpa had them on, he wouldn't be able to use his ability. We'd be able to see which one was Trevor.

Laila gave me a small shake of her head and said under her breath, "Not unless you want to turn Trevor's brain to mush."

So the cuffs must be bad for Norms. Great.

"Kids, won't you have a seat? I just need to grab some report forms and we'll move forward," the Mass Manipulator said, then left the room. He thought the two Trevors would stop us from following through with our plans. He was right.

"Look, we're not filling out your stupid forms. So stop with the formality," Laila called after him. She watched the other man in the room warily, the one who hadn't spoken. He leaned against the wall in the far corner, his eyes boring into each of us in turn. He was thin and tall, his arms seeming too long for his body. His face was gaunt and his eyes empty. He had to be the Memory Eraser. I knew that Laila feared her own ability in others. Probably because she knew how much power she held.

"Addie, can you tell which one is real?"

"Oh yeah, let me put on my girlfriend glasses and study them real close."

Couch Trevor ran a hand through his hair. "I'm real."

Chair Trevor, not to be outdone, stood. "No, I am."

Their voices sounded exactly the same, and I wondered if that was why Fake Grandpa had really recorded Trevor's voice on his black box, so he could perfect it.

"I'm Trevor," Couch Guy said again.

I sighed. "We just need a few more and we can change your name to Spartacus."

Laila huffed. "Nobody gets your weird book references, Addie."

"It was made into a movie," I said. Why couldn't I tell the difference? Shouldn't I be able to? "Eli? What are their thoughts like?"

"Very similar, unfortunately."

There was a pounding on the door, and the skulking guy in the corner answered. Duke walked in. "You're all still in here . . . talking?" He noticed the two Trevors, and his eyes went wide.

"Duke, we see you've switched sides," Skulking Guy said.

Hearing out loud again that he was what started all this made anger surge up inside me. I could feel my energy building. Recognizing its presence had changed everything. Before, I'd let my emotions take over and push it into use, but now that I felt it, I could hold it back, let it build.

"Sit," he said, and started walking toward me. I had absolutely no desire to sit, but lots of desire to run. Laila started backing away.

"What are you waiting for?" Duke asked me.

I pointed to the two Trevors, and he rolled his eyes. He probably wished I would just leave both Trevors here. Laila had backed all the way to the wall, but then a pair of strong black arms reached through from behind her, followed by the entire person. He grabbed hold of her. She jammed her heel down hard on his instep. He grunted but didn't let go.

"You know what the difference is between us and you guys?" Laila asked, looking directly at the Memory Eraser.

He tilted his head as if curious about her answer.

Suddenly, the guy holding Laila dropped to the ground, followed by the Memory Eraser. Neither moved a muscle. "We don't have to follow protocol," she said.

"What just happened?" I asked.

Both Trevors jumped up, but then Couch Trevor sat back down, and I couldn't decide if that was the real one trying to show he wasn't concerned about the enemy or the fake one just pretending not to care.

"I Erased everything," Laila said.

"You what?" Duke asked.

"I shut every path."

I stared in horror at the guy nearest to me. His lips were turning blue. "Laila! Restore them! They don't remember how to breathe."

"I'm trying, I'm trying. I didn't expect that to happen. I can't concentrate with everyone freaking out at me."

I turned to Duke. "Help her relax."

He nodded.

The Mass Manipulator near my foot came to first with a sharp gasp of air. I backed away. It took a few more long seconds for the Memory Eraser to take a breath, and I wondered if Laila did that on purpose. But he finally inhaled air, the color rushing back to his face.

I took a breath too, realizing I'd been holding mine.

"See, they're fine," Laila said, crossing her arms. "We should've cuffed them while they were under."

The demobilizer in my hand was the last thing I had thought of when two people were dying in front of me.

"I could . . ." She held up her hands.

I pointed at her. "Don't."

Chair Trevor started to speak, but Couch Trevor interrupted him. "Search it, Addie," he said.

He was right. I should Search it. It would take half a minute. Was that too long? Would they be able to incapacitate me and my ability in half a minute? If not, would it use up too much energy?

Chair Trevor met my eyes. "Addison," he said. "You don't need to Search it. You know."

I smiled. That one word—Addison—was all I needed. I gathered all the emotional energy around me and slowed time. I touched everyone, including Chair Trevor . . . real Trevor. He kissed me.

"Why didn't he wipe our memories?" Laila asked, staring at Memory Eraser, who was still recovering on the ground. Only now recovering in slow motion.

Trevor looked at him as well. "He had to touch my head to do it."

"He can only do it by touch?" A proud expression came over her face, as she must've realized how talented she truly was.

"Okay, the second you touch them, they're going to come into the moment with us," I said.

"The second we touch them or the second *you* touch them?" Laila asked.

I furrowed my brow. "I'm not sure."

Laila held cuffs at the ready and nodded Eli over to help her. "On the count of three," she said. "One, two, three." They each grabbed a hand of an agent, and nothing happened. He stayed in slow motion.

"Nice." Duke slapped the cuffs onto Memory Eraser's hands and threw him over his shoulder. Laila bound the Mass Manipulator.

Eli moved on to Fake Grandpa turned into Fake Trevor and dragged him to the couch with Trevor's help. "So we're resetting the night, right? Should we just arrange him like he fell asleep on the couch?"

"Yes. Put one of his tech devices on his chest."

Eli did. My head started to pound with trying to hold the time so long.

"Hurry and Erase him."

"Three hours?" Laila asked.

"Yes."

As Laila Erased him, Trevor's face faded from his, revealing the dark-haired man.

Trevor followed Duke's example and threw Mass Manipulator over his shoulder, probably not quite knowing what we were doing.

"Hurry," I said, my head screaming at me.

We left quickly. Halfway down the stairs I knew I couldn't hold it anymore, and time started returning. They might not be able to use their abilities, but that didn't mean they wouldn't try to escape. Trevor must've felt the man picking up speed, because he said, "What should I do?"

"I'll buy us some time," Laila said. "Confuse the crap out of them."

She must've started Erasing the time little by little from both the prisoners, because they began making the oddest sounds. I never thought we'd make it to the van, but we did.

Connor threw open the back doors for us, and the guys plopped down their loads onto the seats like sacks of potatoes.

"Hello, boys," Connor said with a smile. "Let's get you settled in front of your equipment." The computers were up, and prisoner number one looked like he was just now coming to from Duke's earlier knockout. He pushed against his bindings, then kicked Laila in the chin. She kneed him in the gut. "Connor, why don't you just Heal all of them? That would solve everything."

"Laila." His voice was a low warning.

"No, seriously, these guys are scum. They've totally abused their power. They made Addie think her grandpa was still alive. You Heal them, then I'll Erase their memories of it. They won't know what hit them."

"What do you mean, Heal them?" I asked.

One man thrashed and yelled something vulgar.

"You don't like that idea?" Laila asked. "It sounds just as good as the ideas you guys come up with in the name of justice." She turned to Connor. "What do you say?"

Connor shot her a look of death, then without looking away from her, waved to Duke and me. "Duke, get ready to do the night over. You and Addie go drive around. Pretend like you're seeing her for the first time tonight. And end up here with Fake Grandpa."

I nodded.

"Laila." Connor's voice was measured, like it took a lot of effort to keep it level. "Three hours for these guys, and then we need to do some Thought Placement while they come to. Direct their memories."

"How are we going to do that?"

"We'll hide in the alley around the side of the building."

"Is that going to work?"

Connor nodded to Eli. "It will because we'll know what they're thinking and what thoughts will make them believe what we need them to believe."

"Where should I go?" Trevor held Mass Manipulator by one arm and Duke was on his other side. Duke must've been working on his emotions, but he still looked like he wanted to rip out someone's heart with his bare hands. It probably wouldn't be too hard for him either, if he could use his ability.

"Home," Laila said. "Connor, Eli, and I will follow you there in a little while and hang out just in case this doesn't work." She put her hands on my shoulders. "I know you're a horrible liar, Addie. But you can do this."

I laughed. "Thanks for making me feel nervous."

"Let's go," Connor said. "Oh, and everyone. We can never speak of this again after this moment, or this is all pointless."

There was a moment of silence, almost like we all knew that silence was the correct response to the statement. Laila took care of Mass Manipulator first. Then I nodded to Duke, and we took off running toward the Hummer.

"Addison!"

I stopped and turned. Trevor stood on the other side of the street. My heart jumped and I ran toward him. We met in the middle and he scooped me up in his arms. "Be careful."

"I will. I'm so glad you're okay."

He reached into his pocket, pulled out my phone, and handed it to me. "I'll see you later."

I nodded. Then Duke grabbed my hand and dragged me away.

After driving around for a while, he opened his glove box and took out a small metal device. *Showtime*, he mouthed, then stuck it to his skin. It immediately started blinking. He pulled over, rolled down his window, and yelled, "Addie," as if I were outside. Then he opened his door. "Get in."

I opened, then shut, my door and took a deep breath. I could do this. "What do you want?"

"I need to talk to you. I can't believe you told him."

My heart hammered in my chest. "What are you talking about?"

"Trevor. You told him about the Compound."

Shock, anger. I tried to embody those emotions. Anger came very easily. "I did not. Why would I ever do that?"

A sadness seeped through my body, and I wondered if it was Duke projecting or if the night was catching up with me. My anger melted away.

"I don't know. You tell me," he said.

I grabbed his hand, trying to diminish the ache in my heart

or his. "I didn't. I signed the contract in the Tower. There's no way I'm telling anyone about the Compound. Did you read the stuff they can do to you?"

He gave a halfhearted smile and squeezed my hand. "You're staying here, aren't you?"

I wasn't sure if this was still part of the act or if we were now to real questions, but I met his eyes. "Yes. I love him." There were so many more reasons I was staying here, though, reasons I couldn't say out loud. I had found out so much about the Compound tonight, and I knew I couldn't go back to a place like that. I knew now why my dad chose to leave.

"And you can live out here with no abilities and be with a man who has no abilities?"

"Love makes you do strange things."

"It does, doesn't it?" He sighed. "So Trevor really doesn't know anything?"

"Really."

"Okay. I'll take you home."

"No. Will you take me to my grandpa's? My dad and I are in a fight, and I don't want to go home tonight." My dad and I *were* in a fight, and I felt terrible. I'd accused him of some awful things when he had been telling the truth the whole time.

"It's kind of late."

"He'll want to see me. He always wants to see me."

I was scared to go see Fake Grandpa alone, but I kept reminding myself the Containment Committee had no idea what we had done. Or at least I hoped. And Fake Grandpa said he was root-ing for me, so he wouldn't hurt me.

"Addie," Duke said as I grabbed onto the handle of the car door.

I paused and looked back. He pulled me into a hug, pressing his cheek against mine. "I'm sorry," he said. "Good-bye."

When he drove away, I took a deep breath. Inside, I opted for the elevator. I was tired. I didn't even want to look at the stairs. My nerves were making my legs shaky as well. This was the moment of truth. The opportunity to see if everything we had just done had worked.

Fake Grandpa opened the door after I knocked. He looked a little out of it. "Addie, it's late."

"I know. Sorry. My dad and I got in a big fight. You think I could hang out for a little while?" I looked past him, trying to see if any of the guys from the van were in there. His apartment seemed empty.

"Of course." He opened the door wide and I went in and sat on the couch.

"You had that dance thing with Trevor tonight, right? How did it go?"

"It was nice." It *was* nice. I wished I were back there where my only problem was Stephanie and her reaction to Trevor and me.

He smiled like he knew something he wasn't supposed to. "You like that Norm boy, don't you?"

"I do." Loved him.

"That has to be hard to have such a big secret you can't tell him."

"It is."

"You really should think about using the box."

So the box was another part of my test. First they gave me back my grandpa so I had someone to confide in, trust . . . and love. And then the man I trusted gave me a supposedly secure place to tell all my secrets.

"No, Grandpa, I'm not going to tell him. I wouldn't want to put the Compound in danger like that." The boys in the van would probably like that added bit of patriotism.

He sat next to me on the couch and put his arm around me. "You seem down tonight. Are you down?"

I leaned against him, letting myself believe for one last second that this was my real grandpa. That he had come back from the grave and was a part of my life again. My mind wouldn't let me believe all the way, though, so a sadness settled in my chest.

"I think you passed," Fake Grandpa said.

"What?"

The front door opened and shut. I sat up quickly.

"Who's that?"

"Just someone who's going to help you feel better."

Memory Eraser from the van walked in. His empty eyes took me in. I tried not to let the fear that shot through me show on my face. Duke must've delivered the news to the van that I hadn't confessed to anything like he'd claimed I would. Memory Eraser didn't know what we'd done. Laila would restore my memory later. I just needed to relax. I repeated those three phrases over and over as he walked toward me. I pretended to be confused, looking back and forth between the two of them. And then his hands touched my head and I was enveloped in blackness.

CHAPTER 42

Laila: Real feelings are much better than fake ones.

Eli slept in the cab, so Connor and I lay in the back of his truck, under some blankets, staring at the stars. Everything looked hopeful. Addie had just texted Trevor to come pick her up from the dance. She was confused as to how it had gotten so late and about where everyone had gone, but otherwise seemed to have her memories. Which meant they really had only Erased Fake Grandpa from her mind.

Now we were waiting for Trevor to return so we could restore Addie's memory before heading home. We had only applied for a twelve-hour pass—it was the quickest way out of the Compound. We wanted to get back sooner rather than later to avoid more people investigating this area. That was the last thing Addie needed.

Connor lay a couple of feet away, his arms crossed firmly over his chest, his hands tucked beneath them. I knew he was angry with me for suggesting he Heal the CC guys of their abilities, but I was pissed too. Those guys had been playing Addie like she was a piece in some game, and they had absolutely no remorse. But I couldn't say that out loud. I had to be careful with what I said out loud. "I was just trying to scare them."

He didn't say a word. Didn't move a muscle. Was he really going to be a baby about this?

"What do you want me to say?" I asked. "Sorry?"

He stood then, vaulted out of the truck, and stalked away from me. I closed my eyes and sighed. Yes, he needed to walk it off. Get it out of his system. Wait, no, that meant I'd sit in this truck angry.

I ran up the street after him and caught him by the arm just as he entered the circle of yellow created by the streetlight overhead. I cut off his retreat. "Connor, you have an ability. Use it."

"I will use it when I feel it's necessary, not when you do."

"You never feel like it's necessary, so I was just making a suggestion."

"More like a demand."

"Oh, and you weren't demanding that I use mine?"

"Considering you use it when someone looks at you wrong, I didn't think you'd have a problem with it."

"Why do you care when I use it? Are you my father now?"

"Someone needs to be. Yours couldn't care less about how you abuse your ability. Or anything else you do, for that matter."

I whirled around, but he caught me by the wrist before I could leave and pulled me to face him. He clasped my wrists against his chest, and I used my forearms to keep him from pulling me any closer.

"I shouldn't have said that. I was angry."

I shrugged. "It's true."

"I shouldn't have said it." He moved his head in front of me, forcing me to look at him. "I thought you understood how I felt about what I did."

"You used your ability. You shouldn't feel ashamed of that."

His eyes shifted back and forth between mine, staring at me intently. "I took away my father's ability. You really think I should be proud of that?"

Maybe I felt this way because I was so angry with his father. "You saw what you were capable of. If you're going to bury your ability for the rest of your life, you might as well stay here." I pointed to the ground, letting it represent all the Norm world. I was breathless now, and my eyes stung. When I focused on Connor again, his intense stare had softened.

"Is that what this is about?" he asked.

"What?"

"You wanting me to use my ability. You're worried that if I don't depend on my ability, I won't need the Compound? You're worried that after spending time here, I won't want to leave?"

I shook my head. "No. I'm not worried about that. You can do whatever you want."

"Do you want me to stay here?"

With clenched teeth, I shook my head no.

He pulled me close, and this time I wrapped my arms around him. Then he kissed me like this was good-bye. It scared me. What if being here *had* made him realize how much he loved it? What if it had tilted the scale in favor of the Norm world? I, alone, couldn't add much weight to the Compound side of the argument, even if I jumped up and down on the scale. Especially after everything we'd seen tonight. Maybe I was stupid for wanting to go back. But I did, and I didn't want this to be good-bye. I tried to memorize the feel of his lips, the pressure of his arm on my back, the texture of his hair, as if he was going to slink away in the night as soon as the kiss was over.

When his touch turned electric, I pushed away. If he was going to leave me, it needed to be now, while I could still breathe through the tightness in my chest.

"What is it?" he asked.

"You're staying, aren't you? You're going to send in your application from here. Or maybe you won't even let them know. You'll just disappear and dare them to find you."

He laughed a little. "Why won't you just let me love you?"

His comment caught me so off guard that I sputtered a little.

"I've made Laila speechless. Is this a first?"

I smiled. "Shut up."

"You still want to go back to the Compound after . . ." He

trailed off, probably not wanting to say too much about what had happened tonight.

I nodded. "If everyone left, who would challenge the system? Who would change things? Besides, you're the spokesperson for the new free-market society there, right?"

He gave a little smile at my sarcastic comment, the same one I'd used on him a few weeks ago. "I'm coming home with you. We'll see how long we can stand each other."

"I'm pretty stubborn, and if this is a competition, I can so outlast you."

He seemed willing to accept that challenge.

I put my arms around his neck. "I don't know about this throwing around the *L* word. That was pretty reckless."

"I know, shocking, coming from the king of responsibility."

I laughed. "You were pretty brilliant tonight."

"I try."

A set of headlights lit the street, then faded to black when the car parked. Trevor stepped out, then opened the door for Addie. He didn't say a word, like we had all talked about. He just led her to me, and I restored her memory. We hugged, and that tightness that had left my chest when I found out Connor wasn't staying here returned when I remembered Addie was. Only Addie could make me cry. I wiped my face as she pulled away. She left her tears there, streaming.

"Bye," I said to Trevor.

He took Addie's hand in his and smiled. Trevor was perfect for Addie. I never would've thought a Norm could make her happy, but she was constantly proving me wrong.

"We should go," Connor said.

I hugged Addie again. "Don't be a stranger."

"My mom would never let that happen."

The sound of Connor's keys jingling together drew my attention, it was such a foreign sound. The only person who didn't turn at the sound was Trevor.

We all walked together to the truck. Connor placed a hand on Trevor's right shoulder. "Good to meet you." Then he put a finger to his own lips. "Try not to scream."

Trevor's look of confusion was quickly replaced by a look of sheer pain. It took me too long to realize what Connor was doing. He was healing Trevor's shoulder. Addie must've realized it too, because her tears came back in full force. Pride coursed through my chest. Something that had been stolen by an ability was now returned by one. Without another word, Connor let go and climbed into the truck.

Addie wouldn't have it, though. She opened the door and threw her arms around him in a big hug. "Thank you so much." He laughed a little.

When she returned to Trevor's side, she grabbed his hand. His face was pale. I gave him a one-armed hug and whispered, "A wrong was just righted. Take care of my best friend."

He nodded, and I watched them walk back to Trevor's car together. Then I went to the driver's side of Connor's truck, opened the door, and pulled him into a kiss. I could tell I'd caught him off guard, because he took a sharp breath through his nose. But then he relaxed into it and kissed me back.

"I kind of love you right now," I said.

"Now look who's throwing around the *L* word."

I smiled and climbed into the car. He started the engine and pulled away from the curb.

Addie waved until we turned the corner.

I was overwhelmed by the conflicting emotions of what Connor had just done and having to leave Addie.

"You good?" Connor asked, taking my hand.

"I will be." I leaned my head back against the seat and let the warmth of his hand travel up my arm. I would be fine with Connor in my life.

"Ugh," Eli groaned from the backseat, sitting up. "If I have to listen to your mushy thoughts all the way home, I might have to crawl into the back."

Connor raised one eyebrow.

"Don't get a big head. They weren't that mushy." I laid my head on his shoulder and put his hand on my knee.

CHAPTER 43

Addie: I miss you already.

"Are you okay?" I asked.

Trevor rotated his arm in a big circle several times. He might've been experiencing some shock symptoms, and I was seconds away from making him lie on the ground and raise his feet in the air. Then he said, "I'm perfect," picked me up in a big hug, and spun me around. He slowed to a stop but didn't put me down. Instead he buried his head in the corner between my shoulder and neck. "I'm perfect."

I clung to him, so happy for what Connor had done.

He lowered me to the ground, then pulled back a little. "Are you okay?"

I wiped my face to make sure it wasn't streaked with tears and nodded. "When I came here, I wasn't sure if I could ever really forgive Laila for everything that happened with Duke."

"And now?"

"Now, I don't know how I'm going to live without her."

"This isn't just for me, right? Staying here?"

"You would be enough, but no, my dad's here too." And I could not go back to the Compound now that I knew the lengths they were willing to go to in order to make sure their citizens were all mentally capable. The lengths they were willing to go to in order to fulfill their agenda. "Speaking of, it's almost one a.m. I think I'm going to be in big trouble."

"I'll take you home."

"Thanks."

He walked me to the front porch. "It was an interesting night."

"I never got to ask you about Steph. Is she going to murder me in my sleep?"

"She's just humiliated. She'll be fine." He took my hand and started drawing circles on my palm with his finger.

"And if she's not?"

"Addison, you are the only person I'm concerned about now."

"Good answer."

He gave me a half smile. "Where were we the first time I kissed you?"

"In my dream, we were in your bedroom."

He nodded once, seeming to understand why I had said it

358

like that. "In my bedroom? Was it a mess?"

"For once, I wasn't thinking about the less-than-organized state of your room."

He inched closer until our lips almost touched. "What were you thinking about?"

"I don't remember right now," I whispered as his familiar breath filled all my senses. He kissed me then, his fingers gripping my waist until I barely stood on the ground by the tips of my toes.

The front door opened, and he let go of me. Without his support, I stumbled backward and nearly fell. "Dad." I meant to say it with excitement, but it came out like a sigh.

"You're late, Addie. Get inside."

"I'm sorry, sir," Trevor said. "It was my fault, but unfortunately necessary."

My dad analyzed his statement, nodded, then escorted me into the house, effectively cutting Trevor off by shutting the door. Without waiting for a verbal berating, I hugged him. "I'm sorry about our fight, Dad. I'm so sorry for accusing you of lying. You're right, I've been very selfish. I'll go home for Christmas, but then I want to stay here with you."

His mouth opened, as if everything I'd just spewed had made him speechless for a moment. He regained his composure enough to say, "Really? Are you sure?"

"I'm positive."

As if he thought my speech was an attempt to get out of trouble, he said warily, "You're still grounded for two weeks."

I laughed. "Fine."

He analyzed my face, then smiled. "Maybe one week would be better."

"If you think so."

He put an arm around my shoulder as he walked me to my room. "Or maybe I'll give you a warning. This was your first offense, after all."

I was so glad to know the truth. It was amazing how much perception could change my opinion about a situation. All things considered, he was very kind to me in the midst of all this. I smiled and hugged him again. "Good night, Dad."

I shut the door, and almost immediately there was a tap on my window. I threw back the curtains, and Trevor stood there with a grin on his face.

"Are you grounded?" he asked when I opened the window.

"No. But if my dad sees you, I will be."

He put his hand on the screen, and I put mine up against it.

"Thanks for choosing me, Addison."

ACKNOWLEDGMENTS

Sequels. Sigh. They're hard. Everyone has this new scary thing called expectations. And the added pressure of knowing that everyone who is reading the sequel must've been a fan of the first is anxiety-inducing. What if they're all disappointed?? But there's also a comfort in writing a sequel because anyone reading it must love the characters and is already rooting for them before they turn back the cover. Yes, I'm rambling (and contradicting myself). My point? If you are reading the sequel, I love you. I hope you love it as much as I do. To all those who supported *Pivot Point*, who wrote me letters, reviewed my book, and encouraged me, thank you so much! I love readers.

Thanks again to my amazing agent, Michelle Wolfson, who makes writing fun and always knows just what to say. To Sarah Landis, my editor, thanks for the encouragement and wisdom. Thanks to the whole team at Harper and all the support they give me. Especially Mary Ann Zissimos, my awesome publicist, and Alice Jerman, for all her behind-the-scenes work.

I couldn't write at all without the support of my family: my husband, Jared, who after sixteen years still makes me laugh every day; my kids, Hannah, Autumn, Abby, and Donavan, who I am so very proud of; my mom, Chris, for all her support;

and my parents-in-law, Vance and Karen, who love me like their own; my siblings, Heather, Jared, Spencer, and Stephanie; plus my extended siblings, Rachel, Zita, Kevin, Dave, Eric, Michelle, Sharlynn, Rachel, Brian, Angie, Jim, Emily, and Rick (yes, I have a lot of siblings, and they're all great).

Thanks to the girls who help make my manuscripts shiny before my agent gets them: Candice, Stephanie, Jenn, Renee, Natalie, Sara, Julie, Misti, Linda, Jenny, and Nicki. Love you girls and I could never do it without you. And also, thanks to the Friday the Thirteeners, who helped get me through the crazy year leading up to publication: Erin, Ellen, Elsie, Jenn, Natalie, Renee, Shannon, Megan, April, Mindy, Brandy, and Alexandra. These ladies are talented and fun (and give pretty epic pep talks).

To my friends who try to remind me that there is life outside of writing—I know this is a hard job—thanks for caring: Elizabeth, Claudia, Candi, Neal, and all my church family.

If you just read through this entire acknowledgments expecting to see your name and didn't, then I have failed. I'm sorry. Because I know I am forgetting people. Thanks to all who have supported me and continue to support me.

SEE WHERE ADDIE'S STORY BEGAN.

ONE GIRL. TWO FATES. ONE CHOICE.

PIVOT POINT

KASIE WEST

MORE FROM KASIE WEST

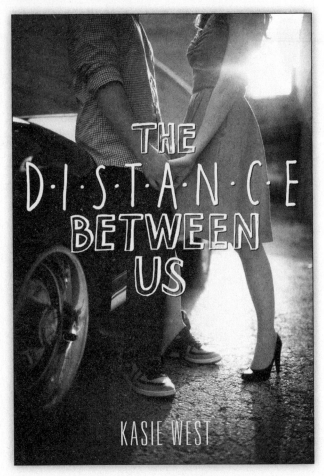

Seventeen-year-old Caymen Meyers learned early that the rich are not to be trusted. Enter Xander Spence—he's tall, handsome, and oozing rich. But just when Xander's attention and loyalty are about to convince Caymen that being rich isn't a character flaw, she finds out that money is a much bigger part of their relationship than she'd ever realized.

With so many obstacles standing in their way, can she close the distance between them?